Totally Bound Publishing books by Makayla Roberts

The Royal Gordanos
A Royal's Touch
A Royal's Pursuit
Craving a Royal

I0658888

The Royal Gordanos

CRAVING A ROYAL

MAKAYLA ROBERTS

Craving a Royal
ISBN # 978-1-83943-816-5
©Copyright Makayla Roberts 2019
Cover Art by Erin Dameron-Hill ©Copyright October 2019
Interior text design by Claire Siemaszkiewicz
Totally Bound Publishing

Published in 2019 by Totally Bound Publishing, United Kingdom.

Totally Bound Publishing is an imprint of Totally Entwined Group Limited.

CRAVING A ROYAL

Dedication

To all five of my siblings. I love you maniacs.

Prologue

They say a vampire finding his or her truemate is the most wonderful, glorious of all occasions. Two souls find one another after years, even centuries of searching. Two become one and spend an eternity in endless love.

Such was not the case with us. Though you are my truemate, our love was never meant to be. Not in this life. It was my decision to make, and, though I can never claim you, I do not regret choosing this path. It was necessary for the world to survive. For you to survive.

And so, I will continue to watch you and your family from afar. Though you cannot see me, know that I am there. I have always been there.

Vivinna

Chapter One

The suburb in the village of Hinsdale just west of Chicago was the type of neighborhood that made Naomi cringe. Each house she passed was bigger and more lavish than the last, as if the residents were in competition to show off who had the most fortune.

And it was clear that the owner of the sprawling mansion at the very end of a private road won the award for Top Over-Compensator.

Beyond the large wrought-iron gates was a Mediterranean-style mansion that looked like it'd been plucked straight from the Hamptons. It stretched over a piece of property that could house an entire subdivision of equally large homes. And stepping out of the elegant double doors making up the entrance was a mere waif of a woman who looked as out of place as Naomi felt.

Her closest friend and ex-comrade of many years wore plain yellow scrubs and a white lab coat that was far too big for her small frame. The sight made Naomi snort behind the mask that covered the lower half of her face. She stepped out of the rental car as Siovon strolled up to her.

"You look comfortable," Naomi drawled.

Siovon grinned. "I wouldn't live here if I couldn't feel comfortable in my own home." She waved a slender hand toward the entrance. "Come in. I'm surprised you showed up this time."

Naomi snorted again, following Siovon with caution. It wasn't that she didn't trust her. Quite the contrary, in fact. Siovon was like a sister to her, one she trusted with her life.

No... Her hesitancy had everything to do with the fact that Siovon wasn't alone in that mausoleum of a home. She was the mate of Lucian Gordano — a powerful clan chief who ruled more than a fourth of the United States. Not only was he a ruthless badass whose very word was law, but he was also the firstborn child of Cyrus Gordano, the almighty vampire king. That made him one of the most feared demons around.

And with that grand title came a horde of devoted clansmen assigned to protect every inch of his property. While they were good about staying out of sight — no doubt following Siovon's commands — Naomi still sensed their eyes on her. She'd never ventured to a vampire's lair, not unless it had been to kill one of them.

Something she'd promised Siovon not to do tonight. *Damn it all.*

"It's not like you gave me much of a choice," Naomi grumbled, studying the layout of the grand mansion. She lightened her voice to mimic a higher pitch. "*Come over and get the medicine yourself. I have sooo much work to do, what with pleasing my hubby and groveling at his feet.*"

Siovon chortled. "First off, I do *not* sound like that, nor have I ever said any such nonsense. Second, I wanted you to see my lab. The contractors just finished the repairs last week, and Cyrus ordered a shipment of all sorts of herbs and ingredients and… Well, everything, really." She led them down one hall that had a single door at the end. "And the best part? No one is allowed to enter without my or Calysta's permission — not even Lucian." She punched in a series of numbers on the touchpad. Seconds later, a metal latch unlocked and she swung the door open.

Naomi raised her brows, amused at her friend's excitement. The vast room was like a laboratory from a sci-fi movie. Multiple shelves lined the perimeter, all filled with large glasses of herbs, plants and other earthy products. A portion of another wall contained a refrigerator with glass doors that held all sorts of vials. The steel door next to it was what she assumed to be a walk-in freezer. There were also a half-dozen rolling tables, metal slabs jutting from the walls and glass cabinets encompassing cauldrons, ceramic pots, beakers and lots of scientific equipment that was clean and ready for use.

"This is impressive, Siovon," Naomi murmured in earnest. "Frosty really went all out for you, didn't he?"

Siovon beamed with pride. Her hair was styled in the same short pixie cut she'd had when Naomi had first met her decades prior. That, plus her short stature, dainty features and wide eyes, made her look like she couldn't harm a fly if it bit her on the nose.

Unbeknownst to others, she was all warrior, despite her wish to be peaceful. The battle with Sierra and her zombie Rogues a few months prior had proved that Siovon's new life of peace hadn't corrupted her deadly skills. Since then, her life had just…evolved.

For the better, of course.

She had been reunited with her sister after a ten-year absence, found the love of her life — in a vampire, of all things — moved into a lavish house and had her mate's family to call her own. It wasn't too bad for someone who'd once been an empty shell of an assassin.

Naomi was happy for her. She truly was, but she couldn't halt the twinge of envy that always pierced her heart every time she spoke to Siovon. Naomi didn't have any illusions of a perfect life with a perfect mate and an even-more-perfect family. Still, she couldn't help but wish she could trade spots with her dear friend, if only for a day.

Hell, for just an hour.

She wondered how it felt to be worshiped by a loving companion, someone who'd dedicate his entire existence to pleasing her and keeping her happy.

An image of silver hair and pale blue eyes flashed in her mind, followed by a longing that she ruthlessly squashed.

I am not *going there*, she growled to herself. *I am so* not *going there. Not again.*

Shaking off the depressing feelings she'd been forcing away for weeks, she hopped on to one of the steel slabs. Her feet dangled from the floor as she waited for Siovon to retrieve the vial of medicine she'd come for.

When Siovon paused with a raised eyebrow to look over her shoulder, Naomi only then realized that her friend had been talking the whole time. She gave a slow blink. "What did you say?"

Siovon huffed. "Are you listening to me?"

Naomi shrugged. "No. Sorry."

"I asked if you wanted to stay for dinner. Calysta is still with Keegan, looking for a jinn, and Lucian will be working late."

Naomi widened her eyes in mock surprise. "The leech isn't going to be glued to your side? I'm shocked."

"Oh, trust me. It wasn't his choice. I told him he'd have to find somewhere else to sleep if he shirks his duties again."

"Ah, the old no-cooch-for-the-pooch threat. Works every time." Naomi glanced around the room. "Thanks for the offer, but I have things to do. Maybe next time."

"A job, huh?"

"Nah. My contract ended a week ago."

Siovon looked shocked and froze in the middle of pouring some kind of liquid into a vial. "Really? Why didn't you tell me?"

"It's not a big deal."

Liar, her mind whispered.

The assassin's guild had been her home since she'd been age nineteen. Though their methods of dealing with insubordination and failed missions were rather gruesome and painful, they'd saved her life. The vigorous training she'd endured had helped her become stronger, bringing her a long way from that frightened, weak little girl she'd once been. Killing targets for a living had become the only life she knew. And for a while, she'd been content, though that wasn't something she wanted to do forever.

Oh, she didn't share Siovon's tender heart that craved a life of harmony and cupcakes and rainbows, not even a little.

Her past held a noose around her neck, and it was high time she faced it.

"Are you going to sign another contract?" Siovon asked.

"Probably not."

"Well, what are you going to do?"

Naomi shrugged again. "Dunno."

Siovon let out an annoyed huff. "You should consider working with me and Caly. We're going to open a clinic-slash-pharmacy soon, so extra hands are always welcome. In the meantime, Cyrus is paying us an assload of money to find a way to reverse Rogueism among vampires."

Naomi lifted an eyebrow. "You think you can do that?" Rogues were the class of vampires who had given in to their bloodlust. They were nothing short of rabid beasts, and since there was no way of restoring their sanity, Cyrus' law demanded the execution of them on sight. Siovon had conveyed her surprise to Naomi about his request for her to seek a solution that would help those lost souls find their way back to their former way of being.

Frustration caused Siovon to frown as she glanced at a table holding several beakers containing different color liquids. "I'm not holding my breath on it, but I'm doing my best. From what I've learned about Rogues, there's always some kind of trigger to make them snap—losing a mate, starving from lack of blood, being tortured, et cetera. I think it's a brain function that clouds the mind with only the most basic needs remaining—hunger and attack mode, like how rabid animals are. I hope I can create some kind of anti-rabies vaccine and modify it to work the same for Rogues. If I can—"

Naomi opened her mouth on a wide, obnoxious yawn. "I get it. Nerd talk here, rabid Rogues there. Let's skip the schematics."

Siovon tsked. "Well, you asked."

Several minutes ticked by while Siovon worked the finishing touches on Naomi's medicine. It was a mix that suppressed her succubus needs. While she didn't require daily sex to survive, like full-blooded succubi, if she went more than a couple of days without it, her body would start to turn on itself.

She always chose to suffer through it until the pain became too unbearable. She'd rather that than to give into the needs that had caused her so much misery in life.

Yeah, a sex demon who hates sex. Go freaking figure.

"I'm done," Siovon murmured. She plugged a cork into the opening of the bottle and handed it to Naomi. "Seriously… What are you going to do now that your contract is over? You can teach a martial arts class, you know — show others how to fight and defend themselves. Luc's brother Cassander owns a popular demon gym that's always looking for skilled instructors. They even have cage matches once a month that have large-award prizes. Well, those fights are for men, but I'm sure I can talk Cass into at least considering holding some for women."

When Naomi said nothing, only stared at the six-inch bottle in her hand, Siovon's smile faded. She was calculating, and it wouldn't be long before she found whatever it was she was looking for.

"Something's wrong, isn't it?" Siovon questioned.

Naomi pulled a small piece of paper from her pocket and handed it to Siovon.

She studied the drawing with a frown, twisting and turning it several ways before glancing up. "What am I looking at?"

Naomi returned the paper to her pocket. She didn't even have to glance at it. She'd spent countless hours eyeing the image, trying to figure out its meaning. It was an eye of Horus, the ancient Egyptian symbol for peace and prosperity. However, the eye itself was backward and flipped in a way that made it near impossible to tell which side was correct.

"It's a symbol." Dread settled like a cold weight in her gut. "A few years ago, I came across a man who had it tattooed on his shoulder. We were after the same target, so, of course, he and I got into a brawl. I won, in case you're wondering, but he ran away before I could get any information out of him. I just let it go."

She tapped at the paper tucked away in her pocket. "My last mark had the exact same tattoo on her inner wrist. She was a member of some demon group that was distributing goods on the black market."

Siovon tilted her head. "Okay, so she and that guy had the same tattoos. They could have been from the same group and that symbol is their insignia. But what does that have to do with *you*?" She narrowed her eyes in suspicion. "Don't tell me you want in on the underworld scam. The black market has some pretty twisted shit going on, Naomi."

Naomi snorted. "I may be a killer, but I have morals — hypocritical as that may sound." She shook her head. "I thought perhaps it was all just a coincidence — and maybe it still is — but I've seen this symbol years ago." She sucked in a deep breath, steeling her nerves for the worst part of her revelation. "My mother had a pendant just like it."

For several long moments, the two of them just stared at each other in silence. Siovon's shock had been expected.

Naomi had once lived with her mother in a small corner of Tartarus that was solely inhabited by furies. All furies were female and pureblood, so long as they reproduced with humans, yet Naomi was an anomaly. Her mother had been impregnated with incubus sperm, though no one had known the truth until Naomi had reached maturity and her succubus side had come out. Her mother had been deemed a traitor to their kind and had been executed, while Naomi had been sold into demon slavery.

She'd been a snooping child when she'd found the pendant, but her mother had scolded her with a strict demand to never bring it up again. However, after coming across e same mark on people who might or might not be linked to a group of black marketers, she had to know if it was all tied together.

"I don't know what to say," Siovon murmured.

Naomi blinked up at her with a wry smile. "If you say something pitiful, like you're sorry for my loss, I will hit you."

Siovon flicked her bangs out of her eyes. "This is bizarre. Are you sure it's the same symbol? If your mother was associated with outsiders —"

"Then it's likely her death wasn't because of me being born."

"That's not what I meant. If you go down this path, you might discover answers that are better left covered."

"I'm aware of that." She hopped off the table. "Siovon, I have lived with guilt for so long. I've spent years blaming myself for her death. I need closure or else I'll never be able to move on. And even if don't find the answers I'm looking for, at least I can say I tried."

Siovon flattened her palm over her heart. "Naomi Sofia Morales, that was the longest I've ever heard you talk without mentioning death, torture or kicking someone's ass. I'm so proud of you."

Naomi rolled her eyes, though her lips twitched in amusement. "I'm serious. I need to find the truth."

Siovon nodded and shrugged out of her lab coat. "Very well. I'll go with you. It could be dangerous."

"Oh, no, you're not."

Siovon paused mid-strip. "Why not?"

"Is that a serious question? For one, you have your own life here, and if we come across any danger, you'll only sulk and complain if you have to ruin your newfound pacifism. For two, the moment you step foot outside Chicago, your pet vampire will come after us with his entire clan—and I, for one, have no desire to be in the company of Frosty throwing another one of his temper tantrums."

Siovon's cheeks tinted pink as she gave a small smile. "I suppose he can be a bit overbearing at times." Her smile waned. "I just don't think you should go alone. There's a chance that other furies are involved, and if they catch you snooping around for answers, they may try to kill you."

Naomi already knew that but hearing the words aloud stung. The only family she'd ever known had turned their backs on her when she'd needed help and guidance the most. After her exile, the council had threatened her demise if she ever tried to return—not that she'd wanted to anyway. There was nothing left for her there.

Good riddance to every one of those bastards.

"Don't worry about me," she said on her way out of the door. She pocketed her medicine and threw her hand up in a casual wave. "'Careful' is my middle name."

"The hell it is," Siovon grumbled, following her. They walked side-by-side until they were back on the driveway.

Naomi used the key fob to unlock her car door. "Have you ever heard of The Lotus? Chè tracked down an elf who's a frequent customer there. He wears the same symbol. I'm on my way to see if I can locate him."

"The Lotus?" Siovon asked incredulously. "That's—" She broke off her words, a strange expression crossing her delicate features. It had been there one minute and was gone the next, far too fast for Naomi to analyze it. Siovon then smiled and stepped back. "I've heard of the place. It's a popular nightclub that was opened a few months ago."

Naomi narrowed her eyes. Siovon's smile sent chills down her spine. It was far too wide, her tone overly sweet, as if she were plotting something. "I mean it, Siovon. You'd better not try to join me."

Siovon laughed, waving her away. "I promise I won't. Be careful and call if you need anything."

Naomi still didn't trust her friend's sudden change of heart, but she nodded and slid behind the steering wheel. Seconds later, she was headed down the long drive toward the outer gate.

Siovon's smile fell when Naomi's taillights were no longer in sight. Still, she stood on the gravel of the wraparound driveway, staring off into space.

Fear and worry became a living force in her chest, but not because she doubted Naomi could protect herself. No, it was because her friend had been through so much hurt and betrayal that her journey could quite possibly be the one to tip her over the edge of sanity.

However, there was no use trying to change her mind. Naomi would forever be tormented by her past, and if facing her people was her way of finding peace at last, then Siovon had no right to try to intrude.

Still, the voice of reason always won in those types of situations. Naomi was her closest and dearest friend. She couldn't sit back and let her endanger her life on a mission that could take a turn for the worse. There was no talking her out of it, and she'd just given her word to not interfere.

But someone else can.

18

"Please, don't let me regret this," she grouched as she retrieved her cell phone. She scrolled through her contacts until she found the number she needed. She swallowed her pride and crossed her eyes in frustration. "*Please.*" Then, she hit Call.

A suave voice that could charm the scales off a snake answered on the second ring. "Yes, sister-in-law. How can I help you?"

She rolled her eyes at his sarcasm, knowing full well her mate's brother had been annoyed with her the last few months. However, she needed his help, and she knew he above all others would see to Naomi's protection.

She drew in a deep breath before letting it out. With false cheeriness, she said, "Salvator, darling, how would you like to be reunited with my dear friend Naomi?"

Chapter Two

After living well over three thousand years — *Or has it been two thousand? Hard to remember* — it took a lot to make Cyrus Gordano lose his temper. Clan wars among his people were easy to settle. Even the occasional death threat from an irrelevant opponent didn't faze him, so long as his children weren't brought into the mix.

However, after his long-awaited meeting with the Imperials — the oh-so-powerful justice dealers of the demon world — it was a struggle to keep a calm attitude. They'd made him wait for several months just to turn him away, as if his problems were insignificant. As it was, an array of tiny sparkles fizzed around him, a sure sign that his elemental power to call on lightning was ready to be unleashed.

And he'd like nothing more than to spark every last one of the Imperials' majestic asses. *Damn the repercussions.*

Anais, a Royal child who'd been wandering lost and alone, had been taken in by his daughter, Ava. It had been due to Ava's ability to see memories that they had found out the girl was from a dimension in Tartarus, where she and many other Royals have been held captive for what could have very well been centuries. She was only ten years old, but she was a pureblood, which meant that up until at least a decade ago, the Gordanos weren't the only Royals, as they'd believed.

Yet, because the others were being held in another world, Cyrus and his family had no further information about them, nor were they able to travel outside the human realm.

That was the entire reason Cyrus had demanded a session with all the Imperials. If anyone would know what was happening in other realms, it would be those bastards. Hell, for all he knew, they'd known for a long time, yet had never once stepped forward to assist the other Royals or, at the very least, inform Cyrus. His people were his responsibility. It didn't matter if they were Royals, Aristocrats, Turnbloods or even Rogues. If they were vampires, they were under his care.

To his annoyance, the Imperials had merely treated his demands as a trivial matter, as if the missing Royals were of no concern. First, they had accused him of making up the story. Next, they'd demanded proof by encountering Anais and Ava, but he'd declined out of concern for his daughter's and the child's mental stability. Ava was too far pregnant, and having the Imperials digging through her brain would only stress her out. As for Anais, the girl was so fragile. Ava had been working hard during the previous months to wipe her memory little by little, so what little she still remembered wouldn't be very helpful.

However, after a good bit of arguing back and forth, the Imperials had conceded by saying, in the simplest words, *'We will look into it.'*

And that had been the end of it. It pissed him off to no end, yet he'd done all he could do. *Damn the gods*.

Fuming, he stormed through the cavernous walls making up the tunnels leading to the Imperials' courtroom. Though they traveled far and wide across the globe to host their sessions, this particular chamber was located deep within the rocky bluffs lining the Mississippi River somewhere between Illinois and Missouri. Though he walked without a guide to lead the way, it didn't take long for the sound of the river's flowing waters to reach his hearing. He hoped the fresh air would calm the slow rage burning in his gut.

The night sky soon became visible at the end of the tunnel, making him move a bit faster. He'd almost made it, too, until a white puff of smoke appeared before him. Scowling, he stopped in his tracks.

"*Merda*, give me a break," he growled.

Merisl, one of the eldest of the Imperials—and that was saying something—stared straight into him with eyes that never failed to make his skin crawl. They were a solid white. There was no pupil and not even the faintest of color in the irises. They were just pure white, along with her eyelashes, eyebrows and floor-length hair. Her skin was so pale that it was damn near see-through, and the full body robe she wore didn't make her look any less demonic.

"You and I go a long way back, Cyrus," she murmured in a soft tone, as if trying not to be overheard. "I have known you from the time you were still a bean in your mother's womb."

He scoffed. "I'm aware of that. Yet it seems every time I need your assistance, you turn your back on me."

She didn't so much as flinch at his accusing words. "Quite the opposite, in fact, but let us not waste more time on the past."

"What is your point for being here, Merisl? If you aren't going to help, then I have nothing more to say to you."

"Do not be so arrogant, Cyrus. You may be feared among others in this world, but do not forget that I am an Imperial."

Though she still spoke in that whispery-soft voice, he wasn't fooled for a moment into believing he'd ever be able to take her if it came down to a fight. It was true that he was one of the most powerful demons in the human realm, but she had the type of power that could wipe out an entire country with just a lift of her finger. It was almost god-like, which was one of the things that made the Imperials so frightening.

Not that he was afraid in the slightest, but he was a wise man.

Taking his silence for fear, she took a step forward. "I am forbidden from revealing any information pertaining to your...situation."

At that, Cyrus snapped his teeth together, narrowing his eyes. "So, you *do* know what's going on."

She didn't give any indication of a yes or no, which confirmed his suspicion and further pissed him off. "I cannot say. There are forces even greater than me that prevent it. However, I will give you this." She waved her hand and from out of nowhere, a black binder floated before them.

Cyrus didn't like magic, and caution made him take a wary step back. "What is that?"

She pushed the binder with her fingertip and it floated toward him. Still unsure, he tensed and held the object away from him, as though it would explode at any given moment. "It may or may not help you," she said. "Keep an open mind."

With that, she disappeared in another puff of white smoke. Annoyed and fearing the worst, he flipped the cover over, revealing a stack of really old letters inside. He scanned over the first one with a concerned frown. The words were written in his native tongue, a long-forgotten language that had died long before the Romans took over Italy.

"Vivinna…" he murmured under his breath. "Who are you?"

* * * *

Chicago, Illinois

After three hours of lingering inside a demon nightclub Naomi hoped never to return to, she fought her way through three hundred writhing bodies dancing to the deafening electro music — a sharp jab in the side, an elbow to some ribs and a yank on a ponytail that slapped her in the face.

It seemed her abusive efforts to make a break for the exit were ineffective, which had her temper flaring. When someone grabbed her ass, she whirled around and socked the bastard in the face, causing his nose to crunch under the force.

His howl of pain couldn't be heard over the music, but a quick glance around showed that one of the bouncers had witnessed the incident and was charging right for her.

Shit. The last thing she needed was to be deterred even more than she already was.

She returned to shoving people aside, performing all kinds of painful maneuvers on them to urge them out of her way. Subtlety be damned. She was on a mission, dammit, and these bumping and grinding idiots were delaying her progress.

Just as she was about to break free from the crowd and make a dash for the exit, someone grabbed her from behind. Before she could throw another punch, her joints turned to jelly and the world around her disappeared.

When her feet touched solid ground, it took several moments for her muscles to stop spasming. Glancing around, she realized she wasn't in the middle of the crowd anymore, and the music from the DJ's booth wasn't thrumming through her chest. It was quiet, and the lights weren't as dim — nor did it smell like sweat and lust.

"My, my… You don't peg me as the partying type, dove," a smooth voice said from behind her. The words were coated in an ancient Italian language. Latin, if she could remember correctly. "I must say I'm rather surprised to see you here."

Naomi stiffened. That silky voice mixed with the intoxicating scent of aged whiskey and rich cologne washed over her, blanketing her in a warm embrace that was foreign to a solitary creature like her.

Foreign, yet oh-so-familiar.

Time seemed to stand still as she faced a man who was far too beautiful to be human. He was tall and lean, with solid muscles hidden beneath a dark red suit she assumed cost more than most people had in their savings account. His long silver hair, as straight as silk ribbons, was left loose to frame a narrow face with sharp Roman features, though his hair and pearly skin hinted at Norse descent. His eyes were mesmerizing, the blue orbs so pale in color that they reminded her of arctic waters.

And he was watching her with a stark hunger that matched the one she'd done her best to hide for months.

She twisted her lips in annoyance to mask her unease. "You," she grunted.

His lips twitched with humor, as if he knew very well the effect he had on her. "Me."

"Explain yourself."

"What's there to explain?" he asked with a curious lift of his hands. "I teleported you away from my patrons before you caused any more damage to my high-paying customers."

Naomi frowned. "What do you mean *your* patrons?"

He expanded those sinful lips into a cocky smile. "I believe the answer is rather obvious, dove." He waved to indicate the room they were in. It was twice the size of her old apartment and far more lavish, with its crimson walls and carpet, low-hanging chandelier and lush furniture. There was even a hand-carved desk with a computer monitor and neat piles of paperwork. "I am the owner of The Lotus, and you, my sweet, have caused quite a ruckus downstairs."

Then it clicked. No wonder Siovon had seemed so suspicious then wore that enigmatic smile. It had been because she'd known who would be waiting when Naomi arrived.

Oh, she is so dead, she thought. *I'm going to kick her little ass.*

She made a 'tch' sound between her teeth, returning her glare to the silver-haired vamp standing a few feet away from her. "I was just leaving." She turned to stroll toward the door, but, of course, it could never be that easy—not with Salvator. The man put the 'S' in stubborn.

Using that annoying vamp speed of his, he was standing before her in the blink of an eye. "I'm afraid I can't let you off that easily. You see, guests who don't follow the rules are to be reprimanded."

She rolled her eyes, wishing she had a weapon on her. A stake would sure come in handy. Per the rules of the club's entrance, no one was allowed to bring weapons inside, so as to 'keep the peace'. Yeah, because having a dagger at her hip and another hidden inside her boot was *so* dangerous.

Crossing her arms, she remarked in the driest tone, "Oh no. I'm banned from ever coming here again." She stepped around him. "Don't worry, pooch. I don't plan on returning. *Ciao*."

Yet again, an amused Sal blocked her path. "You and I aren't quite through."

"*Si*, we are. Step aside. I have nothing more to say to you."

"Really now?" He flashed out of sight, only to reappear behind her. Goosebumps rose on her flesh when he spoke into her ear, causing her nipples to pucker. "Because I have a lot I want to say to you."

"Tough," she growled, spinning to punch him in that arrogant, beautiful face. He dodged, stepping just out of reach. "I have shit to do."

"Then I'll make this quick," he assured her, straightening to his full height. "Why did you run away all those months ago?"

Straight and to the point.

Naomi stiffened, the question bouncing around in her mind. There were too many answers to it—and they were all embarrassing as hell. Fear was the primary reason, though she wouldn't tell him that. Disgust with herself followed right behind it, for sleeping with him had felt like the worst sort of betrayal to her dignity. "There was no purpose in me staying after the battle."

"That's not what I'm talking about." He flashed to once again stand behind her, using a finger to trace the shell of her ear. "You didn't run away from the fight. You ran away from *me*."

Naomi was frozen in place as Sal's light touch sent shivers across her skin. "How presumptuous of you to think my leaving had anything to do with you."

"But it did, didn't it? After your trembling climax in my arms, you snuck off before I awoke. Then, after the battle in Rochester, you disappeared again without so much as a goodbye. You were running from something, so the only logical explanation is that the something was me."

Naomi lowered her lashes. His fingers felt good brushing against her skin, and she remembered all too well having them touching her in a far more intimate way. "I had things to do," she muttered. "Things that had *nothing* to do with you." She stepped out of his reach and faced him. "Things that *still* have nothing to do with you. Now, are you satisfied?"

He pursed his lips and dropped his hand. The loss of contact made Naomi's chest clench, but she ignored it. She wouldn't dare let the cretin know he had any effect on her, that his very presence filled her with both desire and longing for something she could never have—for something she shouldn't even want to have.

"Hardly," he murmured. "What brings you here tonight?"

Naomi reached for the blade she kept at her hip, only to frown when all she felt was air. It wasn't that she felt threatened, but stroking the hilt of her blades was a habit that consoled her whenever she felt uncomfortable.

And for her, nothing was more uncomfortable than being around Salvator Gordano.

"What business is it of yours?"

"Everything that happens under my roof is my business."

She gave a wry smile, though he wouldn't be able to see it under her half-mask. "This club was made to provide customers with the utmost pleasure, correct?"

He narrowed his eyes in suspicion. "That's what the private rooms are for."

She studied her nails, feigning indifference. "Then what other reason would a succubus have for venturing to a place like this?"

Sal stepped forward. "No."

"No what?"

"You aren't that type of person."

Naomi went still, widening her eyes in shock. "Don't pretend you know anything about me."

He took another step. "I know more than you think, dove. I know you're strong, both physically and mentally. You can rip a man's heart out and bring him to his knees in pleasure at the same time. I know you're an assassin who used to work alongside my sister-in-law, and though you have this detached air about you, your devotion to her is far deeper than that of a mere associate."

As if glued to the spot, Naomi couldn't move as Sal leaned forward, violating her personal bubble. "I know you are a dangerous woman with a shadowy past, so you fight to keep from sinking into that darkness. That makes you a warrior — an admirable one, at that." He pressed his lips to hers, and though there was no skin-to-skin contact due to the filmy mask, she felt the jolt of it all the way down to her toes. "Lastly, I know there's something about me that terrifies you to the point where you push me away. You might be able to hide from the rest of the world, but never from me."

Naomi's heart gave a painful throb, because he was right on the money about everything.

She brought her palms up and, for just a moment, she envisioned gripping him by the lapels of his velvety jacket and pulling him against her. While her tainted blood demanded she seek out the nearest male and ease the painful cramps twisting her gut, she'd been successful in ignoring it, as of late. However, standing before Sal cranked her desire to full blast, and her hands shook with the need to let him put her out of her misery.

Instead, she shoved him away with enough force to send him stumbling backward. She didn't like being analyzed, nor did she care for how vulnerable he made her feel. She stormed away, clenching her fists at her sides.

"Don't flatter yourself, Sally," she growled over her shoulder. "I push you away because I don't like you — plain and simple." She jerked the door open. There was a vampire standing guard outside, so she shoved him aside and stomped down the hall, ignoring his growl of annoyance. She didn't know where the hell she was going, but as she followed the steady thrum of music, she soon found a set of stairs leading to the VIP floor on the second level of the club.

Stupid Salvator. She cursed him a thousand times for making her that way, for making her *feel*. He brought forth emotions she'd buried ages ago. Ever since she'd met Siovon and trained to be an assassin, she'd squashed every one that made her weak. She'd done her best to become a detached, uncaring, cold-hearted killer — to be as inhumane as possible. Siovon was the only person to ever really know her, and even then, it was because she'd saved her from a life of torment that would have killed her long ago.

For years, Naomi had carried the darkness of her past with her, using it to push her until she became a dull shell filled with hate and anger. All that negative energy was directed at everyone—herself included.

Yet the moment Salvator had sauntered into her life, he'd shaken her to her core. Something about him had pulled on those weaker emotions, threatening to break the ice she'd formed around her heart. Though, at first glance, he looked like a pretty boy who'd freak out if he broke a manicured nail, it was all a façade. In truth, he had a lethal prowess that surpassed her own. He was a skilled warrior—strong and proud and fearless.

He was also a man who enjoyed over-indulging in the pleasures of the flesh. He'd made it clear that he'd wanted to seduce her right from the jump—and he'd succeeded. Well, truth be told, she'd met him halfway. He'd been a treat to her succubus needs and, in a moment of weakness back in that schoolhouse, she'd only wanted him. They'd had sex, rough and fast and brief, just like she preferred. Yet it had been far different than with any other lover she'd taken.

She'd felt connected to him in a way that had chipped away at her resolve. She'd even thought she felt his presence inside her, like she could sense everything he felt. It left her exposed and terrified.

So yeah, she'd run away from him—not just from the fight and not from just seeing Siovon being happily accepted into a new family that would cherish her. No, she'd run from Sal, because after knowing him for just one day, he'd almost ruined everything she'd become.

She had even avoided coming to Chicago altogether, just to avoid crossing paths with him again. It was the entire reason she'd refused to meet with Siovon on multiple occasions, in the event he would pop up.

Giving a sharp shake of her head, she found herself on the ground floor. Instead of trying for the front entrance, she spotted a narrow hall with a lit *Exit* sign at the end. Another bouncer stood guard, glaring daggers at her as she approached.

She didn't say a word, merely trotted past him and shoved the door open. She inhaled the fresh summer air, thankful that the veil she wore as a mask to hide her scars was thin enough to allow it. The door led to a short alley between the side of the warehouse and a high fence, so she walked around the gated maze until she found the wide expanse of a parking lot.

It was amazing the things magic could do. To the naked eye, The Lotus looked like any other abandoned warehouse occupying a forgotten neighborhood near the outskirts of north Chicago—dark and creepy, with a wide chain-link fence surrounding the perimeter, an aged parking lot with weeds sprouting from the cracks and boarded windows that had been tagged with gang signs. It appeared to be something straight out of a horror flick, complete with 'no trespassing' signs and blackened walls from a fire decades ago.

Unbeknownst to humans, however, the old building was so much more than that. Protected by dozens of glamour and repulsion spells meant to keep out the riffraff, it was an elegant, booming nightclub with music so loud it could be heard from outside. Even the parking lot was paved and littered with dozens upon dozens of vehicles belonging to the patrons who were partying inside.

Naomi had parked on the end, farthest away from the building and other cars. Her rental was an ordinary black sedan with tinted windows. It wasn't the flashiest of cars—and damn sure not her usual taste—but it was good on gas. And considering the fact that she had no idea how much driving she'd have to do, being conservative would come in handy.

When her car came into view, she pulled the key fob out of her pocket and aimed it. She pressed the unlock button, only to stiffen, her finger still pressing the button downward. Usually it took a single press for the headlights to light up, signaling the driver's door was unlocked.

It didn't happen.

It could very well be a bad case of paranoia, but she wasn't about to take any chances. She backed away several feet, narrowing her eyes and glancing around to see if anyone was lingering in the shadows. Then, she released the button.

For long moments nothing happened and the tension left Naomi's shoulders. Christ, she'd been so on edge lately and now she was even more so, after running into Sal again. She reminded herself not to be so jumpy. Even a novice assassin could sense her unsteady nerves, and they wouldn't hesitate to pounce.

She took only one step when her neck hairs stood on end. She spun around and twisted her lips in displeasure at the sight of Sal approaching her. "What the hell do you want now?"

He shrugged. "I'm a gentleman, dove. What kind of man would I be if I allowed you to walk alone without protection?"

"You personally walk every woman here to their car? How considerate."

He tilted his head at her bitter words. "I'm confused as to why you seem to think I'm some heartless monster who doesn't know how to treat a lady."

Naomi shot him a glare, her words coated with acid. "Because I know men like you. You're all the same."

Sal reared back as if she'd slapped him. "I beg your pardon. Just because you've had bad luck with men doesn't give you the right to lump us all together."

She planted her fists on her hips. "No? Tell me if any of this sounds familiar. You flaunt your wealth and feed women pretty words to make them feel desired, and like mindless sheep, they fall for it. The attention you receive makes you feel good about yourself. It makes you feel empowered, like you're king of the freaking world. But deep down, you know you aren't. You care nothing for those women. You probably won't even remember their names by the next morning. It's all a game to you, but if you strip away the women, the money, the looks and the charm, all that lies beneath is a scared little boy who's using this elegant lifestyle as an outlet, a nice distraction from the reality that you're too much of a coward to face your own fears and insecurities. You're the one who's running from something by hiding behind a wall filled with glamorous lies."

She stepped forward and patted his cheek, as if he were a child she was patronizing. "Tell me, Sally. On a scale of one through five, how right am I?" When he said nothing, only regarded her with shocked, troubled eyes, she simpered. "My point. You said that I hide from the rest of the world. That may be true, but at least I have the balls to stay true to what's inside me. Now, for the love of God, leave me alone."

She turned and pointed the key fob at her car as she made her way toward it. She'd forgotten she already pressed the button, so when she did it again, she'd expected to see the headlights flashing. Instead, time seemed to move in slow motion as a spark ignited from under the hood, traveling the length of the car and sending it into flames.

Before she could react, Sal had thrown his arms around her and fallen to the ground, rolling her beneath him to shield her from the explosion. The result of the blast was deafening, and though Sal's arms took the brunt of the fall, her back was scraped against the asphalt through her spandex bodysuit. The sky lit up with a bright yellow and orange glow, a wave of heat rolling over them.

Long after the flying debris had settled, her ears were still ringing.

She stared up into Sal's face, that was pinched with pain. His lips moved, but she couldn't make out what he was saying. "What?" she yelled.

He shook his head and rose, bringing her with him. Slowly, the ringing subsided and was replaced with the sound of her blood rushing in her ears. "Are you okay?" Sal asked again, squeezing her hand.

Naomi brushed dirt off her ass. "I'm fine, I think. What was...?" She trailed off when she spotted her rental car engulfed in flames, only the framework left behind. Her eyes went round with the horror that had she been a few steps closer, she would have been caught in the blast.

She scanned the area but nothing seemed to stand out. Several of Sal's bouncers rushed toward them, one barking out orders to extinguish the flames. Patrons filed out to see what all the commotion was about. Sal dragged her away from the fire and his men, pulling her to a safe distance on the side of the building. He gripped her chin in a hold that wasn't painful, but it wasn't sweet either.

"You want to tell *me* what the hell that was about?"

Naomi tilted her head toward the burning car, still trying to piece together what had happened. "I don't—"

"Don't fucking lie to me," Sal growled. "Nearly half of my parking lot is demolished, blown up by your car. Do you have such a grudge against me that you thought you could ruin one of my businesses?"

"What?" Naomi looked at him. Her shock turned to anger. "Listen, you piece of shit. I had no idea this was your establishment. I was here to meet someone. That's it." She shoved at his chest, making him release his hold on her chin. "Not everything I do revolves around you. And believe me, if I wanted to destroy a big building like this, I wouldn't do it from the outside, nor would I stand so close to the blast and risk my own neck, thank you very much."

She turned to storm away. *Ha, and go where?* Her car was destroyed, as well as her belongings that she'd packed inside.

"You're not leaving that easily." Sal flashed in front of her. "I deserve an explanation."

"Well, I don't have one," she snapped, crossing her arms. "I'm just as stumped as you."

His nostrils flared, as if he was scenting whether or not she was telling the truth. She was, for the most part. She'd only been inside the club for a few hours, yet, in that short time frame, someone had planted a bomb on her car that would ignite at the push of a button. That had taken some serious skill, and she wasn't fooled into thinking it was a mere coincidence.

"Maybe so," Sal concluded, "but your being here is the cause for it." He lowered his voice and pulled them farther away from the crowd when a few curious patrons glanced their way. "Who wants you dead?"

Naomi let out a disbelieving scoff. "Is that a serious question? I've targeted hundreds of people who had family or close friends who might be seeking vengeance. Take your pick."

"Fine. Then what's your true purpose for being here?"

She grunted and turned her back on him. "As if I'll tell you anything. Go crawl back into your feeding hole and mind your own business. I'll mail you a check for the damages."

Sal flashed before her, causing her to roll her eyes. Damn, but that was getting annoying as hell. *Poof here, poof there. Freaking poofer.*

"I don't want your damn money." He grabbed her wrist. "It may have nothing to do with me, but I take it personally when someone tries to kill one of my lovers."

One of his lovers? Not his lover, *but* one *of them.*

She'd already known he had many women at his beck and call, but the thought that he regarded her as one of many sent her rage spiking. Yet she refused to believe it was due to something as petty as jealousy. No, if anything, she was irritated because of how pompous he was. She hated men like him.

She curled her lips in disgust and fisted the shirt underneath his suit jacket, moving to the tips of her toes to be at eye level with him. "I am *not* your damn lover, and you will refrain from grouping me with one of *them,* like I'm some commoner. *Comprende?*"

After several bewildered moments of silence, he lifted one corner of his mouth, as if she'd revealed some hidden information that pleased him. "You're so pretty when you snap and snarl."

Heat rose in Naomi's cheeks and she let him go, refusing to meet his eyes. She knew he was teasing her, but the words stung. She was far from pretty and they both knew it. "I'm serious. Leave me alone."

When she turned from him, she managed to get a few steps in. She thought, perhaps, that she'd won, that he would let her go at last. It was the crinkling of paper, however, that made her go still. She reached inside her pocket, grumbling under her breath to find it empty. *Dammit.*

"I've seen this before," Sal murmured, studying the symbol with a serious expression.

Naomi stiffened, her heart stuttering as she faced him. "You have?"

"This is…" He broke off with a shake of his head. "Is *this* why you're here?"

For a beat, Naomi disputed against revealing any information to him. Only Siovon and Chè—and old comrade of theirs—knew that Naomi was investigating the origins of that symbol. She trusted Siovon more than anything, even herself, so she knew her friend hadn't set her up. Chè, however, was debatable. While she trusted him to an extent, loyalty meant nothing to him for the right price.

While she hoped Sal wouldn't be foolish enough to betray her and risk getting on Siovon's bad side, she didn't trust him either. Not just with the symbol, but she didn't trust the feelings she had for him. If she did, she'd only be setting herself up for another heartbreak.

Still, she hadn't found the elf—*What was his name again? Maple or Sap or something*—so she was back to square one, with no resources on her side. Whatever Sal knew might jumpstart her investigation.

"I was here to locate an elf who had intel on that symbol," she admitted.

"Why?"

"For personal reasons. I didn't find him, which means he either knew I was coming for him or someone else is preventing me from looking into it." She shrugged. "Now, tell me what it means."

Sal eyed her with an unreadable expression, as if he was trying to comprehend what was going through her mind. She hoped to hell he couldn't. Royal vampires each had a special power, and it was clear that Sal's was the ability to teleport. Even so, she didn't want to take any chances.

He let out a small sigh, glancing at the paper again before handing it to her. "I can't recall its exact meaning, only that I've seen it several times. However, my brother would know more about it."

Naomi tucked it back into her pocket. "If you think I'm stupid enough to fall for your trap to land me in the middle of some vamp dungeon—"

"Don't be absurd," he chided. His previous anger was replaced with amusement. "You really have trust issues, don't you, dove?"

Isn't that the biggest understatement of the century? Naomi snorted. "When all you get in life are rejections, betrayals and lies, you're damn right."

A haunted expression crossed his features, a flicker of hurt that he masked behind a half-smile. "Understood. Cassander prefers to keep his company to himself, so it'll just be the three of us. If not, I'll personally hand you the stake to end my life. Deal?"

Naomi wanted to ask what that look had been about, but she refrained. Why go digging into his past when she didn't want the same done to her?

Mistaking her silence for hesitation, Sal rushed to say, "From the way I see it, you now have no vehicle, no weapons to defend yourself and—if those bits of charred paper flying around are what I think they are— no money. I, however, have all those things at our disposal. I can get you the answers you're looking for. Logically speaking, you need me."

Naomi shifted her weight to one leg. She didn't bother trying to hide her suspicion as she asked, "Why are you trying to help me? What do you get out of it?"

A secretive smile played at his lips and his eyes glinted with mischief. "Would you believe I'm doing it out of the kindness of my heart?"

Instead of answering, she arched a single eyebrow.

He snorted. "Someone's attempt on your life almost killed me, and half of my parking lot is blown to bits. I intend to make someone pay for this."

Naomi rolled her eyes but didn't argue. If she were being honest, the explosion had left her a bit shaken. She wasn't foolish enough to believe she'd leave the guild unscathed. It wouldn't surprise her if there was an entire army of family and friends seeking vengeance. Even if she had been just following someone else's orders, she had been the one who'd committed the deed, making her the target to blame.

No. What made her nervous was the knowledge that there were eyes on her. The thought of someone even more skilled than her tracking her moves unnerved the hell out of Naomi. She always preferred working alone, but for once, she was grateful for Sal's presence. At least he was capable of watching her six, and his teleportation powers would damn sure come in handy.

But, of course, she wasn't going to tell him that. If she so much as hinted at needing his help, it'd just go straight to his head.

"Well?" Sal prompted at her silence. "What do you say, dove?"

Naomi blinked, realizing once again she'd gotten lost in her train of thought. It was a common occurrence for her, a quirk she'd never quite been able to cure. She shook her head, moving past him toward the back of the building where he'd aimed his hand. "Just don't piss me off. Otherwise I'll have to explain to Siovon why her brother-in-law suddenly went missing. And stop calling me that froufrou-ass name."

"Why does it bother you?" he asked, falling in step beside her.

"Because I'm not one of your harebrained floozies. Don't give me some idiotic pet name just because you've forgotten my real one."

Chapter Three

Sal blinked in surprise, slowing his pace as Naomi continued to walk ahead of him. *She thinks I don't know her name?* Did she not know how much he'd sat in misery, mulling over her disappearance? That he'd been unable to look at another woman the same? That he'd spent weeks roaming the streets of Alleman and Rochester looking for a trace of her scent?

"I haven't forgotten your name, Naomi," he murmured. Proving her senses were far greater than a human's, she paused. He tilted his head to one side. "You aren't nearly as easy to forget as you seem to think." With that, he ambled past her with only a backward glance to ensure she was following.

She watched him with a troubled gaze. Her beautiful caramel-colored eyes were so expressive that he wondered if she'd ever be able to hide what she was thinking. *Doubtful.* Though the top half of her face was the only thing she allowed others to see, he was able to read her like an open book. It was one of the things about her that pleased him the most.

Naomi made a 'tch' sound and continued after him. He led her around the back of his club to the private employee parking lot. Among the newer model cars was a shiny red Maserati coupe. It was one of his most prized possessions. His baby.

It was no secret that the Gordano family had enough wealth to fund a small country. Their father was over three thousand years old and the king of all vampires. Lucian was almost two thousand and both Sal and Cass were aged over a thousand years. It only made sense that they'd accumulated a vast amount of wealth throughout the centuries. Nowadays, most of them invested their money in something that would only continue to increase the fortune.

Sal had dozens of nightclubs and smaller businesses all around the world. Cassander owned large demon fitness centers, and two of them held popular fighting cages every month that demons paid small treasures to watch. Darius and Julius were both prodigies, despite the fact that they chose to act like asinine fools. Darius was a world-class chef with the highest-ranking restaurant in Chicago, and Julius was a renowned artisan, whose work was said to rival the most famous painters in history. Andreas had invested his wealth into a PI service that helped both humans and demons.

Sal aimed his fob at his car, hesitating for a fleeting second before pressing the button to unlock it. Relief slid through him when it didn't explode. He hadn't expected it to, but there was no such thing as being too cautious, especially after what had just happened.

He held the passenger door opened for Naomi but frowned when he saw her glowering several feet away.

"What is it?" he demanded.

She turned her nose up at him. "Is subtlety even a word in your vocabulary?"

He snorted with humor. "What's the purpose of having wealth if I can't show it off?"

She rolled her eyes. Like the first time he'd seen her, she was dressed in a full spandex bodysuit that had some kind of leather armor covering her vital areas — upper back, forearms, thighs and chest. Her black boots came up to her calves, she had a dozen empty sheaths that had once housed her blades and two empty gun holsters hanging under her arms.

Even without her weapons, she looked dangerous — deadly and far more beautiful than anyone he'd ever laid eyes on. The skin-hugging getup clung to her slender form, emphasizing her slim curves and muscles. Where his sister-in-law appeared small and dainty, like she couldn't harm a fly, Naomi looked every bit the lethal warrior he knew her to be.

"I bet you're one of those people who name their cars, aren't you?" she asked with a disdainful sniff.

Sal stiffened, pursing his lips. "Don't be absurd."

Actually, he *did* name his cars, all of them. Why was that such a bad thing? And why the hell did it offend him that she seemed to be making it a negative?

Naomi shoved past him and flopped onto the passenger seat. Sal hid a smile. Others might be put off or frightened by her constant attitude, but he adored it. It made him all the more determined to seduce her. The victory would be that much sweeter.

Within moments, they were peeling out of the parking lot. Sal did his best to focus on navigating through the dark streets, but her rich scent of chocolate that filled his car drove him mad with want. He'd missed her scent, missed having it wrapped around him while he made love to her.

By the gods, he was pathetic. He'd never been so enthralled over a woman, so consumed by lust and the need to just be by her side.

The former months had been utter torment for him. After a hot, passionate romp that had ended in him holding her while they slept, he'd awakened to find himself alone—no note, no goodbye, nothing. She'd just vanished off the face of the earth, leaving him by himself, confused and downright grumpy.

He'd been so sure that after giving into his touch, the woman would be butter for him. While he didn't form attachments to lovers, he was accustomed to women seeking him out, begging for the inexplicable pleasure he could provide them. He'd been positive Naomi would be the same, losing that cool façade and clinging to him the way all women did.

So yes, perhaps it had been a blow to his pride that she'd done the total opposite and refused to see him. He hadn't heard from her since, and Siovon had been tight-lipped, determined to keep him from finding Naomi. No amount of bribes or pleas would make her cave in. To add to his annoyance with the entire situation, he'd been uninterested in anyone else. Him— the insatiable lover who'd spent a thousand years sating the desires of the most beautiful women, a man who could spend an entire week indulged in an endless lovemaking session with multiple partners—totally flaccid after an all-too-swift one-night stand with a woman he knew very little about.

Oh, how his family had mocked and tormented him about the woman who'd successfully pulled a 'him' on him. He'd sworn to get back at Naomi, to seduce her until he got her out of his system, then teach her a lesson about toying with his mind. As the months had passed, he'd settled for pretending she'd never entered his life to begin with. Even when Siovon had called him earlier in the evening to tell him Naomi was on the way to his club, he'd been dead set on acting as though she meant nothing to him.

It had almost worked, too.

Except the moment he sensed her presence, all petty thoughts of revenge had flown out of the window. His vision had zeroed in on her until his surroundings had become a blur. It was like a missing piece of him had returned, the hole that had been drilled into his chest stitching itself closed.

The implications of his reaction made him conclude that Naomi could very well be his truemate — the one woman he was destined to spend the rest of eternity with. Every vampire had one. Sometimes it took centuries to find them, sometimes they never got the chance. Sal knew plenty who longed for the day they'd meet theirs, but he'd never been one of them.

'Why settle for one woman when I can have countless others?' had always been his motto. Too many times he'd seen his brethren fall to their knees in despair after losing their mate. His father and Cass were the closest ones to him who had gone through it. He'd almost lost them to either Rogueism or death, for the pain they'd endured had been too much for them to handle.

Sal had never wanted to risk going through that shit, so he'd been content with the thought of never finding his truemate. Yet there she likely was, less than two feet away from him, gazing out of the window at the passing city lights. The signs were all there — constant lust for only her, the driving need to be by her side, the mind-blowing sex, a sudden burst of emotions he could no longer control. Sex played a key role in figuring out whether or not a vamp had found their truemate. After doing the deed, it was said that the two lovers could feel each other's presence in their hearts.

Sal wasn't sure what the hell that meant, but just before he'd fallen asleep with Naomi in his arms, he'd felt something change inside him. It had been like a feeling of peace settling in his chest, filling him with a warmth and comfort he'd never experienced.

The only lingering reluctance was his fear to admit it aloud. Naomi had already rejected him by running away, and even now she continued to push him away. He wanted her to trust and open up to him, but doing so would take patience and determination on his end, two things he had an immense amount of.

However, he wondered how deep Naomi's distrust ran. While he didn't know the details, it was clear that she'd been hurt so many times in the past, perhaps enough to where she'd never completely open up to anyone.

"Which one of your brothers did you say we are we going to see?" she asked, jarring him from his musings.

"Cassander."

He didn't need to look at her to know she rolled her eyes. "No shit. Which one is he? I know he's not Lucy, the ice prince. That would leave either the kitty shifter or the twins, if I remember correctly. And so help me, if we're going to go see Tweedledee or Tweedledum, you can just let me out right here."

Sal tilted his head back and laughed. "Good gods. If any of them heard the names you just tossed out, there would be hell to pay. Lucian would have a damn stroke."

Naomi grunted, shrugging a shoulder. "I'm not good with names. There's too many of you as it is. Honestly, someone should have given Cyrus the talk about contraception."

He flashed her a smile. "Lucian is the ice prince, as you put it. The were-cougar is my brother-in-law, Marc. The twins are Darius and Julius. There's Andreas as well, but you didn't get to meet him back then. Cass is the blond one who—"

"Oh, the Viking," she murmured. "Siovon told me that he's the most bearable one of you all, mostly because he doesn't talk much."

"Did she now?" The information didn't sit well with Sal, but not because of his sister-in-law's low opinion of him. Siovon had made her contempt for him clear the first day he'd met her. He'd been amused, and still was, truth be told.

The annoyed feeling settling in his gut was directed at the thought of Naomi allowing herself to relax in Cass' presence, when all she did was fuss and fight in his. Jealousy wasn't a word that had ever been in his dictionary but, damn the gods, it was tonight—another sign that Naomi was his truemate.

He shook his head, slowing to a stop at a red light. "Tell me about this symbol. Why the interest—and why would someone want you dead over it?"

Naomi was quiet for so long that he feared she wouldn't answer. It just figured. She didn't reveal information, especially if it was pertaining to herself. To her, everyone who crossed her path was an enemy. Even after a steamy bout of rough sex that had blown his entire world away, it seemed to have had the opposite effect on her.

Damn the gods.

However, she surprised him when she heaved a sigh. "My mother had a pendant with that symbol on it long ago, and she refused to talk about it. I've come across a few people with that same mark tatted on them, and each of them were tied to some kind of black-market distribution. I need to know if my mother was involved with them in any way."

Sal pressed his foot to the gas to continue driving. "Your mother—a fury, I'm...assuming?"

A flare of anger burned in his chest, but somehow, he knew it wasn't directed at him. It was due to his connection to Naomi, and whatever memory that had dredged up wasn't a pleasant one. "*Si*. She was killed by her peers after they discovered I wasn't a pureblood."

He sucked in a sharp breath and glanced at her. She glared out of the window, but she wasn't able to hide her sorrow. Though the connection between them had grown faint over their months apart, he could still feel bits and pieces of her emotions. He wondered if she could sense his presence as well. Sex would strengthen the bond, and he had every intention of seducing her soon enough. At the moment, however, he didn't want to overstep his boundaries and have her withdraw back behind her defenses. The fact that she'd even agreed to allow him to come along was a huge step that worked in his favor.

He returned his gaze to the road. "What does learning about this group mean to you?"

She reached for her ponytail. The thick mass fell to her waist and had silver bands spread through its length every six inches. She toyed with the tail at the end, something that had him smiling. His sister did the same thing with her hair when she became nervous or lost in thought. It was refreshing to know that such a proud warrior wasn't as detached as she wanted to think.

Of course, he wouldn't mention it. She'd punch him in the face for calling attention to such a tic.

"Peace," she whispered, her breath fogging the glass of her window.

"Peace? Peace for what?"

She sighed. "If my mother's involvement with this group was the true reason for her death, I can find peace. It would mean that my being born didn't kill her." She sent him a wary glance out of the corners of her eyes. "I know Siovon set you up to try to stop me. That's why she didn't tell me that you were the owner of The Lotus. I don't expect either of you to understand why this is important to me, but I won't change my mind."

Sal didn't bother correcting her assumption. Siovon hadn't asked him to stand in Naomi's way at all. He had been asked to stay with her until the end — wherever that led. She was on a path to confront her past, something that could lead to heartache and self-destruction. However, there had been no need for the request. The thought of Naomi heading into danger made him eager to stand at her side for protection. It was foolish, no doubt, given that she was an assassin with a frightening reputation, but that didn't matter. The need to be with her and lend her his strength was too powerful to ignore.

Placing her hand in his, he brought her slender fingers to his lips to kiss her knuckles. Her breath hitched, and the sweet scent of her arousal spiked in the air. The potent pheromones resulted in his pants growing tight, and he hope to the high heavens that it was too dark for her to notice. While he was confident in his sexual prowess, she wasn't like any other woman who'd been an easy seduction for him. She'd probably call him a sick pervert or some such insult. "I have no desire to stop you, Naomi, just to accompany you and make someone pay for our near-death experience."

It was a slight lie and they both knew it, but to his relief, she didn't call him out.

Instead, she closed her eyes and tugged her hand from his hold. "Just don't get in my way, vampire," she said, turning back to face the window.

The fact that she didn't curse or growl at him was a good sign. At least, Sal took it as such. He assumed it meant she didn't detest him quite as much as she pretended to. "I make no promises, dove." Relaxing into his seat, he wove them through the night traffic.

* * * *

It was a rare occurrence for Cassander Gordano to leave the comfort of his lair. The few times he did was if his father or his clan chief Lucian commanded him to do something — or if he needed to check on the status of one of his gyms.

On this night, it was the latter.

Though his top two gyms held monthly cage fights where customers could bet on the fighters, once a year there was a tournament where the winner earned several rewards, including triple the prize money and a championship title that was considered a great feat. The fights were going to take place in a handful of weeks, and he had to make sure everything was being set up the correct way. Not that he didn't trust his managers to perform the tasks, but every detail needed his approval before they could carry on.

Luckily it hadn't taken long to do. He was eager to return to his lair, as always. Being surrounded by acres of silent land with only his shadow to keep him company was all he cared for. Yeah, he was a recluse through and through.

He loved his family. The past half-year had been far more uplifting than he'd ever expected. Ava had returned to them, making their family complete again. She'd even found her truemate and was due to give birth soon. Andreas had been cured of a disease that had almost claimed his life and Lucian had found his own truemate. In all honesty, his family's happiness was all he could ever hope for.

But he'd be lying if he said he wasn't a tad envious of his siblings for finding their destined loves. He'd already found his truemate, a human named Maria whose memory forever tormented him.

Vampires mating more than once was beyond rare. Only a few were fortunate enough to find a second truemate after losing the first, and Cass had never once believed he was part of that equation. After all the damage he'd caused in his younger days, fate just wasn't in his favor.

Before the depressing thoughts could take permanent residence in his brain, he made his way through the large building that made up Black Iron Fitness. Demons scrambled out of his way, their expressions fearful of his stature. It was nothing he wasn't used to. At six-foot-six and built with muscles upon muscles that bulged with every slight movement, he knew his size evoked fear among the people he came across. Well, that and the knowledge that he was a Royal vampire. Very, very few were stupid enough to try to get on his bad side.

Not that he was anywhere near as violent as he used to be, but if allowing them to believe otherwise would keep them from approaching him, so be it.

The building was three stories high with tunnels leading toward the underground arena. Grunts and growls could be heard from everywhere as men and women put the different exercise machines to work. Cass only spared them a passing glance as he took the stairs to the first floor. The gym had all the modern accommodations gym-goers wanted — updated equipment, an indoor pool, multiple saunas, an array of classes that taught yoga, pole-dancing, martial arts and a wide variety of other things.

What truly made his gyms stand out were the heavy weights and cardio machines that had been specifically designed to be demon friendly. It would take the strength of three human buffs to lift a single barbell.

Cass turned down a hall and passed several rooms with large windows that revealed a handful of classes in procession. He turned another corner that held more rooms, those made for people to rent if they wanted to work out in private. As he strolled toward the exit, he heard a series of angry growls and grunts coming from the last room on the left.

He never lingered to spy on his customers, and tonight shouldn't have been any different. However, there was a faint tint of desperation coating the air that piqued his curiosity. He approached the window. The blinds were drawn halfway, and inside he caught sight of swift movements going at a hanging punching bag.

Cass gave a hard swallow as he eyed the woman. She was tall — at least six feet — and shaped like an Amazon warrior, with tight muscles that flexed with every punch and kick. She wore black-and-orange spandex pants with a matching training bra that revealed a flat, toned stomach with smooth skin the color of nutmeg. Every so often, the overhead light caught the flash of gold, making his gaze drift to the thin bands clamped around her forearms and biceps. Her dark hair was pulled into two French braids that fell just short of her shoulder blades, swinging with every fluid motion of her body.

She was merciless as she assaulted the bag, dodging this way and that, as if fighting a real opponent. Cass dropped his gaze to her ass, and to his amazement, he found his pants growing tight. He grunted and shifted his sudden erection.

That's...new. It had been years since he'd last felt even the slightest of wiggles down there. It had been centuries, in fact. His brothers often teased that he'd been castrated, and in all honesty, he'd begun to believe it. It was refreshing to know he wasn't dead below the waist anymore.

Still, his reaction to the woman in the room surprised the hell out of him. Whether it was her beautiful body or the way she worked the punching bag like a pro, he was turned on from watching her.

And yep, I'm a fucking creep.

With a disgusted grunt, he started to turn away but paused when the woman gave a loud, frustrated growl. She kicked the bag so hard that it rocked beneath the force, the metal holding it above the ground creaking, as if it wanted to give way.

Panting, she placed her forearm on the bag and leaned her head against it. Then, her shoulders shook. Alarmed, Cass realized she was crying.

He frowned as the sour scent of her desperation flared again. For some odd reason, he felt like comforting her. He wanted to pull her into his arms and hold her while she relieved her burdens onto him. It was a devastating feeling, for he'd never felt the need to alleviate anyone outside his family, let alone a total stranger.

As if sensing his eyes on her, the woman lifted her head. Her features hinted at Native American descent, and her teary brown eyes were wide as she spotted him through the glass. Time seemed to freeze as they stared at one another, neither moving a muscle, not even to blink.

Cass' heart must have forgotten how to work, because it seemed to halt dead in his chest. He was stunned, glued to one spot and unable to tear his eyes from her. Likewise, she seemed to be stuck in the same trance as she watched him. An eternity could have passed, for all he knew. As if in slow motion, she straightened to face him. There was a questioning look in the dark pits of her eyes. For a moment, he contemplated going in there to speak to her, but hell if he knew what he'd say.

The instant was broken, however, when his phone chimed. He pulled it out and glanced down at the text message from Sal. It would appear his brother was on the way to his house for some kind of emergency. He gave a one-word reply, tucked the apparatus back into his pocket then peered up at the woman.

To his disappointment, she'd resumed her workout, her back turned to him as she continued punching and kicking the bag. Cass lingered for another moment, silently wishing she'd look at him again.

She didn't.

With a deep sigh, he continued onward and exited through the door. Something in his mind urged him to go back, but he ignored it. Even if he did talk to her, what did he think would happen? Maybe if she were interested in him, he could take her out to dinner, then go back to his lair and indulge in a bit of pleasure, maybe even for a few weeks. Not that he'd ever gone on a date or given himself to anyone since Maria's death, but perhaps that woman would offer a pleasant change for once.

However, it would never go beyond that. Developing romantic relationships were impossible for vampires. Even if they were to fall in love with someone, unless that person was their truemate, it would never last. It would be fun and riveting at first, but the feelings would soon wear off, leaving behind two bitter lovers who could no longer stand each other.

While plenty of demons he knew — *ahem, Sal and Darius* — were comfortable with that type of lifestyle, Cass wasn't. He longed for that eternal happiness only a truemate could provide. He wanted someone at his side, providing him with an endless number of smiles and laughter. Someone he could wake up to every night and kiss

He approached his vehicle, and within minutes, he was on the road heading for him isolated home. The farther he drove, though, the wider the feeling of emptiness spread through his chest.

With a frown, he rubbed at it as his mind returned to that woman. He'd never seen her in his gym before, but that wasn't surprising. He only ventured there once every few months, so it wasn't like he got to meet every one of his customers. Still, something about her made him curious to know more.

Who is she?

Chapter Four

Though Naomi hadn't remembered the name of the imposing male who looked like he'd just stepped off a Viking ship, he was impossible to forget.

Towering over her and Sal, the man was…daunting, to say the least. He was beautiful, like all vampires, but intimidating. The top half of his platinum-blond hair was pulled into a series of braids that tied into a ponytail, while the remaining hair fell down his back in thick waves. He was pale like Sal, with the same Roman facial structure as his brothers, including the icy, pale blue eyes.

Unlike Sal, however, the man looked like he ate scrap metal for breakfast. He also didn't seem as outgoing or flashy. He was dressed in a pair of jeans and a gray T-shirt, his face set in hard lines as he studied the image of the inverted eye of Horus.

He'd been observing the paper in silence for the last ten minutes, and Naomi was close to snapping in annoyance for him to hurry up and say something. She was growing impatient, especially after having to wait on him to arrive for over an hour. Apparently, Sal had assumed his brother was home instead of calling ahead, so when they'd arrived on the private property to find it deserted, they'd had to wait until Cass left Chicago to join them. Of course, she'd given him a piece of her mind over that one, and much to her chagrin, all he'd done was flashed that goofy grin, as if he got off on women berating him. *Imbecile.*

Impervious to her rising irritation, Cass at last lifted his gaze from the paper. "The original sign of Horus means protection and power. With it designed this way, it could very well mean the opposite—a symbol of chaos and death, if you will."

Naomi rolled her eyes. "Yeah, no shit—"

Sal slapped his hand over her mouth, cutting off her sarcastic words. "I've seen it before on a group of black marketers ages ago. Naomi also came across a few of them."

Cass nodded, his gaze shifting between Sal and Naomi with great amusement. He strolled over to a large desk holding four different computers. On the wall adjacent to them, a line of TV monitors revealed cameras located all around his property. "If I recall, not much is known about them. They're very…secretive." He began tapping away at a keyboard, bringing up a list of files on one computer screen. After series of clicks, he pulled up a folder that held a single document containing two pages.

Naomi scoffed. "That's it?"

"As I said, they're hard to get information on." Cass printed out the papers and handed them to Sal. "They call themselves The Oracles."

Sal returned to Naomi's side. "The Oracles?" he echoed. "The eye of Horus is an Egyptian symbol, whereas oracles are a reference to Greek mythology. Is there some kind of cross in religion? If so, I don't see how the two correlate."

Cass shrugged, the muscles making up his broad shoulders threatening to rip apart the shirt he wore. "Your guess is as good as mine."

Still annoyed, Naomi read the entire length of both papers. "Where did you even get this information?"

"A few years ago, Lynx—the lieutenant of our father's Guard—was sent to investigate the sudden disappearances of members from a local wolf pack in Baton Rouge, Louisiana."

"Wolves? I thought you leeches only stuck to leeches," Naomi commented. "Sort of a bloodsucking birds-of-a-feather-type deal."

Cass shot up one blond brow. "*Merda*, you've got a set of balls on you."

Unconcerned, she cracked her knuckles. "Because I can back up what I say. If you have a problem, we can throw down right here."

"I do enjoy a good challenge."

Sal tapped his foot in annoyance. "If you two are done flirting," he growled, glaring at her.

Naomi rolled her eyes. Her statement wasn't meant to be a joke. She'd never been one to bite her tongue. If she managed to offend someone in the process, oh-fucking-well. And if they wanted to do something about it, she was always ready for a fight. "Go on."

Sal huffed. "Our father's influence is widely spread, so he has alliances all over the world that aren't just limited to vampires. If one of his allies has a problem they cannot handle, they'll come to him with a request to intervene, and in return, they are indebted to him."

Cass nodded, adding on, "The local wolf pack had members who were going off the grid, and Lynx was sent to find out why. Turns out, those who had been kidnapped were murdered with their pelts being sold on the black-market channel in New Orleans."

Naomi felt her stomach turn at the thought. Who could be so...cruel to do something so sick and twisted? Hell, she might be a ruthless killer, but at least all of her kills were clean — a single gunshot to the head or a stab in the heart.

The image of pools of blood and loose limbs strewn about a cavern in a distant mountain flashed in her mind, damn near making her lose the contents in her stomach.

Most of my kills, anyway.

She squeezed her eyes shut and forced the thoughts away before opening them again. "What about the symbol? How did he come across The Oracles?"

Sal sent her a look of concern, as if sensing her unease, despite her attempt to hide it. He didn't say anything, though, only sidled closer to her and brushed the back of his fingers against hers. It was an intimate gesture that made her uncomfortable, yet it eased the nausea rolling through her. *Strange.*

Cass returned his attention to the computer. "On his first night there, he was attacked by a group of demons, as if they'd anticipated his arrival. As you can imagine, Lynx didn't earn his spot in Cyrus' Guard for nothing. He managed to capture one of his attackers alive — a Turnblood — and with a bit of...persuading, he'd gotten the sap to spill some information. Unfortunately, he died before Lynx was able to get any more than what's there on that paper."

Naomi didn't have to ask what kind of 'persuading' Lynx had done. It didn't take a genius to know it was far more than idle threats. She looked back down at the papers in her hand. There wasn't much information to go by. The Turnblood—a vampire who'd been turned rather than born—had been a novice and hadn't known much about the group, other than their name and that they made up the darker part of the underworld black market. Or, UBM, as Siovon called it.

Contrary to its name, however, the market wasn't in Hell. It was in a small realm simply called The Shade that sat between the human world and Tartarus, the upper level of Hell that was inhabited by demons. Where Tartarus and other zones were impossible to get into without a special pass from the Imperials, The Shade was far easier. So long as a full-blooded demon knew where to find one of the gateways, they were allowed entrance.

Of course, it wasn't so easy staying alive after that. Naomi had never been there, but the rumors about The Shade were all the same. The demons who ran the darker section of UBM could be quite ruthless, and they were always looking to make a quick buck, regardless of integrity. Honor had no meaning there. It was every demon for himself, which was why no one lingered longer than necessary.

"So, these people," Naomi mumbled, more to herself than the two brothers, "they're some kind of cult who sell living creatures and the remains of the deceased?"

Cass grunted. The grim twist of his lips made it clear that he was just as unnerved by the ethics of The Oracles as she was. "It would appear so."

Naomi remained silent. The entire situation was sickening. It was bad enough that they killed people for their body parts, but to sell living beings as slaves too? She didn't know which was worse — and if her mother had been a part of it in any way...

Dios. She recalled her past, when she'd been sold into slavery by her own people, traded on the black market like a piece of meat at the tender age of eighteen. She'd been young and vulnerable after just having come into her succubus needs. It had always struck her as odd how the furies had chosen to sell her instead of killing her, as they'd done her mother, but what if it had been her mother's will? Or what if there had been others involved in the market, but only her mother had been the one to get caught?

There were far too many questions without answers, and though a portion of her screamed to turn around and find some other way to move on from her past, a stronger voice urged that she find the truth — that it was the only way for her to find the peace she so desperately longed for.

Sal once again brushed his fingers across her knuckles. "Are you okay to do this, dove?" he whispered. It was foolish, considering they were all demons with heightened senses that could hear a flea tiptoeing into the room, but she appreciated his attempt at privacy.

She gave a small nod, straightening her shoulders. She glanced at Cass, who looked confused by the whole ordeal. Though whether it was because of the information they were seeking or Sal's and her seeming closeness, she didn't know. "Do you know anything about the leaders of The Oracles or how I can find them?"

"What's on those papers is all I know. I'm sorry." He frowned, peering at Sal with concern then back at her. "What's this about?"

When Naomi hesitated, Sal stepped up. "Someone placed a bomb on her car tonight and took half of my parking lot in the explosion. We have reason to believe the ones responsible are members of The Oracles."

"*Cazzo*," Cass breathed, scrubbing a hand over his face. "What makes you so sure it was them? She is..." He trailed off, seeming to be worried that he'd offend her with his words.

Naomi waved it aside. "I'm an assassin with loads of enemies. You're right. However, I had information that an elf who carried the Horus tattoo has been a frequent customer of The Lotus. He was supposed to be there tonight, but he wasn't. Instead, someone tried to kill me, as if they'd known I was looking for him."

"You think it was a setup?"

She shifted, unwilling to say the words aloud. However, she wasn't stupid. Tonight's events had been far too extreme to have been a coincidence. As much as she didn't want to doubt a comrade she'd known for years, all signs pointed to Chè betraying her. If that was the case, she was going to have to play her cards right and feign ignorance until she got him in her presence. Which reminded her...

She pulled the burner phone out of her pocket and sent out a coded text message to Chè's primary line, one that was an SOS, asking him to meet her somewhere. Chè was intelligent and would figure out she suspected him of foul play if she'd called him right then, so she had to tread carefully. He was even less trusting than she was, even with people he considered friends. All she had to do was wait for him to respond with a place to meet.

It didn't take long, as usual. Less than a minute had passed when her phone buzzed with the coordinates of where to meet him, along with a time.

Looking up at the two brothers, who were immersed in a quiet conversation, she opened her mouth to say something but thought otherwise. Her business with them was done. She's gained all the information she could from the Viking—*damn, what was his name again?*—and though it had been helpful, all it'd done was confirm the suspicions she already had. She still needed a location or a name, at the very least.

With a shrug, she turned around and headed toward the library door. She'd almost made it there when Sal called out, "Naomi, where are you going?"

She paused, peering over her shoulder with a single eyebrow raised in question. "I'm done here. There's no need to linger."

The Viking quirked his lips into a smile, easing the hard lines around his face. She got the feeling he didn't smile very often. "She doesn't play around, does she, *fratello*?" he asked Sal.

Sal grunted a response and moved to her side. "Do you know where we're going next?"

Naomi blinked in surprise. "We?"

He scowled in annoyance. "Yes, *we*. Did you think I would call it quits here?"

"Honestly, yeah. I did."

Her blunt words irritated him, going by the way his frown deepened. "Why are you so eager to be rid of me?"

Naomi crossed her arms. "Why are you so hard to get rid of? I already told you that this has nothing to do with you. You could get hurt or killed."

Just like that, Sal's frustration was replaced by a smug smile. "Concerned for me, are you?" He stroked the back of his knuckles along her jaw.

That single, tender gesture was enough to send a scorching heat to Naomi's cheeks — that, and the realization that she'd just revealed she truly was concerned for his wellbeing. *Dammit*.

She took a step back. "Don't be absurd," she grumbled. "I just refuse to have Gordano blood on my hands. I don't need your annoying-ass family looking for my head."

"And the balls continue to grow," the blond muttered to himself.

Ignoring him, Sal chuckled and closed the distance between him and Naomi. "You're a terrible liar," he whispered, leaning in to kiss her.

Not for the first time, she wondered how in the hell it was possible for him to make her bones melt with the lightest of touches — and with a mere piece of fabric preventing skin-on-skin contact. As it was, the feel of his soft lips smoothing over hers sent tingles of desire to her libido. He brought his hand up to the back of her neck, massaging as he pressed his lips more firmly against hers. Naomi's knees threatened to buckle as a roaring hunger rose from deep within her.

Someone cleared their throat, interrupting the heated moment between them. At once, she and Sal jerked their heads to look at the forgotten brother with surprised eyes. His expression was a cross between discomfort and amusement. "While I'm pleased the call is affecting you both, there are plenty of spare bedrooms you can venture to for privacy. I don't want any love stains on my carpet."

Naomi blinked, stepping out of Sal's hold. "What are you talking about? What call?"

Sal growled in warning, jumping in before his brother could respond. "Nothing. He's speaking metaphorically."

Naomi knew he was lying, but before she could question them further, Sal was tugging her out of the door. "Thanks for the info, *fratello*."

"Be careful, Salvator," the Viking called out, his deep voice echoing off the walls. "Call if you need anything."

"Will do."

Naomi wanted to dig in her heels and demand he tell her the truth, but the cramps spreading throughout her body made her grit her teeth against the pain. Dammit, she was screwed. Not literally, of course, because that would have solved her dilemma.

No, the medicine Siovon had given her had been in her rental car, now destroyed from the blast. That treatment would have suppressed her needs, making the cramps vanish for several days before she could no longer push her desire away.

Though Sal's kiss had started out innocent enough, it had rocked her straight to her core, jumpstarting the fire in her blood. The cramps would only get worse the longer she went without sex, meaning she had only a few hours before they became full-blown unbearable.

Truth be told, it was miraculous she'd managed to go this long without going crazy. The last time she'd done the deed was four months ago with Sal, as her body and mind had rejected all other men who'd crossed her path. Normally, all it would take was for her to be within a certain vicinity of a horny male and her body would react. And even with the medicine, she could never go more than a couple of weeks without sex.

However, it had been months, and while the resulting cramps had been painful, they'd been tolerable, vanishing after she drank Siovon's potion. The only explanation she could come up with was that Sal had given her a mind-blowing orgasm that had satisfied her urges for weeks.

It wasn't plausible, but she hadn't questioned it. She'd enjoyed not being forced to lie with a male she didn't know or care about, just because her body demanded it.

Now, though, there was no wishing away the cramping of her lower organs. Sal's kiss had awakened the passion that had lay dormant, and it would not be dismissed until she gave in.

With a soft sigh, she followed behind him until they were outside and nearing his car. He held the door open for her, but before she slid in, he caught her wrist and gave her another swift kiss. Then, he walked around to the driver's side.

Naomi swallowed hard. She wouldn't tell him of her needs. She couldn't. The last time she'd given in had resulted in her mental defenses weakening. It had taken sheer determination to keep from seeking him out and curling into his embrace.

No, she couldn't allow herself to sink to that level again. Salvator was no different from Reinaldo, the man who'd made her life a living hell. They were both rich and powerful men who used their charm and good looks to lure helpless women to their beds. While the sex had been great, there was a monster beneath that suave beauty that would show its true colors soon enough. She wouldn't fall for the tricks—not again.

Steeling her resolve, she nodded to herself. She'd allow Sal to travel with her, but only for his resources. It was just business — nothing more, nothing less.

Movement out of the corner of her eye caught her attention, and she blinked at Sal in confusion. "What?"

He frowned. "I was talking to you."

She tilted her head. "You were?"

"I asked what's our next destination. Do you often zone out like that?"

Yes. "No," she lied. "How long will it take to get to Rosehill Cemetery?"

He thought it over for a moment before saying, "About an hour and a half. Why?"

"I'm meeting an old colleague there. He's the one who told me about the elf, and I need to find out if it was a setup."

"I'll rip the bastard's throat out."

"I'll do it myself if he has betrayed me. However" — she narrowed her eyes at him — "it'll be best if you stay in the car."

He scoffed. "You should know by now that's not going to happen, dove."

She rolled her eyes, having already expecting he'd say that. "Just don't do anything that will cause alarm. I can handle him on my own. You just sit back and look pretty."

Sal made a choked sound of shock. "Excuse me? Sit back and look — "

She waved her hand. "Come on. Time's ticking. Oh, and give me a blade or a gun. Thanks to your stupid club rules, I had to leave mine in the car, which are nothing more than melted metal by now."

"By the gods," he grouched, starting up the car, "you're so demanding."

She shrugged, not caring in the least bit. "As if you have much room to talk."

He grumbled a series of Latin curses before buckling in. Then, he pulled off.

Chapter Five

It was nearing two a.m. when Naomi and Sal pulled to a stop at the west entrance of Rosehill Cemetery. The Gothic-style entry gate and gatehouse were a beautiful sight, giving one the idea of being teleported centuries into the past. Though graveyards weren't to Naomi's usual taste, she had to admit there was a certain calm about the vast landscape, along with a historical feel that made her want to pick up a book and research the history of the place.

Another day, she promised herself. Tonight, she had to be alert. Chè had been in the guild even longer than Siovon, so one had to keep all defenses in place when meeting him.

The gates were locked, but that was to be expected. Sal slid an arm around her waist and teleported them onto the concrete path inside. She still wasn't used to the feeling of her bones turning to jelly, but at least it didn't make her head spin anymore like it used to. It was a sign that she was growing used to his powers poofing them around.

Or it was a sign that she was just getting used to him — his touch, scent and overall presence. Despite her best efforts to pretend he meant nothing to her, every passing minute made it harder to keep up the pretense.

Sal lingered longer than necessary, seemingly not wanting to withdraw his arm. Naomi meant to glare at him, but at the close proximity, all she did was gaze in awe. She couldn't see very well in the dark, but the sky was clear and there was an old-fashioned lamppost shining down on them. He looked like something out of a cheesy romantic flick, what with the light spilling over his pale features in an ethereal glow. What was even more trite was the piercing way her heart constricted in her chest, bringing forth all the emotions she'd refused to analyze for months.

He curved his lips into a small smile. "You're beautiful," he whispered.

So are you.

The words almost slipped from her mouth, which would have been embarrassing as hell. Salvator Gordano didn't take anyone or anything seriously, so she doubted her complimenting him would mean much. He knew he was beautiful. Every woman who crossed his path knew it. They fawned over him all the time, and he took great amusement in the attention he received.

Even his words to her had been a mockery.

Naomi clenched her fists and stepped out of his hold. She wasn't beautiful, and a bitter voice in her head taunted that he was only teasing her. He'd seen the ugly scars on her face, as well as the ones marring the rest of her body. She was too skinny, her breasts were too small and her attitude was less than appealing. There was *nothing* beautiful about her. Reinaldo had made sure of that.

Gritting her teeth, she forced back the hurt that threatened to surge and turned her back on him. "Let's go," she commanded.

"Naomi—"

But she'd already started walking away. She didn't want to hear his lies or listen to whatever smooth lines he had to say. They were all just to get in her pants. That was the type of bastard Sal was. He used pretty words to make women feel desired, but it was for his own gain, not because he meant them.

Naomi straightened her shoulders and marched onward. She had to rely on the distant lamps to light her way, following the winding paved walkways that wove throughout the cemetery. More than once, her attention was drawn to a statue she passed by or a grand crypt with beautiful images carved into the structure. After about twenty minutes of walking, they came upon a small pond with a fountain in the middle, the perimeter surrounded by tall willow trees.

"Who is this comrade we're meeting again?" Sal asked from beside her, seemingly not as impressed with the landscape as she was. He lived in Chicago, so of course he must have seen or heard about the large cemetery plenty of times.

"A gargoyle named Chè," Naomi responded, stroking the hilt of a blade resting in the sheath at her hip. "He's even less fond of leeches than I am, so don't do anything stupid."

Sal had kept a stash of weapons in the trunk of his car, proving he wasn't as impervious to the constant dangers of the world as one would think, given his appearance. He'd handed her a half dozen knives and daggers to replace her lost ones, for which she'd been grateful. Where some people felt comforted by wearing a lucky charm or a family heirloom, Naomi felt at ease when armed.

"Chè?" Sal repeated, slowing his pace.

Naomi paused and glanced over her shoulder at him. "Problem?"

"Hell yeah, there's a problem. Back in Alleman when you were…you know, you said you needed Chè. Is he a lover of yours?"

Heat rose in Naomi's cheeks, and she hid her embarrassment by crossing her arms. "*Dios*. What business is it of yours?"

He growled, stepping up to her. "Is he — or is he not?"

She rolled her eyes. "I'd hardly call him a lover. There was no meaning behind what we did."

"Oh, darling, surely our fun nights together meant more than just physical release," a deep voice drawled.

Naomi tensed, turning to spot Chè stepping from under a willow some yards away. Though he didn't hold the surreal beauty vampires had, the man was a looker in his own right. He was wearing a black wifebeater and low-riding denims, and nearly every stretch of skin on his arms and chest was covered with tattoos. His dark hair was in a short military style, and his jaw bore a five o'clock shadow that only emphasized the hard, no-nonsense look in his eyes. He looked human enough, but in his true form, his resemblance to the sculptures of the grotesque beasts wasn't too far off the mark.

"Chè," Naomi said with a tilt of her head.

"Naomi," he replied, returning the gesture. "I wasn't aware you were bringing a friend."

She gave an indifferent shrug and faced him. She made sure to keep her tone and expression neutral. "*Si*, well, my current means of transportation is now melted into the ground somewhere. I don't suppose you'd know anything about that?"

His face was its usual stony mask, giving nothing away. "I don't."

"*Cazzate*," Sal growled.

Naomi held her arm out, stopping him from attacking. She stroked the hilt of her blade, narrowing her eyes on the gargoyle. "I'll only give you one chance to answer truthfully, Chè."

He raised an amused brow. "Or what? You'll sic your vampire on me?"

She lowered her arm and stepped forward. "No, but I'll kill you myself and drop your remains in a pit of hellhounds." She took another step, lowering her voice. "And you *know* I mean it."

His lips twitched as he fought to keep from smiling. Despite the fact that they both knew she would carry out her dark threat, Chè was skilled enough that even if he were facing death, he would never show fear. Whether it was true bravery or arrogance, it made him a fearsome adversity.

Chè closed the distance between them, ignoring Sal's warning growl. He took her chin between his fingers and moved to be eye level with her. "I had nothing to do with what happened to you tonight. After I found out about the explosion, I went looking for the elf myself. I did not — nor have I ever — betrayed you."

Naomi released a breath of relief. He was telling the truth, something she felt all the way down to her bones. While she wasn't the best at reading emotions, she knew Chè and Siovon well enough to figure out when they were lying or keeping something from her.

Before Naomi could step away, Salvator pushed Chè, sending him back a few steps. "Don't touch her," he growled, his body tensed and poised for a fight.

Chè righted himself, smirking at Sal. "What's the matter, vampire? Can't stand a little competition?"

"Competition my ass. She said you weren't lovers."

"Ah, so she did," Chè boasted. "Nah, we weren't lovers. We just like to fuck like wild beasts."

The words hadn't even left his mouth when Sal dashed forward, swinging his fist at Chè's face. The resounding crunch of bone made Naomi's stomach turn, though it was hard to tell if it was from Sal's fist or Chè's jaw. *Probably both.*

Chè threw his own punch at Sal, and just like that, the two went at it like dogs fighting over a piece of meat.

Naomi grimaced, not liking that description, since the piece of meat in question was her. Rolling her eyes in annoyance, she padded over to a nearby bench. She made herself comfortable as she watched the two alpha males engaged in a flurry of lightning-swift punches and kicks.

She pulled up the Internet on her phone. She went to the primary search engine and typed in *How to make two dogs get along*.

As she scrolled through the links, she read over the options. "Take a long walk together. Use two separate feeding bowls. Reprimand the aggressor." She paused in her reading to glance up at them. Sal had thrown the first punch, but Chè had goaded him. It seemed like they were both aggressors.

She shrugged and changed her search. *How to reprimand bad dogs*. She clicked on the first link. "No hitting. Damn," she muttered, disappointed. "Time-outs, take their toys away, refuse treats."

With a sigh of resignation, she returned the phone to her pocket. *Man, what a nuisance.* She wasn't one of those pathetic-ass women in the movies who cried and begged the two guys to stop fighting. *Who wants to get in the middle of that?* Not her, because the moment one of them hit her, she would be tearing them both a new asshole. It didn't matter if it'd been an accident or not.

Instead, she shook her head and watched the melee as though it were a rerun of one of those boring, old-timey movies. Despite her knowing Sal and Chè were both expert, elegant fighters, there was nothing graceful about their brawl. They were grappling on the ground, throwing punches and yelling curses at each other. It seemed to be a pretty even match, though.

Not that she was surprised. Salvator was a master vampire — a Royal, at that. His kind were the most powerful in existence. And Chè was a master assassin who was a gargoyle, one of the toughest demons anywhere. He could manipulate his skin to turn into stone, making him close to impenetrable. Not only that, but he was able to wield ancient magic that was no joke to play around with.

It was hard to tell which would be the victor. Sal was teleporting out of sight and reappearing in a way that was disorienting. However, Chè was what he called stone-skinned, so Sal's attacks weren't doing much harm, if any.

Naomi let out a wide yawn, glancing at the time on her phone. At this rate, they'd be there until dawn. Royal vampires didn't burn in the sun, but it sapped at their energy, she knew. And gargoyles reverted to their stone structure in a type of sleep paralysis until the sun set again.

Naomi was also tired during the daytime, but it didn't drain her energy. She was just accustomed to staying up at night and sleeping during the day. It was a good thing they had a few more hours until sunrise, but those two idiots were wasting precious time.

"Naomi, get your fucking bloodsucker off me," Chè yelled.

She blinked. Salvator had Chè on his back and was pummeling him, while Chè had his forearms covering his face in defense. "I'm not his handler," she replied. "You should have never taunted him to begin with."

"I was just speaking the tru — Ouch! The fucker bit me."

Naomi let out a long-suffering sigh and stood. "That's enough, Sal. We have work to do."

Sal continued as if he hadn't heard her — or maybe he was ignoring her. She crossed her arms in annoyance. "Salvator Gordano, get off him right now or I'm leaving without you." *And you won't get your Scooby snacks*, she silently added.

That got Sal's attention. He froze with his fist raised and swung his head at her. His eyes were flashing silver, not unlike a cat's in the night. With a frustrated growl, he shoved off Chè and moved to her side.

His suit was ripped and dirtied, and blood trickled out of one corner of his mouth. Even his hair had fallen from its immaculate ponytail and was lying in strips around his face. Naomi glared at him. "Was any of that necessary?" she demanded.

He wiped his mouth with his torn jacket sleeve, and Naomi caught sight of his bruised knuckles. Instead of answering, he pulled her into him and yanked her mask down. He cupped the back of her head, fisted her hair and, before she could protest, he crushed his lips to hers in a kiss that was rough and possessive.

Naomi was wide-eyed, unsure about what to do. Her body knew, however, for it to melted into him. She grasped the lapels of his jacket and held on for dear life while she kissed him back.

Just as her toes started to curl, he pulled away, leaving them both breathing hard. "Yes," he snapped, "it was necessary. I won't let anyone disrespect you like that. You're not some damned animal to be compared to."

Naomi could swear her heart skipped a beat at his words. The look in his eyes and the seriousness in his voice left no room for discussion. He wasn't teasing or mocking her. He really meant what he'd said, and the realization made Naomi feel…strange, like something inside of her had cracked. Perhaps it was the stone wall she'd erected around her heart. A fissure in the structure broke free, allowing a tiny bit of room for light to squeeze through.

"Jesus Christ, dude, I was only joking," Chè grumbled. He rose as well and wiped blood from his nose. He looked even more disgruntled than Sal, having taken his first ass-whooping in years. It was evident he had been unable to turn to stone in time to protect himself from Sal's blows.

Naomi tugged her mask back into place and turned her back on Sal, though she didn't protest when he pressed his body against her. She was sure that if she looked up at him, he'd be glaring daggers at Chè.

Reinaldo had been possessive, as well, but somehow, his and Sal's reactions were different. If another man had so happened to glance her direction, Reinaldo would throw a fit and take it out on her. Sal, however, had defended her, even though Chè hadn't been serious. It was the first time she had been able to separate the two of them, having been so focused on her undesirable opinion of Sal.

The revelation made her feel conflicted. It was the very first time she was able to see Sal in a positive light. Hell, it was the first time in decades since she'd been able to see any male in a positive light.

Naomi pushed the clashing thoughts away, not wanting to dwell on them. It terrified her far too much. Instead, she looked at Chè, who glared back at them with disgust—specifically Sal. "You said you went looking for the elf after the bomb went off," Naomi said to him, trying to change the subject. "Did you find him?"

He fixed her with a hard look. It was true what she'd said. She and Chè weren't lovers, and they weren't friends. What they had was a business deal. He'd help her when she needed sex, with the understanding that no feelings were to be involved, and in return, she aided him in gathering intel on his missions. Plus, they'd saved each other's lives a time or two, so there was a small line of mutual trust and respect between them. It was a very small line, given that she refused to trust anyone.

Except Siovon, of course, but that was under different circumstances.

Chè spit out a mouthful of blood. "Yeah, I found the prick in his house down south. He was dead before I could question him, though. Someone must have known he was going to spill the beans. However"—he pulled something out of his back pocket and tossed it through the air—"you might find this a bit useful."

Naomi caught the box that was no bigger than the palm of her hand. She opened it and froze. Inside was a golden necklace with the inverted Horus' eye pendant hanging at the bottom of the chain. With shaking fingers, she pulled it out. "Where did you get this?"

"Brancher had it clutched in his hands before he turned into pixie dust."

"Who the hell is Brancher?"

"The elf? Who else could it be?"

Oh, right. So his name wasn't Maple or Sap as she'd first thought. Still, 'Brancher' was pretty close.

"Is that…?" Sal started, only to trail off at Naomi's nod.

"It's just like the one my mother had," she stated. She glanced back up at Chè, who was frowning down at his appearance. "Did you find anything else?"

Without looking at her, he said, "There was a calendar in his room that had a circle around the date for Sunday."

"That's convenient," Sal grumbled.

Chè flipped him off. "Whatever. I had to do a bit more digging and calculations, but Sunday is the first night of the full moon this month."

Naomi tilted her head in confusion. "The full moon could mean anything to a demon."

"Yeah, but the black market is only open during the nights of the full moon. According to my research, The Oracles spend the entire time between phases gathering their prizes to sell when the doors to The Shade open. They meet in different areas, but Montreal holds the largest distribution center, so the majority of them can be found there."

When Naomi twisted her face in thought, Sal touched her shoulder. "What is it?"

"Montreal…" she murmured, shuffling through her memories. "That's where I first encountered one of The Oracles several years ago. And one of my last targets was a French-Canadian woman with the same Horus tattoo."

"Hm-m. Their headquarters could be in Montreal then—or somewhere in that area."

Naomi nodded, peering at him over her shoulder. "That's what I'm thinking. Is there anything else?" she asked Chè.

Chè shoved his hands into the front pockets of his now-ruined jeans. "A thank you for my hard work would be nice." Then, he smirked. "Or, a thank-you kiss would work just—"

Naomi didn't need to look up to know Sal had bared his fangs. "Don't test me, gargoyle."

Chè shrugged. "Are we even, Naomi? Now that you're out of the guild, there's no need for us to remain in contact. Nothing against you, but you know how it goes."

Naomi gave a solemn nod, not offended in the least bit. Chè wouldn't admit it aloud, but his words had been meant for both of their protection. "*Si*, we're even. *Adios*." She threw her hand up in a careless wave then walked away.

Sal placed an arm around her shoulders and flashed them to his car. "Are your goodbyes often that casual?" he asked.

Waiting for the brief disorientation to subside, Naomi shrugged, returning the pendant to its box. "Did you expect a teary farewell or some such nonsense?"

He snorted, trailing a finger along her jawline. "No, but friends tend to show some sign of emotion. Neither of you even batted an eye."

Naomi opened her door and took a seat, then waited for Sal to slide into the driver's side before responding. "We weren't friends. We worked together and had a business arrangement—nothing more, nothing less."

Sal let out a low whistle. "Heartless, Naomi. You are one cold woman." He started the car, lowering his voice to a grouch. "Well, at least *he* got a goodbye."

"Careful," she drawled. "You almost sound envious."

"So what if I am? You claim he was nothing to you except a business arrangement, yet you told him goodbye. However, I didn't even get a word. You simply disappeared without a care. That tells me what you and I did was less than—"

She slapped her hand over his mouth. "That was…" She shifted in her seat, uncomfortable. "That was different, Sal. You were…"

Dammit, she was not good with such things—confessions and heart-to-heart moments and comforting people. That was always Siovon's strong suit. Naomi never felt the need to do any of it.

At the moment, however, she did. Sal sounded hurt by her actions, as if her running away was far more than a blow to his pride. Not too long ago, she would have scoffed at the belief that such an arrogant playboy would feel that way. Hell, little over an hour ago she would have, but something just felt…different between them.

She shook her head and withdrew her hand from his mouth. "Chè has never made me question my own feelings. Let's just leave it at that."

Sal's jaw went slack, and Naomi was sure that her flaming cheeks were the color of a stop sign beneath her mask. She angled her body toward the window, not wanting him to see the uncertainty and confusion he made her feel. For long moments, she sensed his eyes on her, but he said nothing. In truth, she didn't want him to say anything. She feared he'd make her feel even more ridiculous for her admission. She didn't think she could withstand it if she was only seeing things that weren't there.

So she almost sighed in relief when he put the car in motion. She didn't question where they were going. She simply trusted his judgment. Montreal was several hours away, but with Sal's powers, they could flash there in seconds. And since the first night of the full moon wouldn't be for another day and a half, they could use that time to devise a plan and gather proper weapons in preparation for a fight.

Or she could spend that time convincing him to just leave her be and let her complete her quest on her own. The longer she stayed with him, the more he chipped away at the block protecting her heart.

Well, if she had to be honest, a piece of him had already managed to wiggle its way inside.

And for the first time since killing Reinaldo and joining the guild, the thought wasn't quite as terrifying as it once had been.

Chapter Six

St. Charles, Illinois

With a sigh, Andreas leaned back in his father's desk chair, lowering the binder containing a collection of letters addressed to no one. Reading every heartbreaking page had given him a headache, making him feel sorry for the writer.

He glanced at Cyrus, who sat across the room in his favored wingchair playing Candy Crush. Every so often he'd mutter a string of Etruscan curses after losing a level.

"Who is Vivinna?" Andreas asked.

Instead of responding, Cyrus focused on moving his fingers with rapid speed, swiping the screen of his smartphone over and over. When the game chimed with victory, he punched the air in excitement. "*Bene*! It took me three weeks to beat this round." He flashed Andreas a triumphant grin. Then, seeing his son's annoyance, he forced a serious expression. "My apologies, son. Was I being too loud?"

Andreas refrained from rolling his eyes. "You know, for a man who's lived for an indeterminable amount of years, you're pretty childish."

Cyrus returned his attention to his phone. "Say what you will, but this is not a child's game. It's a challenge made for those of the utmost intelligence."

"It's a puzzle game with candy, bright colors and cutesy phrases — the very description of what children like." When Cyrus waved that aside, Andreas snorted. "I asked who this Vivinna is."

"I'm not sure. That's why I called you."

"Okay, but why is this important? Where did these letters come from?" When he received no answer, his temper spiked. "Father, if you do not give me some kind of information to go by, I'm not doing it."

That time, Cyrus lifted his head a fraction, fixing Andreas with a stern look. "You are refusing a direct order from your king?"

Andreas tilted his chin to a stubborn angle. "So what if I am?"

"You will receive the same treatment as lesser vamps who disobey me." Those pale blue eyes narrowed, giving him a look that would have others peeing their pants — even his children.

Andreas, however, had an ace up his sleeve. With exaggerated calmness, he reached for the desk phone and punched in a number.

"Who are you calling?" Cyrus demanded.

Andreas ignored him and waited until a woman picked up on the other end. "Ava? Hi, sis. You'll never believe what Dad just said to me —"

Before he could continue, Cyrus was at his side in the blink of an eye, snatching the phone away. "Don't listen to him, Ava," he said on a nervous laugh. "Get back to doing whatever it is you were doing. Kiss Anais for me. Love you, *cara*. Bye-bye." He hung up and glared at Andreas. "That was dirty."

Andreas just chuckled. Cyrus was one of the most frightening demons on the planet, yet he had the biggest soft spot for his daughter. Had Andreas finished snitching to her, she would have given their father absolute hell. Cyrus loved all his children equally, but Ava was the only one he would risk looking like a fool over to make her happy — more so ever since she'd become pregnant.

Plus, none of the Gordano men wanted a pissed-off Ava on their hands. Though she was a general sweetheart to all of them and good at keeping calm, she turned into a true monster when her temper reached its boiling point. At that stage, they all had two options to choose from. Either run for cover and bring her a bouquet of flowers and chocolate when she calmed down or stay and be chewed out in a way that left them feeling emasculated and humiliated so badly that it took days to recover.

"Fine," the great warrior huffed. He placed the phone back on its hook. "I truly don't know who she is. The Imperials were as unhelpful as ever when I met with them."

Andreas nodded. While finding Anais was still a complete shock to all of them, even after the prior few months, they'd welcomed the little girl and tried to make her as comfortable around them as possible. In the meantime, they'd all hoped to hear some good news from Cyrus' visit with the Imperials, but the thunderous expression on his dark features had warned Andreas that such wasn't the case.

Cyrus continued. "I know they have some information on the matter, but they refuse to tell me anything, only that they'll look into it." He rolled his eyes at that, making his anger with the powerful justice dealers clear. "It's a load of shit. They have eyes and ears in every fucking realm, yet they feign ignorance toward our people's suffering. By the gods, I'll—" Probably realizing his voice had grown louder, he closed his eyes and inhaled several deep breaths to calm his rising temper.

I don't blame him, Andreas thought. The desire to save the other Royals was shared among all of them. For so long, they'd lived with pain over the belief that one day their kind would no longer exist, but with the revelation that such was no longer the case, they were eager to do what they could to help.

Revealing that everlasting calm that came with his age, Cyrus opened his eyes again and fixed his son with a grave expression. "As I was leaving, Merisl pulled me aside in secret and handed me those letters, saying they might help. Yet all I see is a bunch of sappy-ass words from some woman who probably offed herself a long time ago."

Andreas returned his attention to binder. As unsympathetic as his father's words were, it was true. Vivinna's letters were filled with sorrow. Whoever she was, she had been in love with a man who was her truemate, yet through unknown circumstances, they had been unable to claim each other. Instead, she'd sat back and watched him build a life with someone else. The last letter was her goodbye to the world, which indicated suicide.

"I just feel bad for her," he murmured. "Watching your truemate fall for someone else? Yikes."

Cyrus shook his head as an odd expression crossed his features. It was fleeting, far too fast for Andreas to analyze, but for a moment it looked like...guilt. "While vampires are unable to resist the truemate call, other demons experience the symptoms, but they are able to choose another—humans, especially. Her letters are vague, with no true indication as to who or what she was talking to. Her mate could have been any creature. That's why I need you to find out who she was."

"I don't see how she could possibly relate to what's going on in Tartarus."

"Neither do I, but nothing the Imperials do is a coincidence—annoying as hell, but never a coincidence. If Merisl was concerned enough to go against the rulings of her peers, it must be of some significance. It wouldn't be the first time her cryptic words have aided me. Besides, from scent alone, I can tell that most of those papers are well over a thousand years old. Perhaps this Vivinna could have been a witness to what happened to our people."

"Right," Andreas drawled. "So, you want me to...sniff through some centuries' worth of letters to see what happened to her?"

Cyrus flashed him a wide grin and clapped him on the back. "You've got it. Do your best, son." With that, he sauntered back across the room to his chair, ignoring the glare from said son.

Andreas blew out a loud breath. "*Do your best, son,*" he mimicked under his breath. "You're impossible." Still, he closed his eyes and concentrated his powers. He brought the binder close to his nose and inhaled deeply. He refrained from cringing at the stale, musty scents and dust tickling his nose, instead channeling his powers into taking him several years back.

Whereas Ava could touch someone and see into their memories, Andreas' ability allowed him to view the history of most scents he caught on to. Though his powers worked better on recent odors, he still saw most of the papers' history.

There was a lot of darkness from them being displayed on a shelf, a few brief glimpses of them being passed around a large table occupied by the Imperials and a bit of them traveling. Then there was a long stretch of darkness, as if they'd been locked away in a box for ages.

He didn't know how much time had passed as he shuffled through the scents. He worked his way backward, starting from the last letter written to the first one. When he got to the beginning, he froze when the darkness ended and a new scene took over.

He popped his eyes open in disbelief. He glanced across the room at his father, who was minding his own business playing Candy Crush. Andreas peered at the first letter, taking in the bold strokes of ink written on a piece of papyrus that was worn and almost completely faded. He and his siblings could all read Latin scripts, but the majority of the first letter was written in his father's native language and would be impossible for them to translate into the modern English. However, there was no mistaking *Cyro* and *victo*, which he assumed translated to 'Cyrus the Conqueror'.

Before saying anything aloud, he focused on the image of that letter once more, just to be sure what he'd seen was correct. The spiderweb of scents took a while to untangle, but there was no mistaking the ancient metallic scent of vampire blood.

My father's and another. He studied that papyrus sheet and held it up to the light. Sure enough, in the bottom corners were two thumbprints that were faded to look like two old stains. It was a blood oath, a type of treaty between demons that could only be broken by death.

The images of the past were blurry, as though history was reluctant to show him its secrets. However, Andreas concentrated hard until a bead of sweat rolled down his temple. When he felt as though a blood vessel was about to pop in his brain, the image wavered into a moment of clarity.

A warrior dressed in bloodied robes lay on a bed of straw. About two dozen candles formed a semi-circle around him, and though there was no sound, it was clear from the amount of blood spilling from him that death was close to claiming him. A woman – Vivinna, Andreas assumed – sat next to him, tears falling from her eyes as she spoke. Andreas' powers didn't allow him to hear anything, so he couldn't make out what she was saying, but whatever it was had to be urgent. And since he was looking at the memory as though he was the papyrus, he could only see the warrior and a portion of the woman's face hidden beneath the shadow of a cloak she wore.

With his tousled hair cut short and much leaner features, Andreas almost didn't recognize the young man as his father. That was, until he raised his eyelids to reveal piercing ice-blue eyes that had been passed down to most of his children. Cyrus' lips moved with painful slowness as he responded to Vivinna. She waved the document in his face, as if to make him see it better.

Cyrus frowned but lifted one of his bloodied thumbs and pressed it against the sheet. Vivinna relaxed, though the tears never once stopped sliding down her cheeks. She brushed his hair from his forehead, and they exchanged more words. He cracked a slight smile and palmed her cheek in a loving gesture. There was nothing but love shimmering in his eyes, even through the physical pain he had to be in. Moving with caution so as to not agitate his wounds, she leaned forward to place a lingering kiss to his lips. Cyrus closed his eyes as if to savor her touch, but then his face turned to the side as unconsciousness overtook him.

Vivinna shook him, but when he didn't move, she used one of her fangs to pierce her thumb, then smeared it onto the papyrus. A sudden gust of wind filled the room, blowing out every candle except one. A lone figure appeared in the corner. It was tall and gaunt, though there was no light to reveal what it looked like in the face. However, it pointed a long claw-like finger at Cyrus.

Vivinna stood, using her body to shield Cyrus from the intruder. She shoved the papyrus at it and yelled something. It grabbed the document with a gnarly hand. After several minutes of nothing happening, the newcomer finally peered at her. It dropped the papyrus and conjured up a metal chain.

Vivinna gulped but squared her shoulders before approaching it. With one final glance over her shoulder at Cyrus, she and the gaunt creature disappeared into the night, leaving the great warrior all alone.

Alone, yet no longer dying.

With a gasp, Andreas opened his eyes and shot out of the desk chair. He stood frozen in place, the shock and confusion of what he'd just witnessed forever burned into his brain.

Alarmed, Cyrus rose as well, concern etched on his dark features. "What is it? What did you see?"

For several long minutes, Andreas could only stare at his father in wide-eyed disbelief. Though the warrior from the past had vast differences with the one standing before him, there was no mistaking it. And though he wasn't able to see Vivinna's face, something deep in his gut told him that she wasn't Camilla or Anna, his father's only two mates.

When words were finally able to form on his lips, he had to clear his throat. "You," he whispered. "*You* were her truemate."

* * * *

Any time there was a family crisis, the Gordanos gathered in Cyrus' library to discuss the matter. In this case, it was more like a gossip group as the latest news of Cyrus' past was discovered.

Either way, the king didn't look pleased.

Cassander's jaw was hanging open, while his siblings — along with their mates — sat with mirrored expressions. Andreas' frantic group text urging that they meet at once had the Viking worried that another threat on their family had been discovered. What he hadn't expected was his youngest brother's startling revelation.

"Come again?" Lucian demanded. He was the first to recover from bombshell that had been dropped, reverting to his signature glare.

Andreas nodded with energy. "Dad had another truemate named Vivinna — long before he met our moms."

They'd all been updated on the situation. Cyrus had pleaded his case to the Imperials, one of them had given him a binder of ancient letters and Andreas had sifted through the scents to discover the writer had been a vampire named Vivinna, who'd watched Cyrus from a distance and claimed he was her truemate.

It was all…bizarre. That was the only word Cassander could think of.

"Is this true?" Ava asked their father. She sat next to Cass, with Marc on the other side of her. He had one arm draped behind her, the other resting over her belly — her very large belly.

"Wait a minute," Siovon said. She sat on the opposite couch next to Lucian, with Andreas on the other side of her. It hadn't taken long for her to fit in with their little family. Likewise, they'd taken a liking to her from the start. Cassander admired her for her skills as a warrior, as well as the way she'd never once cowered under Lucian's menacing glares. "I thought vampires only had one truemate in a lifetime."

"Actually," Julius cut in, "on very rare occasions, we can find another, though ofttimes it takes centuries for that to happen — and that's only if you can survive through the pain of losing one without turning Rogue. Dad had two. Having more than that has never been heard of."

Cyrus remained still and guarded, giving away nothing, yet Cassander knew he was troubled. *Something isn't right.* "Do you remember her?" he asked.

Again, Cyrus didn't respond, only drummed his fingers on the arm of his chair. His slight shake of the head was the only answer he gave.

"Well, who is she?" Ava asked, growing excited. "Have you looked her up? Is she still alive? What happened to her?"

"We don't know anything," Andreas admitted. "All we know so far is what I just told you."

"*Cazzo,*" Darius muttered, running a hand through his short hair. He wore a sleeveless shirt, showing off the colorful tattoos that lined both his arms. "She has to be lying. If she's been around to watch him settle down with Camilla and Anna, then she couldn't have been his truemate. You can't have two truemates at one time. One has to be dead. At least, that's what we've always thought."

"That's because it's true," Cyrus at last spoke, then sighed. He stood and strolled to his desk, where he plucked a vintage bottle of whiskey. It was his signature move for delivering some news he didn't want to share. "I have something to tell you all that I'd hoped to never reveal."

When all eyes turned to him, he took a long swig of the drink, cringing at the bitter taste. "Oh, that's good," he murmured. He cradled it and returned to his seat. "What I'm about to say has been something I've kept in for so very long, for everyone's sake."

"I think I know what it is," Ava claimed. When Cyrus narrowed his eyes on her, she gave a helpless lift of her hands. "I've had a peek inside your memories plenty of times. Though I had to Purge afterward, I can still recall them."

Lucian leaned his elbows on his knees, fixing her with a hard stare. "Say it—" When Ava shot him a glare much like an aunt would a troublesome nephew, he cleared his throat. "Ah, what is it that you saw?" he tried in a more polite tone.

Cassander snorted. Ava and Siovon were the only two people in the world who could ever put Lucian in his place. It was always humorous the way they could give him a particular look or a piece of their mind and he'd act like a decent man.

Ava nodded to Cyrus. "When we mate, the ancient runes binding us together appear, and if one mate dies, the mark fades until it becomes faint. It is hardly noticeable, but still there if you look in the right lighting. Dad's been mated twice, yet his neck is bare."

Cass straightened, resisting the urge to touch his own faded mark. It didn't matter where two lovers chose to bite each other. Once the mating was complete, the old runes would appear as a series of tribal-like loops forming a small circle at the base of their throats.

Ava was right. Cyrus didn't have a single mark on his neck, though how none of them had ever noticed was beyond him.

"Father, explain," Lucian demanded, glaring at Cyrus.

Cyrus took a long—long—swig from his bottle. "Now, children, this may be very hard to hear, so please save any questions or insults until I finish." He took another drink. After a dramatic pause, he said, "I've never found my truemate."

As expected, no one believed him. Julius rolled his eyes. "I call bullshit." Everyone murmured in agreement.

Their father sighed, his eyes filling with sorrow that had his brood quieting down in seriousness. "It's true. Neither Camilla nor Anna were my truemates."

Andreas made a sound of surprise. "But—"

Cyrus cut him off with a raised hand. "Don't. Please save all comments until the end. As I've said, this isn't at all easy for me to explain."

When everyone nodded, he continued. "I cared for them both, and we *were* mates, but they were not my truemates. When I met Camilla, it was shortly after the war with the Ancients. It wasn't love at first sight, there was no compulsion to be with her—none of the signs of a truemate, but we still developed an attachment to one another and fell in love. It's possible for vampires to mate anyone who isn't their truemate, but because of how sacred a ceremony it is, not many choose to do so. Plus, you do not want to mate just anyone, then afterward meet your truemate. It's just not fair to either party. However, Camilla and I had a delicate situation. We were close, but when she became pregnant with Lucian, I had to do what was right. Besides, we were still young by vampire standards and the world was so much smaller back then."

A small, fond smile curved his lips in remembrance, and for a moment, Cass got the impression that Cyrus had truly loved her. It was just a passing love, though, not one that would last a lifetime.

"She was with me as I reshaped our people. Despite how burdened it must have been for her, she was always supportive of my desire for peace. She was a wonderful mate and an even better mother. I loved her for it. But she was *never* my truemate. We both knew that beforehand, but the lack of a mating mark proved it. Yet, we were...content. We were happy together." He shook his head. "Over time the love faded, but we were still very close friends. I didn't blame her when she found interest in another, nor did I become angry that she told me he was her truemate. Unfortunately, our bond prevented her from being with him, which is something I will always regret. As I said, we were young and hadn't thought we'd ever find our truemates."

He shook his head in sorrow. "I was devastated when I lost her to those raiders. Centuries later, I met Anna, your mom." He nodded at Darius, Julius and Andreas. Though they all knew Andreas wasn't their blood brother, Anna had raised him as her own. "Unlike Camilla, the feelings we had for one another were instant. Every day I wanted to be with her, and it didn't take long for us to fall for one another. The feelings mimicked the truemate call, and we foolishly rushed into a mating. However, the lack of a mark told us otherwise. We were so disappointed, but it was too late. We still had feelings, but I was always afraid that she would find her own truemate and grow to resent me. However, that time never came, for she died far too soon. Like Camilla, she was very special to me, and she will always hold a place in my heart. I mourn both of their deaths to this day. However, it's true. Neither of them was my truemate, and the lack of any markings on my neck is proof of it."

He sighed again and gulped a big drink from his bottle. "You all have grown up thinking your mothers were my truemates, and I should have been honest with you before allowing it to carry on this long. However, I'd be lying if I said I regretted keeping this from you. It was a secret I would have taken with me to the grave if I could have."

There were several minutes of stunned silence, ones where no one quite knew what to say. Anger at being lied to for so long burned in Cass' chest, and from the looks dawning on his siblings' faces, they were feeling much the same.

Then, at once, all hell broke loose. Lucian, Cass, Julius and Darius were on their feet, screaming curses at Cyrus. Meanwhile, he continued to drink from his bottle, absorbing the hateful things they said to him. Cass didn't know how long it went on for, but he was shaking with fury by the time Ava stood up. She was still slender, though her protruding belly always made her wobble when she tried to walk.

"Hey!" she snapped. She stood in front of Cyrus, as if fearing they would attack. Given the way Cass was feeling, he most certainly wanted to throttle his father. When they didn't quiet down, she stuck two fingers in her mouth and whistled as loud as she could, making every demon with sensitive hearing wince with pain.

When everyone quieted down to glare at her, she glared right back. Her thickened accent was the first sign — and warning — they had before realizing she was pissed with a capital P. "What the hell do any of you have to be so angry about? Huh? Sure, he lied for years, but what difference does it make if they were or weren't his truemates? They still loved each other, clearly. At least you were all raised in a home with *two* parents. Some of us didn't get that luxury as kids." Sweat beaded across her forehead and her face burned red with rage.

Marc stood. "Love, please calm down."

She swatted him away and continued glaring at her brothers. "You all got to see what it was like growing up with two parents who loved each other. Andreas too, but I'm sure he's always wondered what the hell happened to his birth parents, and I was the result of a late-night hookup between two strangers who never became anything more than that. You don't see us complaining about that, now do you? You all want to jump down Dad's throat about a choice he made — and for what? What is it going to change? Absolutely nothing, you sorry jackasses. If you want to be mad, go bitch about it somewhere else. We're here to find out who the hell Vivinna is and what role she has in our people going missing. Or did you all forget we have problems bigger to deal with than your daddy issues?"

As expected, her words sliced them to pieces. It was the primary reason none of them ever did anything to try to piss her off. It would have been laughable, given how they were all centuries older—and larger—than her, but the brutal accusations she shot at them were enough to shift their anger into regret. At least, that's how Cass felt, but judging by the guilty looks on his brothers' faces, they, too, sympathized with the truth behind her argument.

"But, Ava," Julius stammered, shuffling his feet like a child, "he—"

"Don't 'but, Ava' me. I don't want to hear it. If you want to complain, do it on your own time." She threw her hands up in exasperation and turned her back on them. "By the freaking gods... I'm going to get some juice, and by the time I come back, you assholes better have a kinder attitude."

Everyone was shocked into silence as she waddled away, though she paused halfway with a grimace. Shaking it off, she continued until she reached the door. She paused with her hand on the handle and breathed a curse.

"What is it, Ava?" Marc asked, going to her side.

She turned accusing eyes on her brothers when a puddle of liquid pooled at her feet. "See what you cretins did? My water just broke."

Just like that, the tension in the air shifted to panic.

Siovon gasped and was the first to spring into action. "Marc, take her upstairs. I have a room ready for this exact situation."

"What do we do?" Julius asked, flapping his hands with worry. "We need towels, right? And hot water. I've seen this in a movie somewhere. We can—"

"I said the room is already prepared." Siovon rolled her eyes. "You bickering idiots aren't going to do anything but stress her out even more. Go get some balloons or something." With that, she darted behind Marc and Ava, only stopping to glare at Lucian, who was hot on her heels. "Oh no you don't. This is an emergency situation for trained professionals only. Stay."

"What? She's my sister and I'm not a mutt—"

"Lucian, stay. I mean it."

The great clan chief snapped his mouth shut and watched in reluctance as his mate disappeared beyond the doors. "That was painful," Andreas chuckled, standing. Though it had been months since he'd recovered from his near-death experience, he still needed the aid of a cane to walk as his muscles continued to regenerate themselves. "She has you whipped."

Darius followed that up by mimicking the sound of a whip snapping.

Anger replaced by humor and worry for his sister, Cass chuckled and returned to his seat. He blew out a long, deep sigh and leaned his head back. Everything had changed so fast that it was hard to stay mad at their father. Plus, Ava was right. Sure, Cyrus had lied to them for centuries, but it didn't matter one way or the other if Camilla and Anna had been his truemates. What was really sad was the fact that he'd lived for three thousand years without ever meeting his real one. It was quite depressing and didn't give other vampires much hope.

"I am not whipped," Lucian grumbled, planting his hands on his hips. "I just respect her authority."

"Oh please," Julius commented. "You don't respect anyone's anything. If she tells you to jump, you turn froggy. You've changed, old man. Admit it."

Instead of responding with a snarky comeback, Lucian flopped down into his seat. "Don't you have some balloons to find? Get going."

"On a serious note—and to change the subject," Cass drawled, "we need to discuss Vivinna." He peered at Cyrus, who stared after his daughter with a concerned frown. "It's clear you two were very close. You were probably lovers before she saved your life. How do you not remember her?"

Cyrus turned his attention to his sons. "I'm well over three thousand years old, Cassander. I cannot remember every face and name that has crossed my path. Vivinna doesn't ring any bells. As for that night...? I don't recall it ever happening. I remember fighting the Ancients and being dealt a nasty blow, but my clansmen carried me to safety. The next day, all was well."

"But she has an Etruscan name," Lucian added. "She could have been a part of your tribe when you crossed the sea to Italy."

Their father gave a helpless lift of his hands. "I was just a babe then. I wouldn't remember." His expression turned thoughtful, as if he were trying to recollect, but then he shook his head.

"Perhaps you can contact some of your clansmen from back then. Some of them are still alive, correct? One of them is bound to know something." Lucian shook his head. "Andreas, you saw her, right? What does she look like?"

Andreas snorted. "It was quite dark, *fratello*. I was facing our father most of the time, and what bit I did see of her was shrouded in shadows."

"Fine, then Ava can—"

"Do you want to send her into another Purging episode?" Darius demanded. He pulled a stick of gum from his pocket and popped it in his mouth. "Andreas said father wasn't much older than his twenties. You know how many memories she'd have to sort through to find one that *might* help?"

"I don't want to send her into anything," Lucian growled. "However, she's the only one who can give us an idea of what this woman could look like—or if there's a memory she can uncover. The Imperials gave him that binder, so there has to be some kind of connection between her and our people. Besides, Ava is much stronger now. Ever since running into Anais, she's been working hard to become stronger and control her powers better. The last few times she touched the child, she didn't even Purge, not even a little."

"You make an excellent point, Lucian, but it's up to her." Cyrus placed his bottle on the coffee table. Half of it was already gone. "I won't force her if she's not comfortable, but we can always find another way. Until then, this is a precious time for our family. Baby Gordano will be here soon, so let's try to focus on the positive."

The brothers all nodded in agreement. Despite how eager they were to find out the truth, welcoming their new niece or nephew was more important.

"You do realize that he or she will actually be Baby Lewis, right?" Andreas asked. "Children tend to take their father's name."

Cyrus dismissed the statement as if it were nonsense. "A child under our care will always be a Gordano." He glanced at Lucian. "How's Siovon settling into her new lab?"

Their grumpy older brother replaced his frown with a smile. "She loves it. She spends more time in there than she does outside."

"Has she started on the search for a cure to Rogueism?" Andreas asked.

"At the moment, she's just studying and trying out different potions. I've notified my clansmen to capture a Rogue alive, if they happen across one. Though she isn't happy with the idea of experimenting on a 'poor creature', she'll need to draw blood to see what works and what doesn't."

"I'm sure she'll figure it out in no time. She's wonderful," Andreas stated.

Lucian narrowed his eyes on his little brother. "Indeed she is. She's also mated." At that, he puffed out his chest like a rooster, ready to fight.

Darius chortled at Andreas' blushing cheeks. "So what if he has a small crush on her? She saved his life and she's pretty. That's his weakness."

Andreas sputtered, even as his face turned a dark shade of pink. "I don't have a crush on her! I know she's off limits. I'm just…grateful. That's all."

"Don't worry. Her sister is free. They look just alike, so you can try your hand at getting her."

"I don't—" Andreas cut himself off with a sigh and covered his face with his hand.

Cyrus joined the fun and grinned at his son's embarrassment. "I wouldn't say that, Darius. Calysta seems rather smitten with that imp."

Everyone laughed, making Andreas turn his back on them. Cass shook his head in amusement. Though they all knew he didn't really harbor any romantic feelings for Siovon, they enjoyed teasing him over it. He was living proof that not all vampires were smooth-talking Casanovas. For as long as they could remember, he'd always been shy and would get flustered when it came to dealing with the opposite sex.

"Come on," Julius said to his twin and Andreas. "Let's go get some balloons and teddy bears. We can be the fun uncles."

Cass snorted and stood. "I'm going to check on my gym. Call me when the baby gets here."

"Didn't you already go there today?" Darius asked with suspicion. "Two times in one day is a new record for you."

Cass shifted to face the door to hide his unease. "The fights are starting soon. My presence is required more often than not. Mind your own business."

He rushed out of the room before his family could scent his lie and pester him with questions he wasn't comfortable answering. How could he tell any of them that he'd been lurking around his own gym in the hope of finding that mysterious woman again? They'd never let him live it down.

Chapter Seven

Montreal, Quebec

Since Sal had been to Montreal several times in the past, he'd been able to flash them to the city with ease. That made sense, of course, because he owned yet another large nightclub there. It seemed he had quite a handful of businesses and wasn't limited to Chicago.

And surprise, surprise, this club was just a lascivious as his other ones.

Naomi rolled her eyes at the thought. Just when she'd acknowledged that she had a tiny batch of feelings for him, the thought of him surrounded by an array of floozies knocked them right out of the way. While she no longer compared him to being a replica of Reinaldo, the way he flaunted his wealth and had women desperate for his attention was far too similar.

And as if that weren't bad enough, the upper floors of the club doubled as a hotel, where privileged guests could rent a room for several nights. Sal had a suite for them to stay in, but the scent of lust and arousal from such a large group of demons nearby had her blood rushing with anticipation. The cramps were brutal as her gut clenched in pain in retaliation for her neglecting her needs.

She'd done everything she could to distract her mind. Showering hadn't helped, as the water pelting down on her had felt like gentle hands caressing every inch of her body. Throwing her clothes in the wash had been too swift. Pacing across the floor with just a silk robe rubbing raw against her puckered nipples only made matters worse. The longer she stayed in the room, the more amped up her sexual hunger became.

Salvator had been gone ever since they'd made it to the city, claiming to be checking the perimeter and alerting his security and whatnot. It'd been hours, but she'd tried to give him the benefit of the doubt. However, there was no way in hell it should have taken so long. She was sure that he'd gotten distracted by the bimbos downstairs and decided to entertain them.

The thought was far more unsettling than it should have been, and the more Naomi lingered on it, the more annoyed she grew. Frustrated with herself and him, she scrubbed her hands over her face and jerked her mask over her mouth. With a growl, she snatched the door open and stormed for the elevators.

She couldn't care less that she was dressed in nothing more than a pair of fuzzy slippers and a flimsy robe that displayed that hard peaks of her nipples—or that her pheromones were seeping from every pore of her being, beckoning any unmated male who'd cross her path. For a moment, she thought about searching for Salvator and catching him in the act, but she refrained. As much as she prided herself on her strength and detached attitude, she didn't trust her heart enough to not fall apart if she saw him hooking up with another woman.

Besides, what did it matter anyway? He owed her no loyalty in that department. He wasn't her lover. He wasn't her man. What he did in his private time had nothing to do with her.

She cursed under her breath and tapped her foot with impatience as she rode the elevator to the ground floor. She needed to get away from the damn building. It was nothing but a sex pit, and within moments she'd be trapped spending the rest of the night sating the annoying cravings that came with her heritage.

She cursed her father for her succubus side. She cursed his rotten soul to hell and back, as well as whatever god was responsible for creating her — for making her some abomination that needed sex to survive when she was meant to be a pureblood fury.

Her rage only fueled her lust. The agonizing cramps tightened until her knees almost buckled. Warring against it was a wave of desire flooding through her that had dampness sliding down her inner thighs. She fought through it until she reached an exit door, pushing away the few people who tried to help her out of concern when she staggered. Fortunately, they were women. She didn't trust herself around a male at the moment. She didn't trust herself not to jump his bones and beg him to fuck her until her legs gave out and the pain subsided.

She stumbled down a narrow alley, not caring about stepping on garbage and broken glass. She pressed onward, getting as far away from Sal's club as possible.

Even when she was a safe distance away, it didn't help. Once her senses latched on to a large crowd of sex-craving fiends, she was stuck in its grasp until she sated her needs. If she didn't find a man soon, her hold on reality was going to slip until she was a mindless shell, screwing anyone she saw.

As if the devil was provoking her, she spotted two men at the opposite end of the alley, leaning against the brick wall and passing a bottle of alcohol between one another. Before she could turn away, one of them glanced at her.

In a thick accent, he whistled and said, "Whoa, baby. Where'd you come from?"

Naomi inhaled a deep breath, though she wished she hadn't. Their arousal was thick in the air, propelling her forward. As if moving on their own, her legs crossed, one in front of the other, meeting the two men halfway. As she got closer, her consciousness registered the smell of cheap beer and marijuana. The combination made her want to gag, but her succubus side ignored it, instead focusing on the potent aroma of their desire for her.

When they were in arm's reach, the one on the left circled behind her and threw his arm over her shoulders. He leaned in close. He was already inebriated from the beer and drugs, but her pheromones added an extra kick that had his eyelids drooping low. He licked his lips. "You shouldn't be out here all alone, little lady."

The other one reached for the button of his jeans. "Nah, you came to the party just in time."

Before Naomi could utter a throaty response, a feral growl sounded — one that had her hair standing in fear. The three of them turned to the mouth of the alley. Her heart dropped to her toes at the sight of Salvator, looking angrier than she'd ever seen before — even angrier than when Chè had taunted him.

His fangs were bared, reminding her of a snarling wolf getting ready to strike. Rage rolled off of him in waves, causing the garbage littering the ground to flutter. "Remove your fucking hands," he rumbled, taking a threatening step forward.

Naomi could have sworn a waterfall ran between her legs, though she wasn't sure if it was due to her consciousness or her succubus side. Sal had gone from looking like a beautiful, sensual playboy to a frightening demon who'd rip them all apart, yet he was still the sexiest creature she'd ever seen.

The man holding her let her go and took a wary step back. "Who the hell are you?" he demanded, though his voice held a tremor that revealed he was terrified.

The other hadn't moved an inch. He pulled out a switchblade and pointed it. "Back off, mate. Don't make me use this."

Sal flashed behind him, eliciting a shriek of surprise from one of them. It had all happened so quick that if Naomi hadn't been a demon, she would have never seen it. Sal had the man disarmed with his wrist twisted behind his back, while he had the other man by his neck, hanging above the ground. They struggled, but it was clearly no use against the silver-haired vamp.

"Get the fuck out of here before I kill you both." When they gave jerky nods, he released them. The two tripped over each other trying to run away.

Naomi rolled her eyes. Her bet was that they'd stumble into the nearest diner and frantically ask for the police to be called over a vampire. Then, seeing how plastered the two idiots were, they'd get to spend the rest of the night in detainment.

Movement out of the corner of her eye had her facing Salvator. She didn't even twitch as he stalked her, closing in on her personal space. He took her chin in a grip that could have been bruising if she weren't a demon. "What in the ever-loving shit do you think you're doing out here?" he demanded, his voice rough with emotion. His anger thickened his accent, almost sounding as though he wasn't speaking English.

"What did it look like I was doing?" she retorted, her voice dropping to a throaty drawl. "I have needs, Salvator. Needs only a man can fulfill."

His nostrils flared, though whether it was in anger or he was scenting how close to the edge she was, she'd never know. "And you thought you could just get it from any man?"

She tried to jerk her chin away, but he held fast. "Any male who isn't bound by mating, *si*. I can."

He growled and leaned to level her with a dark glare. "You said it yourself, that I make you question your own feelings. Were you lying to me? Did you only say that to toy with my heart? By the gods, Naomi, if you —"

"If I *what*?" she demanded, her own anger spiking, giving her a moment of clarity from the lust-filled cloud. Oh, it was still there, with no intentions of leaving until she gave in, but for a moment, she was able to give him a piece of her mind. "I can smell blood on you. While you were off sucking on some broad's neck, I was left alone in a room with hundreds of demons nearby filling the air with their lust. Do you know what kind of havoc that wreaks on my body when it's been so long since I've had sex?" She scoffed. "You screw dozens of women on a weekly basis. I've heard the stories about you. As if you have any right to stand between me and any man I choose to be with."

His pale eyes flashed with fire. He stepped back and shoved his hands through his loose hair. "By the fucking gods, Naomi. Ever since I met you, I've been unable to even look at another woman, let alone touch one. You've failed to leave my mind for even a moment."

She scoffed again and crossed her arms. "That line must work for you all the time."

He muttered a string of Latin curses and threw his hands in the air. "Of all the people in the world." He backed away until there were several feet between them. "There's been a connection between us since day one. I know you feel it too." When she opened her mouth to deny it, he cut her off. "You do. It affects vampires more than any other species, but you still experience it. You can pretend to despise me and continue treating me as if I mean nothing to you, but we both know it's just because you're frightened of your own feelings. And honestly, so am I. I never asked for any of this, but there's nothing I can do but accept it."

"What do you have to be afraid of?" she questioned.

She had to restrain herself from touching her heart. Ever since she and Sal had had sex, she'd felt something…different. It was as if a piece of him had filled some unknown void in her chest. Even long after she'd run away, the hole had only gotten bigger. Some days it was almost to the point where she couldn't breathe, and she'd felt the urge to go to him. She'd thought it was all in her head, a taunting reminder of her craving something she could never have — peace and a lover she could claim to end her lonely existence. Mating was something she'd never even thought twice about, but ever since seeing how happy Siovon was with Lucian, a piece of Naomi had wanted to experience what that was like.

Sal dropped his hands from his hair and fixed her with a stare that was impossible to look away from. There was so much pain behind those pale blue eyes. "You've proven to be a flight risk. How am I to know that in the morning you will still be there when I wake up? That if I slip away for two minutes, I will return only to find you nowhere in sight? You've tried to get rid of me plenty of times since you entered my club in Chicago, and even now, you left the suite without notice. How is it not frightening that I have such a strong attachment to you, yet in the blink of an eye you can leave me with ease?" He paused to give a dry snort. "And that's ironic, because I'm the one with the teleportation powers."

He shook his head. "I know you have trust issues, Naomi, but I'm telling you the truth. I haven't touched another woman since you. My family has given me so much shit for that, mind you. Even now, I didn't feed from a live host. I used bagged blood, and I can prove it if you'll let me. But if you still can't find it in yourself to trust me, to trust what I feel for you, then…" He swallowed hard, and Naomi realized it must have been the first time in his spoiled life that he'd ever wanted something he couldn't have. "Then I won't stop you."

She had to clear her throat from the lump that had formed from his confession. "What?"

He waved, as if shooing her away. "If you desire another male, I will not stop you again. I can't promise I won't kill him afterward, but I will not interfere."

For what seemed like an eternity, Naomi just stared at him in shock. He looked as calm as always, though his clenched fists tucked into his dress pants told her otherwise. He obviously hated the thought of her being with another man, but he was willing to put aside his own emotional state. He was giving her a choice — a freedom Reinaldo had never once allowed.

She had so many questions she wanted to ask, most of them pertaining to the 'connection' between them. The way he spoke about it, saying vampires were more affected than others, told her that he knew far more than what he was letting on. However, she wasn't sure she wanted to hear the answer. She knew a great deal about vamps, including the bit about them having a destined truemate. She didn't dare hope she was Sal's — or anyone's, for that matter. It was a commitment she wasn't ready for, since there was never a guarantee she'd survive the next few days.

If the furies were involved with the black-market scam and found out she was still alive, they'd kill her, even if she didn't step onto their turf. The fact that she'd survived all these years and was looking into her mother's death would be enough to make them wary.

So yeah, it was best if they didn't make any vow to each other.

If Sal thought she was his truemate, he would only be setting himself up for heartache. She couldn't promise him forever. However, she couldn't keep denying that she cared for him. Maybe she could lie to him but she couldn't lie to herself. She only needed him long enough to get close to the answers she wanted. After that, she'd have to let him go. There was no way she was willing to let him risk his life for something that was her problem. The furies, as a whole, were far too powerful for even a Royal vampire to take on.

With her mind made up, she took slow steps toward Sal, putting a little swing in her hips. As expected, his eyes darkened with hunger and his Adam's apple bobbed on a swallow.

She'd give him something she'd never given anyone after Reinaldo. Most of the times when she'd needed sex, she took it from behind—even with Chè. The feeling of detachment was always welcome, giving her the mindset of 'get in, get out'. With Salvator, however, she wanted more. Giving herself to him freely was the only way she knew how to make him see that if things had been different, perhaps in another life, they could have been together. Yet just for tonight, she could pretend she was his. It would be a small taste of what she'd never have but could claim for a few hours.

When there was no space left between them, Naomi slid her palms over his shirt, feeling the hard muscles lying beneath. "I don't want another male," she murmured, going on the tips of her toes to bury her nose in his neck. He shuddered. "Just you."

Sal made a low growl in the back of his throat and wrapped his arms around her. Her limbs tingled as he flashed them back to their suite. He scooped her into his arms and carried her across the glossy bamboo flooring, past the beautiful black dining room set and living room, to the master bedroom. Instead of setting her on the bed like she expected, he crossed the room and headed for the attached bathroom.

"Here?" she questioned. During her shower earlier in the guest room, she'd been blown away by the French-inspired décor that gave the bathroom a too-pretty-to-touch look. The master bathroom was tripled in size with a claw-foot tub separated from a shower that could accommodate ten people.

Sal set her on the countertop and went to work turning on the shower head. "Their scents are all over you," he muttered, facing her. He kicked his shoes off then reached for the buttons on his shirt and undid each one before dropping the garment to the ground.

Naomi bit her lower lip, her hunger returning with a vengeance as she took in the smooth pale skin stretched over a physique that had her mouth watering for a taste. Next, his pants fell to the ground, followed by his boxer briefs. Freed from its confines, his cock pointed at her, as if begging for her touch. When he held his hand out to her, she hesitated, suddenly feeling shy, despite the way her body urged her to leap to him.

"Have you changed your mind?" he asked with a frown, lowering his arm a bit in what looked like self-consciousness.

She glanced to the ground, not wanting him to see the insecurity in her eyes. "No, it's just... I have scars. A lot of them."

"I've seen them. Are you ashamed?"

She grunted and rubbed one of her arms. "They aren't ladylike. I don't think I'm your usual type."

There was a moment of silence before Sal closed the distance between them and tugged her mask from her face. She made to protest, but he leaned forward to kiss her, pushing his tongue past her lips to taste her. When he pulled away, she almost sighed in disappointment. He hooked a finger under her chin and forced her to meet his gaze.

"You are beautiful, dove. Every inch of you is...perfect, just perfect." As if to prove his point, he held her gaze while lowering his head. Her nipples were still poking through the silk robe, and without missing a beat, he latched onto one of them. She jerked as shockwaves of pleasure rolled through her while he teased the sensitive peak with his teeth and tongue. He smoothed his hand down a path to where she needed his touch the most.

She opened her legs wider to allow him better access. He toyed with her clit, applying pressure before easing up. He repeated that until she moaned. Needing something to occupy her hands, she tangled them in his loose hair, loving how the silky strands felt, sliding through her fingers. Somewhere in her distant mind, she wondered what kind of shampoo and conditioner he used — or if he had a private salon he went to every week.

When Sal moved his attention to her other nipple, he slid that clever finger along her folds to where she was dripping wet for him. Without warning, he pushed the digit inside, making her arch into him. He didn't halt his movement as he stroked her, pushing deeper and deeper until his knuckle met her entrance.

He released her nipple, breathing hard. "Do you like that?"

Naomi couldn't form a coherent word, so she moaned in response. No longer feeling insecure, she shoved the robe off, allowing it to pool around her waist. Sal chuckled in delight, flashing his fangs in a way that made him look like a feral beast.

A sexy feral beast, one that she was more than eager to allow ravish her.

Her panting breaths grew shorter and shorter until her release was close, but she'd never be able to achieve it until he was buried inside her. She couldn't bring herself to orgasm, and though the foreplay felt fucking amazing, her needs called for full penetration.

So when he withdrew his finger and didn't fill her right away, she cried out in frustration.

"Patience, dove," he murmured. He picked her up and carried her into the shower. The steamy water pelting down on her skin would have felt good if she weren't shaking from the need to be put out of her misery.

Sal turned her to face the wall and busied himself with lathering up a sponge. With deliberate slowness, he scrubbed her back, taking extra care with her ass and thighs in the process. Instead of spinning her around to tend to her front side, he pressed against her back. His dick was hard as a rock as it nestled between her soapy cheeks.

With one free hand, he covered the base of her throat and tilted her chin over her shoulder to kiss her while using the sponge on her tender breasts and stomach. It was a slow, lazy kiss, but the heat behind it sent electric shocks of fire straight to her core. He released the sponge and lathered both hands before running them down to the tops of her thighs.

He broke the kiss and arched her forward. She braced her arms on the cool tile wall and sucked in a sharp breath as he lowered himself to his knees. He flashed her a wicked grin before diving between her legs, licking and sucking her aching clit. He busied his hands with her breasts, kneading the small globes and lightly pinching her nipples in tune with his licks.

"Salvator," she whimpered, once again close to that glorious peak. "Please... I need you."

Without additional persuasion, he rose to spin her around. He lifted her so she could straddle him. "Yes, Naomi," he groaned. In one smooth motion, he pushed inside her warmth.

Naomi cried in ecstasy at being filled, throwing her head back and riding him as the release her body had been begging for caused her to clench around his cock. He remained still until the last tremors of her orgasm subsided, but the vein popping out of his neck revealed that he was struggling to fight his own. When the mild pulses slowed and she was able to recover, she rotated her hips to encourage him to move.

Slowly, he rocked his hips into her, withdrawing to the tip before driving back in. "You're beautiful," he ground out, keeping a slow pace.

Naomi framed his face, taking in the narrow features that reminded her of one of those Roman portrait sculptures. "So are you," she whispered.

His breath hitched and pink stained the tops of his cheekbones. His reaction stunned her. It couldn't have been the first time he'd ever been complimented on his looks, but it pleased her to think that her words meant more to him than others'.

Her thoughts were confirmed when he wrapped his arms around her and held her close while growing more forceful with his strokes. Careful not to nick her skin with his fangs, he nibbled a path along her neck and jaw. He kissed the ugly scar on her left cheek, then the one on the right.

Stupid tears pricked her eyes over the constant reminder of what Reinaldo had done to her, but the fact that Salvator still found her attractive filled her with some kind of emotion she didn't want to name. Instead, she focused on the wonderful feeling of his rigid cock sliding in and out of her. When his rocking grew to be short pumps slapping her against the wall, she knew he was close — and so was she…again.

She drew in gasps of air followed by little keening moans as the pressure of another orgasm made its way through her. "Will you bite me?" she asked between breaths.

Sal went still as death at her words, making her groan at the hindrance. He fixed her with shocked eyes. "Are…you sure?"

She knew giving blood took a large amount of trust from both parties, especially during sex. She wanted it. She wanted to show him in a way other than words that he wasn't just a business arrangement—or some stranger she'd lured off the street.

"I'm sure," she whispered, tilting her head to bare her neck to him.

He breathed a long string of Latin curses, some of them involving a deity or two. He resumed pumping into her at a fast pace. He dipped his head and tasted the warm skin over her vein, shuddering with pleasure. Then, with a seeming impossible ease, he slid his fangs into her.

There wasn't even a prick of pain as he drew in her essence. He moaned a long, deep sound and pounded into her with madness.

Naomi was right there with him. Each pull of her blood seemed to toy with a wired coil until, with one final draw, it snapped. She stiffened and cried to the heavens as another orgasm shuddered through her, sending nerves racing through her body at light speed. An explosion of colors clouded her vision and the water spraying from the shower grew distant, the only sound to be heard was her own heart pounding in her ears.

Somewhere in the background of it all, she noticed when Sal withdrew his fangs and roared his own release, squeezing his eyes shut as he filled her with his seed.

Minutes or, hell, even an eternity could have passed before Naomi's subconsciousness returned. Sal looked down at her with a half-lidded gaze, though wariness lingered behind them, as if afraid she'd come to her senses and rip him apart.

Instead, she slid her arms around his neck and held him, burying her nose in his neck. He blew out a small sound of relief and shut the water off. Not once did he set her down as he draped a fluffy towel over her back, and another on his, before carrying them to the grand bed.

He held her close as she snuggled against him. Neither said a word, though it was a comfortable silence. Like the first time they'd had sex, a feeling of peace and contentment settled in her chest, and the connection between them felt stronger. Though she didn't want to accept the inference of it, somewhere in the back of her mind she knew exactly what had just happened. The sex had confirmed it.

She was his truemate. She possessed the other half of his soul. For him, there would never be another.

Yet he'd never be able to claim her.

But that was a worry for another day. At the moment, she just wanted to rest. Letting out a wide yawn, she fell asleep, wrapped in Sal's arms.

Chapter Eight

It wasn't the first time Salvator had woken up to find his bed empty. In fact, he'd always preferred it that way. At his age, he no longer had awkward morning-after encounters with lovers who'd lingered after a passionate night ended. They all knew beforehand that sleeping over was a no-no.

However, when he rolled over on the bed to find it cold and empty, fear struck his heart. He sat up with a jerk, dread settling like a lump of coal in his gut to find Naomi nowhere in sight. He shouldn't have been surprised, but her abandoning him again was far more painful than any blade slicing through him. Somehow, he'd thought that something had changed between them—that her defenses had finally fallen, allowing him to see the vulnerable woman hiding behind a hardened shell of daggers and scars.

Instead, the bed beside him was wrinkled and cold, telling him she'd left hours ago. Bitterness and an emotion he'd never felt before weighed him down, and he dropped his head in his hands in dismay.

By the gods, I'm pathetic. He'd fallen for a woman he'd known could never trust him. She'd made that clear from the start, yet, for some reason, he'd thought that if he pushed her hard enough, she'd cave in. His pain was well-deserved, that was for sure. While he'd never set out to break a woman's heart, it had happened so many times in the past. Despite his warnings to them, several of his lovers had begged for there to be something more between them, yet he'd had to let them down. Perhaps Naomi was the gods' way of getting back at him.

The scent of rich chocolate washed over him. "What the hell are you crying for?"

Sal jerked his head up to peer at the source of the husky Hispanic accent. Naomi leaned against the doorjamb, wearing nothing more than a fresh silky robe. Her long legs were crossed at the ankles, while her hands cradled a small white coffee mug. Though she hadn't done so the night before, sometime after she awoke she'd let down her hair. It was a tousled mass of dark brown curls, falling to her waist, framing her features in a way that made her look like a fallen angel. A battle angel with her multitude of scars, but they did nothing to take away from the sheer natural beauty of her presence.

For a moment, he was able to picture her several years from now, greeting him every morning with a warm smile in their lair. He'd never before thought of such a thing, never even had the desire to settle down and share his existence with some woman for the rest of eternity.

Yet ever since meeting Naomi, he'd had to accept that she wasn't just some woman. She was his truemate —

the one woman the gods had created just for him, the one who would put an end to his life of blood-induced alcohol and faceless women.

His breath hitched and he had to fight back the embarrassing tears pricking the corners of his eyes. Though he'd never wanted a truemate, he couldn't deny that just being at Naomi's side was a joy he'd never take for granted. He'd give up everything he had if it meant keeping her as his own.

"Oh my God," she breathed, straightening from the door. "You really *are* crying."

Sal discreetly wiped his eyes and stood, fixing her with a soft smile. "I don't cry, dove. Some dust just fell into my eye."

She raised a dubious brow, but her gaze dropped to where his cock stood at attention as he closed in on her. "Sure it did," she murmured, distracted. Red seeped into her irises, swallowing the caramel color whole. It was a sign of her being just as aroused as he was.

When he was close enough to touch her, he was pleased when she didn't back away as he trailed his fingers down her cheek. "I was worried you'd be gone when I awoke."

Her lips twitched, and Sal realized it was the first time he'd ever seen something close to a smile on her—without her mask, of course. "You should have been more worried about finding a stake protruding from your chest."

"That wouldn't kill me."

"No, but I'd get a kick out of it."

Sal grinned and traced a line from her jaw to the other side of her cheek. He touched the X there too. "What made you change your mind?"

She tilted her head, pretending to think it over. Her smile turned mischievous. Instead of answering, she placed her cup on the bookshelf next to them then lowered to her knees. Sal drew in a sharp breath when she grabbed hold of him, stroking his erection with a tentative touch.

"Naomi," he breathed, prepared to stop her. However, when her lush lips parted and draped over the tip of his shaft, all forms of cohesive thought were thrown aside. He threw his head back as she drew downward, taking in as much as she could before he felt the back of her throat. "Gods, woman."

She made a soft sound, almost like a chuckle. She pulled away, only to take him in again. With her hand, she gripped his base and worked it until she found a smooth rhythm. The sight of her sucking him off was the sexiest thing he'd ever seen, and though it was clear she was inexperienced, no one else he'd ever known could compare.

All too soon, he was nearing an orgasm. While every nerve in his body screamed to shoot his load down her throat, more than anything, he wanted to be buried inside her. He pulled away and jerked her to her feet. She didn't protest as he tossed her on the bed, but when he made to cover her body with his own, she shoved him onto his back.

"Let me," she growled, smoothing her hands up his torso. Without waiting for a response, she shifted above him and impaled herself on his dick. They both groaned as she wasted no time riding him, grinding her hips in a circular motion that had Sal digging his nails into the comforter to keep from coming.

When she slowed in anticipation of her climax, Sal gripped her hips and pumped while her sex clasped him. She let out a low, sexy moan and that was it for him. With one last lurch, he arched into her as deep as he could go and bit his lower lip until his shaft stopped twitching from yet another powerful release.

Naomi collapsed on top of him, breathing hard. "Damn," she whispered, her breath fanning across his nipple.

"Agreed," he huffed, feeling drained of all his strength. She had that effect on him. Making love to her left him weak in the best way. He had just enough energy to drape his arm over her back. "You're incredible, Naomi."

He didn't see it, but he could feel her smiling against his chest. "You aren't so bad yourself, bloodsucker."

He laughed at that. Though she still tried to act tough, a wall between them had fallen, for which he was thankful. He enjoyed her badass side, but he also enjoyed this playful one. It made him feel as though she was beginning to accept him more. He'd still have to tell her about their truemate bond, but he wanted to hold off on that as long as possible. He wanted her to come to him of her own free will, to fall for him without thinking it was some magical energy forcing them together.

However, he had no doubt she'd soon be questioning their connection. Though he'd hinted at it the night before, sex always strengthened truemates, making them feel each other's presence, even if they were in separate parts of the world. By now, she'd be able to feel his every emotion, just as he was able to feel hers.

She was happy but stressed. Yet beneath it all was a deep sense of worry that had him wondering if it was more than finding out the truth of her mother's death.

"Why haven't you asked about the scars on my face?" she questioned, her voice soft.

Sal peered down at her. She didn't meet his gaze, instead focused on drawing small circles between his pecs. "It seemed suicidal," he joked. She didn't smile, which made him sigh. "I'm not a complete ass. I know when not to cross a line. I don't want you to ever feel pressured into telling me anything you don't want to."

She snorted, but it was a humorless sound. "You pressured me into telling you why I was at your club last night—and why I was looking for my mother's pendant."

"That was different," he defended. "I feel as though your scars are more...personal."

She nodded. "When I was young, barely out of my teen years, my...*needs* made themselves known. The furies only reproduce via human sperm, and even then, they are forbidden from making physical contact. It's their most sacred law."

Sal thought about that for a minute. Furies had their own community in a small corner of Tartarus, though he'd read about it being no bigger than the size of New York. Anyone not of fury blood who crossed into their plane was killed on sight. They weren't the nicest demons in the world. "You mean they use artificial insemination?"

She nodded again, her soft hair rubbing against him. He couldn't help himself as he toyed with a lock between his fingers. "So long as they use human men, all babies are born pureblood fury—and always female. As the story goes, my mother was seduced by an incubus pretending to be human. No one knows for sure if she really had sex with him or just used his sperm, but either way, it was against their rule. Up until

I reached maturity, no one ever suspected I was anything more than a pureblood—not even me. So when my urges first started, everyone thought I was sick. For weeks I was under constant surveillance by the village doctors, but nothing they did ever made the cramps go away. When I'd go out to train with the others, none of my wounds would heal. I was just…an anomaly."

"Furies have wings, don't they? Surely you not having any must have been—"

"We aren't born with them," she cut in with a dry laugh. "It's kind of like a badge of honor. You earn the wings. You go through a special training course for a few years, and after proving yourself worthy at around age twenty-one, there's a ceremony using old magic that'll bind the wings to your back. It may seem strange to others, but that's the fury way."

Sal nodded and continued playing with her hair while stroking his free hand across her back. While Cyrus had texts about fury life in his library, they weren't seen very often in the human world, so no one really cared to study them. Well, Sal hadn't, anyway.

Siovon had told him bits and pieces about Naomi's past, but never the full story. The fact that she was opening up to him about it without persuasion was another positive sign, though he knew her story was about to get ugly.

"When the pain becomes too much, I'm forced to seek out the closest male to satisfy my needs," Naomi explained. The memories of her past threatened to send her into a panic, but she reminded herself over and over that she was safe, that it had been a long time ago.

Furthermore, she wanted Sal to know the truth about her, to understand why she was the way she was, why she did the things she had to do. Because once the time came for her to let him go, she wasn't sure she'd be able to move on to the afterlife—or wherever it was the deceased went—if she didn't at least explain her reasoning. To him and Siovon, she was just trying to justify the reason for her mother's death. What they didn't understand was that in order for Naomi to find true peace, to finally be able to wake up and breathe without being crushed by guilt, she *had* to know the truth. It was the only way.

Even if it killed her.

"Remember that I was young then. I had no idea what was happening to me, but when my needs reached its peak, I couldn't stop my legs as I took off. I had no idea where I was going or how I knew to go there, but somehow, I'd crossed planes and all but attacked the first man I saw. When the other furies found me, they were disgusted at my actions. *I* was disgusted, too, but I couldn't stop it."

Sal smoothing his hands over her hair and back were comforting, giving her the courage to relay her past to him. "They learned the truth of what I was that day — and my mother was tried and executed for it."

"Even though she was tricked or unaware of what you were, they still killed her?" Sal demanded, bewildered.

Naomi nodded. "I didn't understand it, but what was more disconcerting was the way my mother never tried to fight them or plead her case. It was as though she'd expected the outcome, as if she knew it would be pointless."

"That's...strange."

"Agreed, but at the time, I was just devastated over losing her. I never thought it could possibly be anything more than that. Her only wish had been that they'd banished me instead of me facing execution. I was angry at her for a long time. I had no one to care for me and nowhere to go. I would have preferred death." Sal stiffened at her statement, but she patted him as if *he* needed comforting. "I was forbidden from ever returning there, and if I ever tried, the council promised to kill me without question. They sold me on the black market to the highest bidder, and I never saw or heard from any of them again."

"Did you not have any blood relatives?" he demanded. "Did they not try to fight for you or your mother?"

"My mother had only one sister named Elvira, but she was a member on the council. She was one of my mother's accusers."

"What a bitch," Sal growled. Naomi snorted with humor, not offended in the least bit. "So, what happened after they sold you?"

She went silent, not willing to answer right away. Despite how tragic her past as a fury was, the bit about Reinaldo was where her life had changed courses. It was more than a touchy subject.

"I was bought by a Spaniard named Reinaldo. He was a vampire. He was a lot like you, actually." She peered up in time to catch him scowling. She chuckled. "Not that you looked alike, but he was very wealthy and handsome. He carried himself with pride, and he enjoyed indulging in life's riches—women, clothes, drinks…all of it."

"I hate him already," he groused. "He sounds like a douche."

At that, Naomi laughed, something she hadn't done in a very long time. *Chuckled, maybe. Sneered, for sure. But laughed?* She couldn't even remember the last time she'd done so.

Sal's expression softened as he gazed at her in awe. "What a lovely sound," he murmured, tucking a strand of hair behind her ear. It was a tender gesture that was foreign to her, but she turned into his touch to kiss his palm. "What was it like with this Reinaldo fellow? What a fruity-ass name, by the way."

She laid back down on his chest and sighed. "For a little while, it was nice. He was a true gentleman and treated me as though I wasn't a slave. He never forced me to do anything I didn't want, he dressed me in the most beautiful gowns and he was patient while I adjusted to a new life. At the time, everything seemed too good to be true. I'd thought he was Prince Charming with fangs. Being young and naïve, I fell for him quite easily. He told me I was the only woman for him, that he desired marriage and all that shit."

Her mood darkened, and Sal hugged her tight. "What happened, dove?"

She still drew circles on his chest, though when she took note of the red mark left behind, she realized she'd dug her nails into him in anger. "Before then, it had been a few weeks since my first encounter with a man. One night, my urges hit me like a ton of bricks, and I needed someone again. Succubus pheromones are quite potent, so being in a large house filled with unmated men had them banging on my door. I was fighting my needs, but Reinaldo came in and... Well, you can guess what happened next."

A blast of anger burned in her chest, but it wasn't hers. It was Sal's, and the implication for why she could feel his emotions was one she still wasn't ready to consider. He tucked a finger under her chin to make her look at him. "Naomi, did he force you?"

She swallowed hard. His brows were pulled together in anger, his lips pressed into a tight line. His piercing stare boring into her was intimidating, but she didn't look away. She couldn't. She'd blamed herself for allowing Reinaldo to use her, for not being strong enough to fight him. Though countless readings from psychology texts and anonymous visits to the guild's shrink had assured her that it was common and natural for a victim to blame herself after being abused, none of it had eased the rage she still felt over what Reinaldo had done.

Not until now, when she was able to relieve her burdens onto Sal. Though he looked ready to rip someone's throat out, sharing her past with him drained her of decades worth of regret and anger.

"Bloody fucking hell," he growled, moving to a sitting position. "Where is he now? I'll stake that bastard in the middle of the Sahara Desert and watch the sun fry his ass."

Naomi sat up as well. "That wouldn't have been a bad idea," she murmured. "Too bad he's already dead." He shot her a startled look, but she nodded with grim satisfaction. "After that night, he dropped his 'perfect gentleman' vibe, and it was then that I was able to see his true colors. I wasn't his only consort, nor was I the youngest." She shook her head in disgust. "I'm not sure how long I was there, but when I denied him and tried to fight him off, he carved these Xs in my cheeks as a way of saying that if he couldn't have me, no one would. It took several more weeks for me to finally get the nerve to escape, and I almost did until I saw him beating on a young girl. She was pregnant—very pregnant."

She rubbed her hands over her face, trying to scrub away the image of that girl, bruised and broken. She'd been so skinny, barely strong enough to stand, yet Reinaldo had been merciless as he struck her with his fists, over and over again. "I knew right then and there that I couldn't leave with a clear conscious, knowing he had other women and girls there against their will, doing to them what he did to me. So, I decided to put an end to his madness."

Sal nodded in approval. Facing her, he took her hands in his. "You have a good heart."

Naomi shrugged, not wanting to reiterate that her life as an assassin didn't make her Mother Teresa. "He came for me the next night. I had to time everything perfectly, so I allowed him to do his business until he fell asleep. His guards were all Turnbloods, so I waited until just an hour before dawn to kill him. It wasn't pretty and he put up a fight, but I made sure that bastard bled."

"Good," Sal lauded, squeezing her hands. "He deserved it."

She nodded. "It was my first time killing anyone, yet I didn't feel any remorse. The feeling of being free and saving those other girls from suffering any longer was just...a relief." She threw her head back and eyed the canopy above them. Then, she smiled. "That was the night I met Siovon. I probably looked like a madwoman covered in ash and blood. I thought she was going to kill me, but she was there for Reinaldo. He was her target, which she later told me was due to a number of young girls and women going missing in a nearby village. Of course, this was long before she became a pacifist."

Sal chuckled, though his shoulders were still tense. "A pacifist who was raised as an assassin. Go figure."

Naomi gave a soft laugh. "It does seem unlikely, but I'm very proud of her. She's come a long way. Believe me when I say you wouldn't have even recognized her back then. Anyway, I thought she'd be mad that I stole her kill, but she wasn't. She just gave me this smile, like she was pleased. When she started to leave, I begged her to help me free the other girls and to take me with her. She was very reluctant at first, but then she said these exact words — *Those guards of his aren't innocent in any of this. Show me you have what it takes, and I'll train you.* I'll never forget that, because I remember how badly I wanted to impress her. I wanted her to help me become stronger, so that no one could ever make me feel weak or insignificant again. So, I joined the guild as her apprentice, and from then on, I became…me."

"A warrior," Sal said with admiration. "A survivor. To go through all of that in a short amount of time, yet still make it out with such strength… You're amazing, dove. Truly amazing."

Naomi's cheeks heated at the compliment, but she hid a smile by peering over her shoulder at a nearby window. "It's only an hour before sunset, but we still have a whole day before the black market opens. Perhaps we should use this time to inspect the gates."

Sal kissed each of her knuckles. "Sounds like a good idea."

She bit her lip when he started to nibble at her inner wrist. "Or?"

"Or we can do that tomorrow and spend tonight inspecting…something else."

He worked his lips up her inner wrist to the crook of her elbow. "What did you have in mind?" she breathed.

Before she could guess his intention, he had her pinned beneath him, settling himself between her legs. She gasped at the feel of his erection pressing against her folds, already slick and ready for him. He pulled apart her robe and dragged his tongue from her collar to the shallow valley between her breasts. "What do you say about this?"

Naomi moaned when he traveled lower to dip his tongue inside her belly button. "I say you're a procrastinator, Salvator Gordano."

He nipped at her navel and continued lower. He lifted his twinkling gaze to meet hers, a smile playing at the corner of his sinful lips. "That wasn't a no."

She relaxed when he placed her legs over her shoulders. "Fine," she breathed, moaning when he captured her clit between his teeth. "But only for tonight."

He hummed in response and went to work pleasuring her in a way that only he could.

Chapter Nine

"I thought we agreed on casual clothing," Naomi muttered as Sal emerged from the bedroom.

He wore a crisp white button-down tucked into pressed navy-blue dress pants. His hair was brushed and left loose to flow in a silver curtain down his back, and there was even a monogram on the pocket over his chest. Even though it wasn't his flashiest getup, everything about him screamed, 'I'm fabulously wealthy'.

He paused in the middle of rolling his sleeves up to his elbows. "What do you mean? These *are* my casual clothes."

Naomi parted her lips, giving him a once-over. "You're kidding, right?" He didn't answer, instead fixing her with a confused frown. "*Dios.* Don't you own a pair of jeans or a flannel shirt or anything?"

Sal cringed in disgust, as if she'd asked him to eat a bowl of cockroaches. "A flannel—are you mad? You said casual, not barbaric. Do I look like I chop down trees for a living?"

She rolled her eyes and stood from the couch. "You should. RÉSO is going to be filled with humans and demons. We're supposed to blend in, yet you look like you're about to go wine-tasting in Prague."

"Nonsense." He strolled toward her with a wide smile. "I think I look wonderful."

"Of course you do. The point is to not look wonderful — to not stand out."

His smile stretched to his ears. He stopped close enough for the smell of his aftershave and soap to fill her lungs. It was a heady scent that made her insides quiver with longing, as if she hadn't spent all night having orgasm after orgasm. "If you want us to match, all you have to do is say so. I believe there's a blue dress somewhere in those bags."

Naomi peered down at herself, frowning. Earlier in the morning, Sal had sent one of his employees out to buy her a change of clothes. She'd argued against it but conceded to the fact that her usual outfit would only draw the attention of everyone around them. While the black spandex allowed for easy movement and blending in with the shadows, wearing it in the daytime when she was supposed to be incognito wasn't the brightest idea. Instead, she'd dug through the bags of designer clothing until she'd found a maroon sweater and ripped denims. To her, it was…cute.

She'd long ago given up her taste for 'feminine' attire. Dark colors suited her, and the hijab covering her hair had a sheer black veil attached that covered her scars. Besides her eyes, hands and knees, she was almost covered head-to-toe. It was a simple style compared to Sal's, but she liked it. She liked the modesty of it, and while looking at herself in the mirror, she'd felt normal for the first time.

"Match you?" she scoffed, turning away from him. "I'll gauge my own eyes out before dressing up in some bedazzled costume."

"Bedazzled costume?" he sputtered. "Gods, woman. Are you determined to insult me all day?"

Naomi shrugged in response and headed for the door. To her dismay, she still wasn't able to bring even one blade, due to the metal detectors in the city. The lack of weapons still unsettled her, but she'd push through it until nightfall when the gates opened. She didn't expect a fight just yet, but if things came down to it, she and Sal could just teleport to safety.

Her reliance on him was another thing that was unnerving. She'd been alone for so long. She always fought her own battles, yet the fact that she'd gotten close enough to Sal to trust him with so much of her past was terrifying. He made her feel vulnerable, like she didn't have to be strong in his presence. She could melt into him and let her walls down, and it'd be okay because he'd be there to hold her.

A small part of her still warned that it was just an illusion and he truly was a monster like Reinaldo. Or perhaps he wasn't as cruel, but he would end up breaking her heart. After all, Salvator Gordano was a name known even across the seas in the demon world. Everyone knew of the prestigious debaucher. Long before Naomi had ever met him, she'd heard his name dozens of times. Even some of the other guild members — the women, of course — would fawn over him, saying how they'd give anything in the world just to spend one night in his bed.

There were hundreds of thousands of beautiful women out there, ones who would be better suited to his taste—ones who enjoyed dressing up in beautiful silk and dabbling in the finest wines and all that garish shit, ones who weren't covered in ugly scars, who had more curves and who weren't reserved assassins with commitment issues. That cruel voice always taunted that even if Sal thought he wanted her now, it would never last. He'd grow tired of her after getting what he wanted. He'd see that past her aloof composure was a woman far too scarred from her past to ever have a decent future.

Whether they were truemates or not, it could never work. Even if she survived her journey, there was no hope for them beyond a few nights of steamy passion.

And the fact that she'd opened up and given such an important part of herself to him was proof that she was already in too deep. She couldn't let things continue going the way they were. For both of their sakes, it was best if she got out while she still could.

When a pale arm waved in front of her face, she blinked to see that Sal was standing in front of her. "Hey, are you listening to me?" he demanded.

She shook her brooding thoughts away. "Nope."

"If you keep spacing out like that, you're going to wind up lost somewhere." He tucked her hand in the crook of his elbow. "Let's get going, shall we?"

Biting back her sigh, she nodded.

Though they weren't going to be in direct sunlight all day, Sal had made sure to pack several bags of blood inside a portable cooler, just in case. It was well-known that Royals and Aristocrats could ingest human food, but it didn't provide them with any nutrients the way blood did. Most of them just skipped eating altogether.

Besides, after having a taste of Naomi's delicious blood, the sweet tooth that had lingered for months had only intensified. He didn't trust himself to not sneak her off in a corner somewhere for a midday snack. Not that he had any delusions that she'd allow such a thing, but it was better safe than staked — which was exactly what she would do if he brought up such a suggestion.

The thought made him smile. Even though he was sure Naomi was more comfortable around him than she'd been previously, she was still her sarcastic, short-tempered self. It was adorable.

He just wasn't going to tell her that. She'd no doubt punch him in the throat, even if he were being honest.

"This place is huge," she murmured, though her voice was drowned out by the thousands of other voices chatting as they passed through.

It was true. RÈSO, aka the Underground City, was an indoor labyrinth of interconnected passageways that made up an integral part of downtown Montreal. Everywhere they looked consisted of stairways and tunnels leading to various shopping centers, hotels, metro stations, restaurants and countless other trades. Though most of the people strolling to their destinations were human, Sal detected a demon every so often, though they didn't look to be up to any kind of trouble.

Making sure to stay close to Naomi so they didn't get separated, he pulled out a map and pretended to study it. It wasn't necessary, for he knew exactly where to go when the gates opened, but in order to not make him and Naomi stand out, they had to give the image of them being mere tourists—just in case someone was watching them.

He pointed to the Eaton Centre Mall. "Here, between the shoe store and the bath store is where the gates will open."

Naomi leaned closer to get a better view of the map. "Right in plain sight, huh?"

"Indeed. So, where do you want to start?"

She shot him a confused look. "Start what? We're just going to take a look around."

"It's still early, dove. We have this entire day to explore this mall—or others, if you'd rather."

Her frown deepened. "What's the point in that? We're not here for fun and games."

"No, but it wouldn't be the worst thing in the world to enjoy ourselves and work at the same time, right? Isn't it every woman's dream to go on unlimited shopping sprees?"

Naomi took a step back. Her unease was evident, but for the life of him, he couldn't figure out why his suggestion made her uncomfortable. "What's wrong, Naomi? Talk to me."

She looked around the open floor, refusing to meet his eyes. "This is… I've never… Well…"

Though she couldn't form what she wanted to say, it didn't take long for realization to hit. Based on her revelation about her past, he doubted there was ever a time when she'd gone out into the world—in daylight—just for leisure. Her insecurity about her scars would have kept her from ever venturing outside just for the hell of it. He could only assume she'd never gone shopping before—shopping for anything other than food and weapons for survival.

He fixed her with a tender look and pocketed the map. "I understand. This is my treat. We can start here on the ground floor and work our way upstairs. Anything you see that you'd like, pick it up."

She narrowed her eyes in suspicion. "Why? So that I can be indebted to you? I don't think so."

Though he knew he should have expected her to say something like that, it was a blow to his manhood that she still couldn't fully trust him. He'd made love to her over and over again, had shown her with his words and touch that he'd never hurt her. He thought he'd proven that he wasn't anything like that bastard Reinaldo.

"This is my treat, Naomi," he said in the most serious voice he could muster. "You won't owe me anything, nor will I ever ask for something you're unwilling to give. On that, you have my word."

She stared at him, as if trying to find a lie written on his face somewhere. She had to know he was telling the truth. Before he ever realized she was his truemate, he'd already been smitten with her. Her beauty, her strength and her blunt honesty in not wanting anything to do with him had only lured him in, causing him to spend excessive amounts of time brooding over her. When he'd gotten that call from Siovon, for the first time in ages, he'd felt true happiness, more so after laying eyes on Naomi again.

She was everything to him. While he still feared the thought of losing his truemate, he was no longer reluctant to settle down with the one woman he was destined to spend an eternity with. If it was Naomi, every bit of pain that awaited him would be worth it, so long as he got to spend these precious moments with her.

It was hard to determine how much time had passed when she finally sighed. She relaxed her shoulders, and all traces of wariness left her eyes. "Okay," she murmured, rubbing a nervous hand over her arm, "just one store."

Sal breathed a sigh of relief and flashed her a genuine smile. He took her hand and laced their fingers together, thankful when she didn't pull away. "Sure thing, dove."

* * * *

One store, huh? Sal thought with a smirk, several hours later. He sat on a bench outside the dressing room of yet another women's clothing store as Naomi tried on the armful of clothes she'd snatched up. Next to him were over a dozen bags filled with all types of apparel—mostly her belongings. There was only one bag for him, a tiny one that contained a striped red-and-black tie she'd picked out.

After entering the first store, she'd been hesitant to grab anything, but she'd frozen with shock when she'd spotted a pair of red leather boots. From there, she'd dropped her detached attitude and flitted from store to store, proving his previous words about women and shopping sprees to be true.

Though other men would be annoyed to be treated as tote machines, Sal took great pride and joy in watching Naomi's excitement over picking up things she wanted for herself.

"I feel silly," she called as she poked her head around the corner. "I don't think that saleswoman knew what she was talking about."

He tilted his head to one side. "When did you speak to a saleswoman?"

"When you left the store to answer your phone."

"Ah." Lucian had called to check on their progress, as well as deliver the news that Ava had gone into labor. Though the baby had yet to arrive, everyone back home was anxious to meet the newest member of their family. As much as Sal wanted to be there for such a special occasion, he knew, without a doubt, that Naomi would insist on making him return without her. Instead, he'd made his brother promise to keep him updated until he could join them.

"Nonsense," he responded to Naomi. "Let me see." So far, most of the items she'd grabbed had been pants, blouses, jackets and shoes, all of which she'd tried on and bought. She had yet to put anything back, and each time a sales rep had tried to help her, she'd declined. It made him curious to see what the woman had suggested.

After some low grumbling, Naomi stepped from around the corner and took nervous steps toward him. He did a double take, dropping his chin to his chest at the sight of her.

A dark red bodycon dress clung to her slender form, stopping just below her knees to reveal her toned legs. The spaghetti straps were thin strips over her shoulders, leaving the smooth skin of her arms bare. The plunge of the V-neck showed a small portion of her cleavage, while the rest was covered with intricate lace designs that only teased at what lay beneath. Though she still wore the black hijab and mask, the seductive slant of her eyes added an edge of mystery and intrigue to anyone who peered at her.

"I knew it," she murmured. "You hate it."

Hate it? Sal damn near choked on his spit and had to swallow several times before he could speak. If he hated it, his cock wouldn't be standing at full attention in his pants, threatening to embarrass him in front of thousands of other people. "Naomi, you are stunning," he whispered, unable to tear his eyes away from her.

His words made her self-conscious, he knew, but the happy thump in their bond let him know she was pleased with his compliment. She turned to the wide mirror and took in her appearance. "It's not my usual style."

He cleared his throat again and rose, making sure to shift himself to make his erection not so noticeable. He moved to stand behind her. "Change isn't always bad. How do you really feel in this?"

She tilted her head to one side, then the other. She smoothed her palms down the material of the dress. "I don't know. It's a pretty dress, but I've never pictured myself wearing something so...girly."

"You look amazing, but you don't need this." When he reached for the edge of her hijab, she stiffened, but he held on to her wrists when she made to stop him. "Trust me. Please."

She was afraid to be seen without the mask. He didn't need to be connected to her in any way to know that. He'd realized it from the start when her mask had fallen during their scuffle in the snow and he'd called her beautiful. She was so insecure about her appearance, but he needed her to know she didn't have to hide from the rest of the world. She was beautiful with or without her scars.

When she gave a slow nod of approval, she squeezed her eyes shut as he released her and removed the hijab. Her hair had been pulled into a low bun, and he freed it to allow the silky locks to cascade down her back and over her shoulders. "Open your eyes."

After a beat, she complied. When she peered at herself, her eyes filled with shock, though the fear had vanished from them.

"I told you," he murmured in her ear. "You are absolutely stunning." The brief flash of red in her irises made his dick jump in excitement, and he wanted nothing more than to pull her into the dressing room, hike the ends of her dress up and take her until the frantic need to be inside her subsided.

"Ah, there you are," a perky voice called. "Have you tried on the— Oh my God." Sal and Naomi turned to the saleswoman, whose jaw went slack at the sight of them. Naomi shied away from her, likely thinking that her gawking was because she was disgusted by the scars, but then the woman said, "I knew it would look nice on you! Your shape is perfect for this dress, and the color goes well with your hair and skin. You look like you could be a runway model."

Naomi's shock ran through him, making him smile as the woman gushed over her appearance. It was true that the scars on her cheeks were noticeable, but they didn't hinder her beauty one bit.

The woman—whose nametag read Stacy—called over a few other workers. Sal was dismissed and pushed aside as they fawned over Naomi, though he didn't complain. Her cheeks were bright red, but their honest compliments clearly made her happy.

While they shuffled back and forth to urge her to try on other dresses with shoes and jewelry to match, he returned to his seat on the bench and watched them with a small smile. She didn't fight the other women or try to ward them off. Deep beneath that tough shell of hers, she was all woman at heart.

He was patient as he waited another hour until they exited the store with three more large bags added to her collection. She had put her casual clothes from earlier back on, minus the hijab. He wondered if the compliments of those other women had given her the confidence to show her face. Whatever it was, he was pleased. Though she was alluring with the mask on, he enjoyed watching her lips move when she talked and smiled.

"Are you enjoying yourself?" he asked her.

Her eyes twinkled with delight as she peered up at him. "I am. I don't think I've ever had this much fun."

His heart expanded at that. "I'm glad. What do you say we get something to eat?"

She nodded. "Yes, I'm famished."

He was too, but he was hungry for something entirely different than food. The sight of her in that dress, coupled with the desire he always had for her, stirred the need in him to be drenched in her heat. He doubted there'd ever be a day when his lust for her would be sated.

Instead of acting on his impulses, however, he gathered her bags in both hands and led the way down to the food court. Naomi stayed by his side, more than once brushing against his arm. Somehow, it felt as though another wall had fallen in the last few hours. The shopping must have relaxed her in a way, allowing her to be free for a while to experience a normal life.

When they made it to the food court, dozens of different smells hit his nose, making his stomach growl. *Huh*, he thought. He supposed he did want regular food as well.

"My mouth is already watering," Naomi said, taking a deep inhale. "Is there anything in particular you want?"

You. Out loud, he said, "You decide. Today is all about you."

She shook her head and took a while to decide on what she wanted. "Let's try that Japanese place."

After placing their orders and receiving their food, Naomi chose a private table that was far enough away from everyone else, yet close enough to where they could view the closed-down store that contained the gates to The Shade. They ate in a comfortable silence until Naomi took the last bite of her noodles.

"That was delicious," she said with a sigh of content. "Thank you for all of this. Really. I didn't know being rich was so much fun. I thought you people were all just stuck up, prancing showboats."

Sal choked on the shrimp he'd popped into his mouth. "I beg your pardon?" he choked out, patting his chest a few times. When his windpipe cleared, he took a deep sip of his drink. "How insulting."

She snorted with humor. "Well, I did."

He shook his head in bemusement. "So brutally honest. Haven't you heard the adage that if you don't have anything nice to say, don't say anything?"

She shrugged in nonchalance and reached over the table to stab one of his shrimp with her chopsticks. "How is it any fun for me if I can't say what I want?"

Sal chuckled. "True enough. Your guilelessness is attractive."

She reached for a piece of broccoli. "Okay, Sally. You know all about my life. Tell me yours."

"What do you want to know?"

She thought it over, as if looking for the right question to ask. "How come a boulevardier such as yourself is so skilled at fighting? The strength and speed are understandable, since you're a vampire, but your battle skills are far more honed than anyone else I've fought. You don't strike me — or anyone, I presume — as a man who can kick ass the way you do."

"Bloody freaking hell," he grouched, dropping his chopsticks. "I have no idea whether or not that was an insult or a compliment."

"It was a genuine question."

Shaking his head in dismay, he leaned back in his seat. His past wasn't something he talked about...ever, not even to his family. Though Lucian, Cassander and their father had forgiven him, the guilt over his mother's death still surged every so often, even after a thousand years. That was why he didn't try to stop Naomi from setting out on her journey for the truth. He knew firsthand how desperate one could feel in order to find inner peace.

And though she'd opened up to him all on her own, he wanted to return that trust. He sighed. "A long time ago, when I was a careless young adult, I was powerless to save my mother from being killed."

Naomi paused mid-chew, her eyes flying wide. "What?"

He gave a grim nod. "At that time, Cass had embraced our Viking heritage by setting out on his own path of pillaging and plundering. Cyrus and Lucian spent most of the time overlooking the gladiator wars for the clan chiefs." At her questioning gaze, he waved that aside. "That's a story for another time. At that age, I'd never lifted a sword a day in my life. Lucian had always urged me to, but being a warrior like him and the others was never something that held my interest. Instead, I preferred reading. I'd spend hours upon hours in my father's library. It didn't matter what it was. So long as there was paper and words, I'd pick it up. That was how I spent most of my days."

The pain he'd buried so long ago came roaring to life. It'd been ages since he'd last told someone about the dark area in his past—a dark area that had molded him into the 'insatiable debaucher' everyone knew him to be.

Though he made sure to keep his tone and expression calm, Naomi must have sensed his pain, for she placed her hand over his on the table. It was a light, tentative touch, as if she wasn't used to comforting people, but it warmed him inside. He flipped his hand over and held on to her fingers.

"Keep in mind that, at this time in history, it hadn't even been a full century since Cyrus had become king. The lands were still in chaos and not everyone was pleased with his new laws. One night, it was just the servants, my mother and me at home. A group of Royals who thought they'd make better rulers attacked us. I was so lost in my reading that I didn't realize what was happening until it was too late. I heard my mother's scream, and when I ran to her, I tried to fend off the invaders." He scoffed in self-derision. "Me...a wiry, pathetic excuse of a vampire. They would have killed me if not for my father and Lucian making it there in time. However, it was too late for my mother."

Naomi squeezed his hand and stroked her fingers over his knuckles. "I'm sorry, Salvator."

He shrugged, though it was stiff, due to the age-old bitterness he felt. "I've blamed myself for so long, and deep down I knew my brothers and father blamed me too. After that, I spent every night and day training, pushing myself to become stronger. When that didn't ease any of the guilt, I turned to women and drink to drown out the pain. That's when I developed this reputation."

He expected to see judgment in her eyes — or for her to say something cruel at the reminder of what type of man he'd become. She'd already made her contempt for it clear, yet as he met her gaze, all he could see was sympathy.

Neither of them spoke, though what could possibly be said? It had happened so long ago, and his brothers and father had made it clear multiple times that they'd forgiven him. However, it had taken centuries for him to accept the fact that nothing he could have done would have changed it. Even if he had been stronger, he and his mother had been the only Royals in the villa. They still would have been outnumbered, and the result would have been the same.

He'd ended his salacious ways for a while after finding peace with himself, yet Ava's running away had pushed him back over that drunken edge, further causing him to sink back into exactly what Naomi had accused him of being — a scared little boy hiding from his own pain and insecurities.

Yet right across the table from him, less than three feet away, sat the one thing in the entire world that made him want to shed those layers that gave him his libertine reputation. Naomi was everything he'd never wanted, yet the one thing he needed in life.

And it was time he let her know why.

Chapter Ten

St. Charles, Illinois

Even after Andreas, Darius and Julius had spent a couple of hours shopping for toys, Baby Gordano-Lewis still had yet to make an appearance. Andreas didn't fret over waiting, however. There was something he needed to take care of, and with every passing second, the anxiety of getting back his test results mounted.

It was something he'd done in secret weeks ago. While he couldn't give two shits over forming some kind of bond with his birth parents, the driving need to give them a piece of his mind refused to go away. That was, if they were even still alive. Even so, he wanted to know who they were and to get some answers.

When he'd been lying on his deathbed, he'd had the recurring dream of a woman holding him as a baby. Though he could never see her face, her arms had felt nice wrapped around him. He'd always felt safe.

However, as the weeks had passed and his illness had grown worse, the dream had altered. It would start with her holding him then shift to her running in the woods for dear life. The scent of her fear would always make him choke, yet he was never able to speak or move. Then, just as she broke free of the tree line, she'd hug him tight and kiss his forehead before setting him on the ground and disappearing into the night. He'd cry and reach his tiny arms out to her retreating form, but she would never return.

He'd never known if it was just a dream or a memory buried somewhere deep inside, but since he refused to tell anyone about it, out of concern, he'd left it alone. That was, until he could no longer get those images out of his head. It made him wonder if that woman had been his birth mother, and if so, he needed to know why she'd abandoned him when he was just a helpless baby. Though he loved Cyrus and Anna for taking him in and raising him as their own, all he wanted to know was the why.

Cyrus had never kept his adoption a secret. He'd told him how Anna had found him crying on the forest floor, swaddled in a blanket—no note or anything. Together, they'd never once treated him as though he wasn't one of them, nor had his brothers. They were the only family he knew, and he'd forever be grateful and love them. However, the burning rage that came with seeing those dreams over and over again made him want to discover the truth of his heritage.

That, and there was always a part of him that wondered why he'd specifically been dropped off nearly at Cyrus' back door. It could have just been a coincidence—or that his parents had trusted the king himself to take care of a helpless Royal baby, but he had a niggling sense that there was something more. Something...personal. Though the only physical thing he likely had in common with his father was the black hair, that was far too common a color to suggest paternity. Still, he wanted to know, just to be safe.

Therefore, he'd gotten blood work done in secret. If he had any living or dead relatives out there, he was going to trace their lineage all the way back, no matter how long it took. Perhaps Cyrus had been a distant family member—like an uncle or cousin or something.

Slipping into his bedroom—they all had individual rooms for when they wanted to stay over—he locked the door and took a seat at the small table near the fireplace. Then he removed the padded envelope from under his light jacket and placed it on the table. Instead of opening it right away, he just stared.

Though he was determined to discover the information, the results hidden inside the orangish package made him nervous. It wasn't like he expected anything useful inside. After all, he was over three hundred years old and there was no proof of his exact birthday, so it was unlikely that there were any existing records to aid him in his search.

Inhaling a deep breath to calm his shaking hands, he reached for the envelope and opened it.

It took only a second to read over the two papers inside. However, in that instant, all the blood in his body ran cold, and it wasn't until he started to grow faint that he realized he'd stopped breathing.

As expected, no direct descendants had been found. However, on the paper containing his DNA results versus Cyrus', printed in clear black-and-white ink, was a chart that depicted numbers that shook his very world.

And at the bottom of the page, just below the diagram, was a ninety-nine percent match that proved Cyrus was his blood father.

What…the hell?

* * * *

Montreal

After lunch, Sal had flashed to the suite to drop off their bags, then returned to take her to a section of RÉSO that had another shopping center. She'd been having so much fun that she hadn't paid attention to how much time had passed, nor had she once remembered their true reason for being there in the first place. When he'd dropped off another load of clothes, he'd mentioned the time and told her there was one other place he'd wanted to see.

Suspicious, yet curious to visit another wonderful sight in the city, she'd followed along without question.

Well, until they got a bit farther from RÉSO to a slightly less crowded area in town.

"Where are you taking me?" Naomi demanded, wondering if perhaps she'd been tricked.

"It's a surprise, dove."

"Have I told you that I don't like surprises?"

"No, but I'll note it for future references." He grinned over his shoulder, making her heart stutter. "I wanted to show you something before we go to The Shade."

She glanced at her wrist as though there was an invisible watch there. "Well, the gates open in an hour. You'd better make it quick."

He chuckled and tugged her along an empty sidewalk. When he stopped outside a stone gate, she frowned up at the name. "*Notre Dame des Neiges*. What is this?"

He grinned and shook his head. "I remember how awestruck you looked when we visited the Rosehill Cemetery in Chicago. You enjoyed the picturesque view, right?"

Blinking in surprise, Naomi peered through the slits in the gate to see that the cemetery beyond was just as spacious and beautiful as Rosehill, complete with tame landscaping and lush trees illuminated by the setting sun in an orangish glow. "Wow," she breathed, stepping around him. "Sal, this is... Wow."

He took her hand again and flashed them farther inside. There were trees everywhere, making her gaze in amazement. She didn't pull away as he led her down the twisting narrow paths leading over small slopes. The statues she spotted every so often held her attention, some of them gold-plated, some painted wood and others made of stone. The headstones of the deceased were beautiful and well-maintained, and more than once she spotted a little fox scurrying across the fields.

The sight made her smile, but when they crested another small slope, she eyed a gorgeous stone mausoleum surrounded by an array of wildflowers and a little fountain with two sparrows sitting on the edge. They didn't fly away when they spotted Naomi and Sal, instead tilting their heads in curiosity at the two strange beings.

Naomi sighed in appreciated at the serene beauty of it all. "Sal, thank you for this."

He turned to her and tucked a stray lock of hair behind her ear. "Cemeteries have never crossed my mind when I considered romantic dates, but I thought you might like it."

She smiled up at him. "I do. This was the best idea you've ever had." At his insulted look, she chuckled and squeezed his hand. "Honestly, I appreciate this. This entire day, actually."

He palmed her cheek, and with a slowness to give her time to pull away, he leaned forward. Instead of doing so, she met him halfway and kissed him. The gentle touch caused a slow burn to build, but she liked it. Over and over, he slanted his lips over hers, teasing the entrance each time until she nipped at his lower lip. When he groaned, she slid her arms around his neck and deepened the kiss.

Her legs went weak when he flashed them to the bedroom, back peddling her until her knees touched the back of the bed. Without breaking away, she kicked her shoes off when he reached for her zipper and she lifted her hips to allow him to tug her jeans down her legs. Once free, he smoothed his hands up her thighs, kneading her skin until he made it to the edge of her sweater.

He finally pulled away to tug the garment free until she was naked before him. His half-lidded gaze was full of hunger as he watched her. Unable to hold back, she went to work freeing him from his clothes as well, starting with his shirt. After popping the buttons one by one, she planted little kisses all over his chest while she tugged his waistband over his hips.

"Gods, Naomi," he breathed, dragging her name out on a growl when she took his dick in her hand.

"You're so hard," she purred in delight, stroking him.

"You make me this way." He gripped her shoulders and pushed her onto the bed.

Before he could cover her, she turned over and raised her ass in the air, waving it at him in a taunting manner. He growled again and settled behind her, but instead of entering her, he palmed her cheeks and kissed each one. She moaned when he used a finger to toy with her clit. Still holding her, he leaned to pressed his lips against her from behind.

"Oh," she murmured, arching her back to bare herself to him more. "That feels so good."

He groaned into her, using his tongue to stroke into her as far as he could go. While he worked it in an in-and-out motion, she dug her fingers into the comforter, gripping it as she panted against the bed.

With one final lick, he pulled back just to slide his cock into her with agonizing slowness. Instead of sinking into her, he only used the tip, pulling out completely and reentering, though never going in all the way.

The way he teased her drove her mad with desire, making her bite her lower lip until she tasted blood. The pleasure-pain only made matters worse, and when she couldn't take it anymore, she shoved her hips back and impaled herself on him.

He stiffened when she cried out, loving how much he filled her. "You're so impatient, dove," he gritted, though the sheer amount of will it must have taken for him to not do the same must have been just as much torture for him as it was for her.

"Don't talk," she commanded, wriggling her hips against him. "Just move. Make me come."

"*Merda*," he said on a low, sexy growl. He gripped her waist. "As you wish." He withdrew to the very tip and slammed into her, then again.

Every thrust pushed out a pant, but he didn't pick up his speed. Instead, he rocked into her with a steady, rough pace. To her surprise, her climax built higher and higher, and when he once again reached around her waist to tease her clit, spasms seized her as an intense orgasm only Sal could bring forth rocked through her.

Her core clenching around him made him breathe a curse, and when another one tore through her, back to back, he froze and unloaded himself.

With weak legs, Naomi pushed herself up before she collapsed. "Oh, my God," she breathed, shoving the loose hair from her forehead. "Wow."

Sal chuckled, but it was a weak sound, as if she'd drained the energy from him. "Agreed. Very much agreed."

After taking separate showers—much to Sal's grumbling--Naomi dressed in her assassin's garb, though she hesitated on whether or not to put her mask back on.

Though the women from earlier—and Sal's encouragement—had made her feel good about herself, her scars were pretty distinct. She'd made sure to keep half of her face covered each time she'd killed a mark, but there was always the off chance that someone out there knew what she looked like underneath. She didn't need any extra attention drawn to her and Sal.

Deciding to wear it, she met him in the kitchen. She double-checked to make sure all of her weapons were in place, relishing in the comfort of having them there. *Hello, my babies*, she thought, as if they would respond.

When she spotted Sal, she couldn't stop her mouth from falling open at the sight of him in the ugliest bit of brown fabric she'd ever seen. "What the hell is *that*? You look like you're about to take a trip to Mordor."

If looks could kill, she was certain the glare he shot her would have melted her to the ground. "Laugh all you want. I have one for you too." He tossed a matching cloak at her.

Naomi pinched it with her thumb and forefinger, holding it out as far as her arm could stretch. "I don't think so."

"Tough," he said with an evil grin. "The wool is enchanted to allow us to pass through the gates. Everyone has to wear it."

It was impossible to tell whether or not he was lying, but if he'd refused to wear a mere flannel shirt in public, she supposed his willingness to don a hideous brown cloak was proof that he was telling the truth. Sighing with dismay, she threw the material over her shoulders and fastened it around her neck. Even through her clothes, the itchy fabric made her uncomfortable, but she forced her discomfort to the back of her mind.

"Is this your way of getting back at me?" she questioned, refusing the urge to scratch at her skin. "I splurged at the malls, so now you're torturing me?"

Sal shook his head and grinned. "I told you that was my treat. The amount you spent isn't nearly enough to tip the scale of what I usually buy."

Yeah, that much was obvious. Everything Sal owned was top-of-the-line pricey. She wouldn't be surprised if he had his own little private island somewhere in the Pacific.

When he eased his way to stand before her, she didn't back away. Had it been a few days prior, she would have had him maimed and incapacitated before he could even think about stepping in her personal space. Not anymore, however. He'd grown on her — like a fungus. He was annoying and hard to get rid of, but not the worst thing to come into her life.

"Do you know what my favorite part about today was?" he asked.

"Holding my bags and carrying them around like a butler?"

He tugged her mask to let it fall beneath her chin. "It was watching the way your eyes lit up every time you smiled. The joy you radiated was contagious. I could feel it in here." He took both of her hands and laid them flat over his heart. "From the moment we met, you haven't left my mind once. I've known for a while now what it meant for me, and while the thought has always terrified me, I don't want to be afraid anymore."

The rising pink staining his cheeks told her that none of this was easy for him, but Naomi was frozen in place, unable to react to the words she dreaded to hear.

"Don't say it," she snipped. She snatched her hands away and backed up to put some much-needed space between them. Though her tone had been harsh, her voice trembled. "You don't love me and we aren't truemates or anything like that. Don't you dare say otherwise."

A stab of hurt pierced her heart, though it was from Sal. His crest-fallen expression made her want to hug him, but the trepidation coursing through her refused to let her accept that they could ever be anything more than what they were.

"You know what truemates are?" he questioned, dropping his hands. "How?"

She shook her head and jerked her mask over her face. Then, she drew the hood of her cloak. None of it was enough, however. None of it allowed her to hide beneath layers of clothing to shield herself from the accusation in Sal's eyes. "It doesn't matter," she said. "All this is between us— It's nothing more than lust, something that will fade sooner or later."

"Naomi—"

"No, Sal," she snapped with rising panic. "Just drop it. Don't say another word. Please."

Their connection throbbed with pain, but she had no idea if it was from her or Sal. Love didn't exist for her. It couldn't. She was on a suicide mission, and even if she survived, there would never be a day where she could fully open up to any man. Though she'd accepted that Sal was different from Reinaldo, the scars the Spaniard had left behind would never go away— neither the physical nor mental.

Sal's expression shuttered, but he didn't look away. Instead, he pulled on his own hood. "Very well, Naomi. Let's just go."

It was on the tip of her tongue to urge him to go home, but she knew he wouldn't. Even though she'd hurt him, he would refuse to leave her side while she charged headfirst into danger. Instead, she had to swallow her feelings and push them away so she could focus on finding the answers she needed. That was her top priority. Hell, that should have been her only priority. There wasn't any room for excuses or distractions.

No matter how much her heart screamed otherwise.

* * * *

Despite her multitude of mental pep talks and self-derision, pretending like her feelings didn't exist was proving to be far more difficult than she'd assumed. When Salvator spoke to her, it was as though nothing had happened between them. She sensed he was upset with her quick rejection, but he didn't treat her any differently than he had beforehand.

It was annoying and confusing. A part of her wanted to ask what was up with that, but she was the one who'd told him to let the conversation go. Another part of her wanted him to be cold to her. It would have snapped her out of her musings and aided her in getting over him a bit faster.

She let out an inaudible sigh. It couldn't be helped, she supposed. Salvator didn't at all seem the type to hold a grudge. In fact, very little ever seemed to upset him, and when it did, he was over it within minutes — including having his parking lot to blown to pieces.

Well, now that she thought about it, even though he'd said he wanted to journey with her in order to find the culprit, she had a suspicion that it was only to cover his true intentions.

Shaking her head to clear it, she focused her attention on their surroundings. The Shade wasn't much larger than a medium-sized town, but the amount of demons traversing about made it seem just as big as one of the major cities in the human world.

All types small buildings lined the sides of the cobblestone streets, and in front of each storefront were open stalls with tables where vendors called out prices and specialty items that they were selling. Just as Sal had claimed, everyone wore cloaks, all from a wide variety of colors.

"This is…not what I expected The Shade to be," she muttered to herself.

"What did you expect?" Sal asked, peering at each stall they passed by. "Lakes of fire, smoggy air and three-headed dogs?"

"Well…yeah. I did."

He chuckled under his breath. "I quite like it. It reminds me of the European markets during the Middle Ages. This takes me back in time."

Unlike his older brothers, who growled and grunted more than they made actual words, he was far more relaxed and tuned into the modern world. It made it hard for her to remember that he'd been born over a thousand years ago. "Remind me again how old you are?"

At his side-eyed glare, she quirked her lips into a small smile. Just like that, the tension between them seemed to drain. She had to admit it was more than a relief. She hated the feeling of walking on eggshells around him.

That didn't mean she was fooled into believing everything was okay between them, however.

When they turned onto a wide street with even more stalls and buildings, he leaned to murmur in her ear, "Keep your eyes peeled for anything out of the ordinary — or anyone who looks to be following us. There's an ominous air around here, but I can't pinpoint its exact location."

"You don't need to tell me that," she whispered back. "Just don't do anything to draw attention to yourself. You're good for that."

He looked taken aback. "What? I do not —"

"You there! Royal vampire," a vendor shouted, approaching them. "I have quite a selection of blood vials that may interest you. You'll find everything from the aphrodisiacal water nymphs to the elusive selkies. For the right price, I'll even toss in a vial of Sugarcain."

Naomi gave Salvator an I-told-you-so look, to which he rolled his eyes. He grabbed her by the upper arm and led her away until the vendor was no longer in sight. When they slowed on a slightly-less crowded street, he released her.

"What's Sugarcain?" she queried, glancing at the group of people standing around a street performer.

Sal grunted in annoyance. "It's a nickname for blood drawn from humans who were high on coke. Vampires aren't affected by common drugs and alcohol, but if it's infused in the blood we feed on, it's far too easy for one to become hooked." He winced and Naomi remembered him telling her about his habitual drinking after his mother was killed. It made her wonder if he'd gotten hooked on such human blood before.

"That's a misleading name," she joked, trying to reduce his dark mood. "I figured it was from an over-indulgence of candy."

Her lighthearted attempt worked. "No, but that wouldn't be a bad idea." He raked his gaze over her in a way that had her nipples hardening. "Your blood has a natural chocolaty flavor. One drop is far more addicting than any drug out there."

Naomi shuddered, but she turned away from him. "Now is *not* the time."

"Unfortunately, you're right," he muttered. "Someone is still following us."

Alarmed, she glanced around them with narrowed eyes. None of the surrounding demons looked out of the ordinary, nor did anyone seem to be spying. Then again, there were far too many of them in one place for her to tell. When in such a large crowd, it was easy for one to blend in with others.

"Come on," Sal said, taking her wrist. "Let's walk around."

Naomi conceded, though her shoulders were tight. It was just like it had been back at Sal's club — the thought of someone out there watching her, yet her being unable to see them made her skin crawl. Not having the upper hand in any situation was always a nuisance.

The streets grew wider, and as the next hour dragged on, the feeling of being watched never once vanished. When they came to a huge, square-shaped corner with over a hundred demons moving from shop to shop, a brief flare of panic rose in her when she and Sal were separated.

She spun in a circle, trying to spot the silver-haired vamp, but with everyone wearing similar cloaks with hoods drawn, it was impossible. Her gaze landed on a lonesome streetlamp, and she pushed through the crowd to get to it. She hoped to get high enough for him to see her — or vice versa.

Just when she was about to break through the horde, someone bumped into her hard enough to make her lose her footing. Though the man's face was half-hidden in the shadow of his hood, he looked to be in his mid-forties with a tiny patch of gray hair at both of his temples. His expression was far from kind and his white scar made him look menacing as he glared down at her with multi-colored eyes. "Watch it," he rasped. With that, he stormed away, disappearing into the others.

"Naomi, are you okay?" Sal questioned, helping her stand.

Relieved, she blinked up at him. "I'm fine. That prick just knocked me over though."

"Who?" He turned a sharp glare into the multitude of bodies.

Shaking her head, she dusted off her ass. "Forget it. He's gone now." Annoyed, she crossed her arms. "Don't you have some vamp buddies in this area that might at least have a map? There has to be a better way to go about this."

Sal grunted. "Montreal is free territory, meaning no chief has the right to claim it." A look of realization dawned on his features but he shook his head.

"What was that?" she demanded. "You do know someone, don't you?"

He grunted again. "Not necessarily. There's a clan just outside of Montreal, but they don't allow trespassers."

"So? You're the king's son. Can't you just stroll in there—?"

"You don't understand," he cut in. "Arson is their chief, yet no one has ever seen or spoken to the man in person. However, no one is granted permission to cross into his land—not even other vampires. Not even my father's Guard can get far without being stopped."

Naomi made a sound of impatience. "Well, we have to try. I'm not taking no for an answer."

Though it was clear he looked like he wanted to argue, her determined expression must have caused him to bite his tongue. He cursed under his breath. "Fine. We can try, but don't expect anything good to come of this. And for the love of the gods, please don't attack anything or anyone."

She snorted and held on to his wrist as he led them back to the front of the gates. "I make no promises."

Chapter Eleven

With Naomi on his heels, Sal tiptoed his way across a grand expanse of land making up a golf course. Though there were very few things he feared these days, venturing into foreign territory belonging to a ruthless clan chief was enough to put any vampire on edge. Even Lucian would be tense with worry.

Though Montreal was considered 'free territory' among the North American vampire clans, everything surrounding it from Ottawa to Quebec City belonged to one man—Arson. That wasn't much of a feat compared to others, but the fact that no one had ever seen him in person was strange. Like all other clan territories, if any demon wanted to linger for more than a few days, they would have to have permission from the vampire chief over that area. Some preferred it that way, while others didn't care one way or the other.

Such was not the case with Arson. No demon outside of his clansmen were allowed to enter. The only exception was for anyone traversing along the highway. For demons who wanted to linger more than a few hours, they were either threatened into leaving or beaten for refusing. That was just a warning. Next came the bloodshed.

Cyrus and Lucian dealt with all issues regarding the clans around the world. More than a few times, the southern Quebec clan had complaints reported against them from outsiders. Yet, because all chiefs were granted permission to run their territory however they saw fit—so long as humans weren't injured or killed without cause—nothing had been done.

Sal wished he could say he had nothing to fear, since he was the king's son, but he doubted that would work in his favor. Even if the clansmen accepted him, he was more concerned for Naomi's sake. He knew firsthand that if she felt threatened, she wouldn't hesitate to attack—something he hoped to avoid. He didn't want to cause a clan war over trivial matters.

The chief over the northeastern states had gone to war with Arson a couple of times over the decades, thinking that with his clan's larger numbers, it would be a swift battle. However, Arson's men held strong and won each time without losing a single life. The same couldn't be said for the opposing side.

That was the biggest fear vampires had about going into Arson's territory. Despite his clan being so small, they were backed by enough strength to fight off much larger ones.

Sal shook his head and continued up a hill. Though it was mid-summer, the weather was chillier than it would be back in Chicago. The golf course was consumed by the stench of whatever fertilizer was used, and he hoped it would do well to mask his and Naomi's scents. While sneaking around would only make them look suspicious, he hoped to at least get close enough to Arson to talk with the man in person. Even at formal meetings for all chiefs, he'd send his clansmen instead of making appearance himself.

Sal's hopes were shattered, however, when he crested the top of the hill. At the bottom was the edge of the bright green grass where it met the surrounding forestry, and beyond the dark shadows of the trees, at least forty pairs of eyes were watching them.

"Leave."

The single command sent a chill down his spine as he shifted to half-stand in front of Naomi. There was a collection of voices that had spoken at once, sounding distorted and gravelly.

"I'm getting a strong *Children of the Corn* vibe," Naomi whispered.

Sal would have chuckled if not for the worry that they'd be attacked. He could flash them to safety, but then they wouldn't be able to get to Arson. "Believe me, dove. These children are far more ominous."

"This is your last warning," came another chorus. "Leave."

By the gods, Sal thought. *Do they actually practice this shit?*

"I am Salvator Gordano, third-born of Cyrus Gordano," he announced to them. "Any harm against me is instant death from your king."

There was a collective silence for several moments. If Sal didn't know any better, he could have sworn they were talking telepathically, trying to figure out what they should do. That would have taken creepy to a new level.

Then, one man stepped from the trees. He was a hulking giant, surpassing even Cassander in height and weight. His expression was hard and he didn't blink once as his stare bore a hole into Sal. It was so unnerving that he wondered if perhaps this was the ghost-like clan chief. He certainly had an intimidating presence.

Not that Sal was scared or anything.

"You have no business here. Even Cyrus is aware of our rules," the man stated.

Sal tilted his chin to a proud angle, though he made sure to stay half-guarding Naomi in case she decided to attack. "I have business with Arson. Are you him, by any chance?"

The male snorted, though it was a humorless sound. "Arson sees no one, Royal or not. *Leave*."

"I'm not leaving until I speak with him. It's regarding the black market in Montreal."

Though it was hard to tell from a distance, even with his advanced vision, Sal almost swore the man stiffened. His expression gave nothing away, but he went quiet again.

Naomi stepped around Sal. "You know something, don't you?" she demanded.

The giant's stare flickered to her. His eyes narrowed when he spotted her hand resting on the blade at her hip. Still, he said nothing. That only seemed to piss Naomi off. Sal felt it in his chest, and he had to bite the inside of his cheek to keep from smiling. Her eagerness to fight something—even giants way taller than her—never failed to amaze him. Though he didn't doubt for one moment that she'd be fearless and take on the entire clan by herself, he hoped she had the sense to know that they needed to be passive in order to get to Arson. If not, they were going to be shit out of luck.

"Well? Say something," she growled, gripping her weapon even tighter. "We don't have all night."

The giant drew his lips back to bare massive fangs at Naomi. "Control your bitch, Gordano."

Just like that, all hell broke loose. Before Sal could even flash to the giant to deck him for disrespecting her, Naomi was a blur of black spandex as she dashed forward. The giant drew a gun from his waistband with lightning-quick movements but Naomi was faster. Like a baseballer sliding into home, she went low to the ground and kicked the man's legs out from under him. He growled but didn't fall. That didn't stop her, however, from taking her dagger and slicing his calves.

Breathing a string of curses, Sal flashed near them and fought off the other clansmen that darted forward to defend the giant. It wasn't a fair fight — dozens of vampires against him and Naomi — yet they persevered.

More than once, someone landed a blow on Sal, though not enough to pierce too deep into his skin. They did, however, ruin his shirt, making him pissed.

"Enough," someone barked from a distance.

The clansmen stopped attacking at once. Sal bared his teeth at the retreating vamps, though several stayed behind to form a semi-circle around him, Naomi and the giant.

Speaking of, Sal peered over his shoulder to make sure Naomi was okay. To his delight, she had the man on his belly with his head locked between her arms. With the force she used to squeeze, it was clear he couldn't breathe as he tapped on the ground for mercy. Sal grinned with pride. "I should have warned you not to piss off a fury."

The giant's eyes flew wide with shock, making Sal nod. His amusement was short-lived, however, when a powerful presence filled the air, one that was ancient enough to make him take a wary step back. Naomi sensed it too, for she released the giant and held her weapons in front of her.

A woman dressed in a full cloak emerged from the tree line, walking with all the grace and dignity of a…well, a queen. That was the only word for the regal aura that seemed to cloud her as she approached. Her bone-straight, dark auburn hair was parted down the middle, highlighted by the moon in a reddish halo. Her skin was all smooth porcelain over a diamond-shaped face, molded with sculpted cheekbones and blood-red lips.

Her eyes were…uncanny, to say the least. A fire burned behind her upturned orbs, making the amber color blaze with light. Though she wore an expression of serenity that didn't look at all frightening, something in Sal's gut told him that she was the clan chief he was looking for.

The elusive man no one had ever seen in person was actually a woman.

Unlike when he'd first encountered the giant, genuine fear slid through him.

"Arson?" he questioned.

Instead of answering, she gave the slightest of nods in confirmation. She trailed her impassive gaze to the ground where the giant clutched his throat and drew in large gulps of breath. One dark eyebrow shot up in a look of sarcasm.

The man stood and moved to Arson's side, glaring at Naomi and Sal the whole time. "Forgive me, Arson. She took me by surprise."

Arson snorted and waved his words aside with a flick of her wrist. She turned her attention to Sal and Naomi. "What business do you have here?"

"Not one for preambles, are you?" Sal grunted. He dusted off his sleeves, frowning at the blood staining through. There was a quiet buzzing in the back of his mind, a slight fluttering as if something was stroking his brain. It was annoying as hell. "I need to ask you some questions regarding the black market."

"And you believe I would know anything about that?"

Sal shrugged. "This is your territory, after all. If anyone should know anything, it'll be you."

"Allow me to rephrase that. You believe I will assist you in any way? My fealty is to the king, not his youngling."

Sal bristled, resisting the urge to huff. No doubt it would only make him look childish. He was well over a thousand years old. *Youngling, my ass.*

Instead, he gritted his teeth. "Surely there must be something I can offer you in exchange. Money? My family and I have plenty to spare."

Arson scoffed. "I have no need for it."

Naomi growled, never one for beating around the bush. She nudged Sal and turned to walk away. "We're not here for bullshit. You were right. This was a waste of time."

The giant leaned down to whisper something in Arson's ear, far too quiet for Sal to hear. Arson raised both of her eyebrows in mild surprise. "Really?" The giant nodded. She called out to Naomi. "Wait."

Naomi didn't falter. Instead, she threw her middle finger up in a salute.

"I will help you."

That got Naomi's attention. She did an about-face and returned to Sal's side, though she didn't look one bit pleased. "What made you change your mind?"

Arson was quiet for a moment, just studying Naomi with a blank stare. "Is it true that you're the fury responsible for the Makalu Massacre?"

Naomi narrowed her eyes, though she couldn't hide her shock. Siovon had told Sal and his brothers about that event, the one where she'd killed a cave full of mountain trolls. Well, killed was a mild way of putting it. The blood-thirsty beasts had been shredded limb from limb. It was a story that had been the highlight of the demon world several decades back, though not many people had known who was responsible for such carnage.

"How do you know it was me?" she demanded.

Arson tipped her head at the giant. "Demetri says you are half-fury. There is only one known around this plane, thanks to that massacre."

"Yeah, but why did that make you change your mind?" Sal demanded.

Arson peered at him. "I once had a clansman native to Tibet who was visiting family during that time. His mate was one of the victims of the trolls, yet had you not intervened in time, he would have lost her." She eyed Naomi. "While I do not aid outsiders, nothing is more important to me than my clansmen. When someone saves the life of one of them, the least I can do is return a favor."

"How noble of you," Sal drawled. He glanced at Naomi, frowning to see the confliction written on her face. "What's wrong?"

She didn't look at him. Instead, she frowned at the ground. "I saved someone that night? I thought... I thought there weren't any —"

Arson's expression softened just a bit. She strolled until she was a few feet away. From the proximity, Sal studied her closer and pondered if he'd seen her before. She looked familiar, but he couldn't place why.

"You saved her, along with her unborn child," Arson murmured. "Though it was a tragic ending for most, there were two lives to make it out of those caves. I'm assuming you weren't aware of such?"

Naomi shook her head in denial, making Sal want to draw her into his arms.

One corner of Arson's lips tilted upward. He assumed it was the closest thing to a smile they were going to get. "You're here to find The Oracles."

It was clear Naomi was thankful for the distraction, but the statement made her suspicious. "How do you know?"

Arson breathed a soft sigh and returned to stand next to the giant. "You should understand by now that I know everything that happens here. Besides, you're looking for the other fury, aren't you?"

Sal and Naomi shared a look of utter surprise. "The other fury?" he asked.

"Of course. The leader of their cult is a fury."

Naomi sucked in a sharp breath. "How do you —?" She cut her question off at Arson's annoyed look. "Who is it? What does she look like?"

Arson made some kind of signal with her fingers. Without hesitation, her surrounding clansmen — along with the giant — retreated to the forest until Sal could no longer sense them nearby. It was impressive how swift their obedience was, but it also made him wonder if Arson trusted them enough to be left alone.

No, he declined. It was more like she knew she could take them both on if they decided to attack. Though Royals were the most powerful vampires around, Aristocrats and some Turnbloods could become just as strong if they'd lived long enough. Arson's cheeks held a bit of pink, telling him she was able to breathe. That let him know that she wasn't a Turnblood, but an Aristocrat.

Still, the ancient aura surrounding her was almost terrifying. It was even sturdier than Lucian's, which Sal didn't think anyone could ever beat — not including Cyrus, of course.

No wonder her small clan was able to defeat the northeastern chief each time he challenged her. If she had aided them on the battlefield, most of them wouldn't have stood a chance.

"I have only seen the fury from a distance," Arson admitted. "Even then, she wore a mask to conceal her identity."

"What did her wings look like?" Naomi asked.

"She had none."

Naomi frowned at that. "What does that mean?" Sal asked. "You told me that all furies gain wings after whatever that ceremony was."

Naomi nodded, though she still looked confused. "They do. Their feathers are different colors, depending on rank. For example, the councilmembers all have dark blue feathers with golden tips. Teachers have purple ones. Students who have completed the training course start out with pale green. To not have wings mean someone either didn't complete the course — or they had their wings removed."

Sal shook his head. "I don't understand. What would make them get rid of their wings?"

"It couldn't have been voluntary. Furies gaining their wings is an honorary ceremony, regardless of status. No one would ever willingly give them up. My only guess is that she was demoted or banished." At Sal's confusion, she huffed. "It's rare that the council chooses banishment over execution, but it happens. When it does, they remove your wings as a public way of forever disowning you. It's considered humiliating."

"I can imagine," he murmured with a grimace. "Do you remember ever seeing something like that as a child? Perhaps it's someone you know."

Naomi frowned. "No. As I said, exile is very rare. The last case before me had happened many decades prior." She focused her attention on Arson. "What else can you tell us?"

Arson lifted on shoulder in a careless shrug. "Lunegris on West Main Street has been reported to be where the most prized possessions are auctioned. The Oracles are harvesters, so their goods tend to bring in the most money." She went silent after that, indicating she was done sharing.

Sal scoffed. "That's all the information you have?" When she only regarded him with a bored expression, he rolled his eyes. "A load of help that was."

"Actually, it was very helpful," Naomi murmured. Sal shot her a surprised look. "Crash told us that when your father's lieutenant went to Baton Rouge—"

"You mean Cass," Sal corrected.

"Whatever... When he went to investigate that shifter pack, the missing wolves had had their pelts removed and sold on the market. The night he went to The Shade, he was attacked. If we go to the auction tomorrow and they bombard us, it'll be our best chance at finding them."

"That's only assuming they know we're looking for them."

She rolled her eyes. "A bomb being planted on my car isn't enough proof?"

Arson's eyes darted between him and Naomi. He didn't know what the hell was going through her mind, but he didn't like that calculating stare one bit. "I've lingered long enough. Consider this a debt repaid, but next time I cannot promise to be so merciful. Take your leave before I change my mind."

Though her threat was delivered with the same melodious tone as before, Sal didn't doubt for a moment that she intended to carry it out—even if he was Cyrus' son. "One more thing I'd like to know," he called to her retreating form. Somehow, he got the feeling it would be the last time he'd ever speak to her. It wouldn't break his heart in the slightest, but he worried he'd never be able to satisfy the curiosity gnawing at him.

She paused but didn't turn around. She waited for him to continue.

"We've met before somewhere, haven't we? You look so familiar."

She drew the hood of her cloak over her head. "Unlikely. I fear you have me mistaken for someone else." With that, she disappeared into the darkness of the trees.

When Sal made to go after her, he paused, thinking better of it. He didn't want to waste any more time, let alone risk another fight. He'd rather save all his energy in case The Oracles found them. He turned to Naomi, only to find her scowling at him. "What?"

"Let me guess. She's an ex-lover of yours?"

Sal cocked a dubious brow. "Did anything about our interaction suggest past intimacy?"

"With you, there's no telling. She was very beautiful, after all."

He sighed. "I don't sleep with every—" At her disbelieving stare, he sighed again. "She's not an ex-lover. She only looks familiar. And to answer your next question, no. I have no intention of making her one." He shuddered. "She's pretty scary."

Naomi shook her head. "Shocking. Even Royal vampires have fears."

"Say what you will, but I've never seen any non-Royal vampire with that much power. The fact that her face remained impassive the entire time didn't help." Then, he smiled. "I can assure you that my past will remain behind me, dove. You—"

"Don't," she breathed, panic causing her eyes to widen. "Don't go there. I don't want to talk about it."

Sal's smile didn't waver, but her reluctance to accept their bond cut him straight to the core. He trailed a gentle finger down her cheek. "We will have to talk about it eventually."

She stepped out of reach. "Let's just find The Oracles. We'll talk after this is all over."

The bitter scent of her lie only added to the pain in Sal's chest, but he dropped his hand. "Very well." Deciding to change the subject, he said, "What really happened back in the Makalu Mountain? The story surrounding that massacre is quite vicious. Those trolls were literally shredded from limb to limb."

She shifted her weight to one leg then the other, clearly uncomfortable. "Long story short, I've seen a lot of death in my career, but never anything dealing with children."

It took Sal a moment to understand her meaning, but when he did, his stomach churned. "Bloody hell."

"Right," she muttered. "Something inside me had snapped. The world turned red, I blacked out and the next thing I knew, I was back at the guild carrying around that horrible reputation. I supposed it helped with keeping people from trying to befriend me, but it's still not something to be proud of."

"Except, now you can be proud. You saved someone."

She was quiet for a long time, thinking it over. Then, her eyes crinkled when she smiled. "*Si*, I guess I did."

Returning her smile, Sal took her arm and flashed them away.

Chapter Twelve

Just as Arson had said, Lunegris was located at the far end of West Main Street, just past a row of small shops. A two-story green building inspired by French renaissance architecture, it had multiple barred windows meant to keep others from sneaking in. Though the structure was an impressive sight, it was clear that it was a come-one, come-all setup. All the demons who entered were dressed in different styles, from tattered cloaks to elegant ballgowns and suits.

After paying a small fee, they followed the crowd to a rounded auditorium with a stage holding a single podium.

They chose two seats in the far back, thankful that most of the eager attendees preferred to be closer to the stage. "Do you think we'll find them?" she asked.

"Lower your voice, dove," he responded, leaning close to her. "I sense we aren't alone back here."

Naomi resisted the urge to glance around when she, too, felt several eyes watching her. However, she trusted her gut enough to know it wasn't just paranoia. Whether it was The Oracles or creatures far more sinister, she didn't want to do anything to cause alarm. The best thing to do would be to feign ignorance.

When the last of the customers entered, the lights flickered on and off, signaling the auction was about to start. Everyone quieted down as a pudgy demon crossed the stage, his beady eyes lit with glee as he scanned the full house.

"Have you ever been to one of these?" Naomi whispered to Sal.

"A few. They always save the more desirable items for last. You may as well get settled in."

Groaning in annoyance, she sank into her seat. "Terrific."

"Ladies and gentlemen and all other creatures of the night, I'd like to thank you all for…"

As the auctioneer continued to give his grand introduction, his words grew faint in Naomi's ears as boredom set in. It hadn't even been a full five minutes, yet his shrill voice made it hard to pay attention.

When another demon rolled a cart containing the first item onto the stage, she closed her eyes and tried to picture herself in a place far away. Daydreaming in The Shade probably wasn't the best idea, but she told herself it was only for a few minutes.

"Wake up, dove," Sal whispered, giving her a slight shake.

Confused, Naomi blinked her eyes open. "What? I wasn't sleeping."

"Check the time."

Letting out a wide yawn, she checked her phone and cursed under her breath. She really *had* dozed off. The auction had lasted well over three hours, and it was nearing four o'clock in the morning. It was beyond her why so many demons practically oozed with anticipation over these events. Other than the handful of poor creatures who'd been sold and a few hides of others that had been put on display, the rest had been boring, senseless items like fairy potions and whatnot.

"For our final sale, we have a special treat for you. As promised —"

Blah freaking blah. She was slumped in her seat in a rather unladylike fashion, but she couldn't find it in herself to care. Three hours of nothing but over-hyped goods and people fighting over buying them… She was ready to call it quits and return to her hotel room. A fresh start would benefit her, along with a hot shower and some blueberry waffles. *Yum.*

Two imps rolled a large wooden display case to the center stage, and the man who'd done all the announcing waved his hand at the drapes hiding whatever lay beneath. With a melodramatic swoosh, the curtains parted to reveal two intricate angel-like wings with red and green feathers.

Gasping in horror, Naomi sat up straight. "No," she breathed, bile rising in the back of her throat.

"What is it?" Sal asked from beside her.

She couldn't tear her eyes from the stage. There was no mistaking it. The silver beads clamped around the base were custom designs that were native only to her people. "Those are fury wings," she whispered on a croak.

The words had barely left her lips when a strong arm wrapped around her throat and hauled her away. She watched as the same was done to Sal, along with a white cloth covering his mouth and nose. She tried to fight against her attacker, but the man was moving far too fast, dragging her into a darkened room. There was a sound of glass breaking, followed by Sal's furious growling.

Out on the stone pavement, the assailants continued down a dark alley behind the other buildings lining the road. With one hand clutching the brute's arm, she blindly reached for the dagger at her hip. The man shook her like a ragdoll to keep her from grabbing it, but when she felt the hilt around her fingertips, she grabbed hold and swung it in an arc.

The blade caught the bastard in the bicep, making him yelp in pain and release her. She was quick to jump to her feet, but her vision was blurred from the lack of air. "Sal?" she called, shaking her head to clear her sight.

Someone hit her over the head but she didn't fall. Instead, she narrowed her eyes on the male, assessing that he was no taller than her, but far heavier in bulk. However, she wasn't one to shy away from anyone during a fight.

She planted her feet and it didn't take long for him to realize he was no match. With three quick moves, Naomi had him disarmed with a gash across his neck. Even with demon healing, he'd be dead within the minute. She didn't bother staying to watch the result as she followed Sal's trail.

The streets had cleared due to the first night of the market coming to a close, so when she at last saw his limp body being dragged away at the end of the street, her heart lurched. "Sal!" she cried.

Three women and one man detached themselves from the shadows, blocking her view. She growled in annoyance, pulling another weapon from her thigh. She wasted no time in attacking the closest one. Her quick moves surprised the girl. These proved to be far more formidable than the first assailant, but only because they outnumbered her. Still, she persevered.

It took longer than she would have liked, but after planting two silver daggers into the remaining girl, her victim slumped to the ground, screaming in agony. Naomi continued after Sal, panic squeezing her heart in the most painful way. She followed his scent all the way to the outer gate leading her back to the mall, but just as she her feet met the cold flooring, all traces of him disappeared.

She glanced around in frantic desperation, tears welling at the corners of her eyes. "Salvator!" Her shout bounced off the empty walls, an echoing torment of her failure to save him in time. She hadn't cried when Reinaldo had mutilated her and beat those other girls. She hadn't cried when she'd been abandoned by her own people. She hadn't even cried when she'd watched her mother executed right before her eyes.

However, the crushing weight of losing Sal, the possibility of never seeing him again, brought forth the type of sorrow that had her curling into herself while her tears pooled on the floor around her head.

* * * *

St. Charles, Illinois

"It's a girl," Ava exclaimed when Cassander, Cyrus and the rest of his brothers crowded into the room.

"It's about time," Julius huffed, holding balloon strings in one hand and an armful of stuffed animals in the other. "You'd think that after rushing into labor, she would slide on out. But no, she wanted to be dramatic and take her precious time."

"Just like a woman," Darius added with a grin, holding multiple bags of baby clothes. The two of them, along with Lucian, crowded in on the left side of the king-sized bed. Cass, Cyrus and Andreas took up the other side, closer to Marc. "Have you picked a name yet? Daria is cute."

Marc snorted in derision. "Yeah, and she'll grow up with half a brain just like her uncle. Julia, Andrea, Cassandra and Luciana are no-gos, as well."

Ava chuckled, relaxing into the pillows. Between her and Marc, Anais sat with the baby cradled in her little arms. "Her name is Selene," the girl chirped. No longer afraid of her new uncles or grandfather, she flashed them all a wide smile that revealed a missing front tooth. Though blind, it never failed to amaze Cass how it seemed like she was able to look right through them.

"Selene?" Andreas echoed. "You mean like from *Underworld*?"

Ava rolled her eyes, though her lips twitched with amusement. "You can guess which one of us named her."

Marc pounded his chest with pride. "Oh, come on. You loved that movie—and our baby is half-vampire, half-shifter. How awesome is that?"

She waved that aside, but her smile only widened. "It *is* a kickass movie."

Cyrus chuckled and leaned forward, eager to see the newest member of their family. "Would you like to hold her?" Anais asked him. When he nodded, she handed the baby over.

With a tenderness that one wouldn't expect from such an imposing man, Cyrus held Selene and gently rocked side to side. "Selene..." he murmured, his eyes shimmering with unshed tears. "A beautiful name for a beautiful girl. Welcome to our family, *piccolina*."

Ava's smile turned watery. '*Piccolina*' had been the nickname they'd called her while she grew up. Due to her being much younger than the rest of them, it had been become a term of endearment that was fitting for her newborn.

Light flashed, making Cass blink in surprise. Julius grinned while holding his cell phone up. "The world's most feared demon going goo-goo-ga-ga over a baby. I had to snap a picture."

Cyrus glared at him, but it vanished when he returned his attention to his granddaughter. "Says the one who splurged on over-sized balloons and fluffy animals. I imagine the clerks at the store gave your strange looks."

"They did," Andreas laughed. Though Cass sensed something was troubling his little brother, he did well to hide it. "You should have seen his face. It was all red and—"

Julius slapped his hand over Andreas' mouth, silencing him. "He's lying."

When Siovon's phone started buzzing, she excused herself and moved to the far side of the room to answer it. Cass peered over his father's shoulder to get a better look at his niece. She was tiny with little tufts of dark hair, but she looked perfectly content while nestled in Cyrus' arms.

For the first time in centuries, genuine happiness filled Cass' heart. Before Ava had come into their lives, none of his brothers had been very close. They'd stayed in contact, of course, but life had sent them all on separate paths. Camilla's death had been a hard blow for him, Lucian and Sal. When Cyrus had found Anna, they'd been pleased that their father had found love again, but they'd never been able to see her as their mother—not even as a stepmother. She'd been far younger than all of them. Plus, they'd only known her for a few short years before she'd died.

After that, Cass had met his truemate Maria, but due to her illness, he'd wanted to spend as much time with her as possible. Lucian had been overseas, continuing to hunt Rogues and setting up clans, and Sal had been far too indulged in his debaucheries to care for anything else. Even with the twins and Andreas growing up, none of them had been around much. Too many deaths of loved ones and wars had pushed them away.

That had been until Ava had come along centuries later. She'd been the glue to pull their family back together. Cyrus had called them all home for a mandatory meeting, and that was when they'd learned of her relation to them—that she was their motherless sister, so young and lost in a new and frightening world. Her innocence and love of everything had pierced the hearts of her jaded brothers and father.

The Gordanos had been whole again—broken by sorrow yet healed by Ava's pure heart.

Cass and his brothers had been devastated when she'd run away, but ever since coming back home—for good—life hadn't been half as gloomy as it previously had been. And with the birth of the newest member of their family, along with the continuation of the Royal bloodline, all there was to feel in that moment was…joy. Absolute joy.

"Naomi, calm down," Siovon pleaded, panic in her voice. "What happened to Sal?"

At once, everyone's head snapped in her direction.

So much for joy, Cass thought with an edge of concern.

Siovon listened to her friend with wide eyes, and though Naomi's voice was frantic through the receiver, it was too muffled for any of them to make out what she was saying. After a while, Siovon pulled her eyebrows together, grim determination settling her delicate features into a warrior's mask. "It's okay, Naomi. Just calm down. Thor will get to you before I can, but I promise to be there as soon as possible. We're going to get him back. I swear on my life." With that, she hung up and murmured something under her breath.

In a display Cass had seen several times over the months but that never failed to amaze him, the elaborate tattoo curled around her arm writhed and shimmered until a miniature dragon, standing no taller than a chihuahua, rose into the air.

"Siovon, what's happened to Sal?" Ava asked, sharing her brothers' panic. She struggled to sit up, but Lucian placed a firm hand on her shoulder to keep her in place.

Instead of answering right away, Siovon spoke to her dragon. "Thor, I need you to go to Naomi as fast as possible. She's at the Underground City in Montreal. When you find her, let me know."

Though Thor was known to have a sharp tongue and the nastiest attitude against men, his reptilian eyes widened with what could only be described as worry. It was hard to tell what lizard feelings looked like. "Dearest Naomi? Is she injured? Bloody saints, I'm on the way." He flew across the room and, in a little shower of black sparkles, disappeared.

Siovon faced Lucian when he rushed to her side. "*Fatina*, what happened to Naomi and Sal?"

"It's too long to explain it all right now, but we have to go. They were ambushed. The attackers must have known Sal could teleport, so they knocked him unconscious first. Naomi fought some and tried to chase them, but she lost Sal's scent after exiting the doorway from The Shade. I've never heard her so distressed before."

"Hell's bells," Darius breathed. "Can we go just one year without someone attacking our family?"

Ava tossed her comforter back. "We have to—"

"No!" Everyone shouted at once, including Anais and Marc.

When she looked like she wanted to argue, Cyrus returned the baby to Anais. "*Cara*, you just gave birth not even an hour ago. You're staying here."

Her emerald eyes filled with distress. "Then Marc—"

"Another no," Lucian commanded, wrapping an arm around Siovon's tense shoulders. "This is a very precious time for the four of you. You need to rest and savor this moment. Salvator will be fine. I promise we will all return soon, along with him."

Ava opened her mouth before snapping it shut. With a defeated sigh, she slumped against the pillows. "Screw you and your big-brother logic," she grouched.

Lucian chuckled, something he'd been doing a lot as of late. He glanced down at his mate. "You're staying here too."

"The hell I am," Siovon growled, jabbing him in the side. "Naomi is my best friend. I'll never leave her hanging, especially when she sounds so helpless."

"Pf-f-ft," Julius laughed. "Helpless? I've met that chick. She's colder than Lucian."

"No, she isn't," Siovon defended. "She's just misunderstood. Besides, she is Sal's truemate. She's just as vulnerable as any of you would be in her place. Plus, if all of you crowd her without me around, she'll go into defensive mode, and I can't guarantee she won't see you all as the enemy."

"But, Siovon," Lucian argued, "it can be dangerous. The people she's looking for—"

"Dangerous?" Cyrus scoffed. "You're saying that to an ex-assassin who charged headfirst into a band of Rogues, took down two of my best warriors and kicked your ass. I think she's good, son."

Lucian glared at him, then at Siovon's smug look. He rolled his eyes. "No need to bring up the past," he grumbled. "Let's take the jet. We can be there in less than two hours."

Cyrus nodded. "I'll call Ritrel to see if his clansmen have seen or heard anything."

"Wouldn't it be wiser to call Arson?" Darius asked. "His clan is far closer to Montreal that Ritrel's."

Their father was quiet for a few moments, making Cass grow suspicious. "You still can't get in contact with him, can you?"

Cyrus sighed. "He's a rather stubborn man, I'll admit. However, he's quiet and doesn't cause trouble unless outsiders touch his land. Those were the terms of our agreement."

"So, it's true? You've met him before? What kind of man is he?"

"No, I still have yet to see him in person. He communicates via his lieutenants."

Lucian scowled. "After all this time, he still remains shrouded in mystery? I should go have a talk with him then…face to face."

Cyrus waved that aside. "Do it on your free time. As I said, he hasn't caused trouble with me, so I have no care. Right now, we need to focus on finding Salvator."

"I'm going too," Andreas announced, using his cane to shuffle past everyone. "I could use a good fight."

When more than one person made to disagree, he cut them off. "I'm not taking no for an answer. I need this. I've been working out since my recovery. This will help. Plus, with my powers, you'll need me."

After glancing at Cyrus for confirmation, Lucian nodded. "Very well, but don't overdo it."

Ava clasped her hands. "It's settled then. Hurry up and bring our brother home."

Chapter Thirteen

Though Siovon had assured her that it would only be a couple of hours before she arrived, Naomi hadn't wanted to wait. She couldn't. Every minute that passed had her fear rising. She worried over what those bastards were doing to Sal.

Is he hurt? Is he conscious? Is he even alive?

The questions refused to leave her mind, but she felt like she knew the answer to the last one. Through their bond, she still felt his steady presence, telling her he wasn't dead. While that should have put her mind at ease, it didn't. She couldn't be positive until he was back at her side.

And so, with a semi-blurry vision from all the crying she'd done, she'd hijacked a car from a nearby gas station and hightailed it across the highway, back to Arson's territory. She didn't hold out much hope that the frightening woman would help her, but she had to at least try.

It was funny how much Sal had changed her in such a short amount of time. For years she'd gone out of her way to avoid relying on anyone. She'd been determined to do everything on her own, right down to hunting down a dangerous group of people who outnumbered her. So long as she did it all on her own, she could go down with her pride intact.

Yet there she was, dashing across the empty golf course with the blind hope that a stranger she knew nothing about would accompany her on a rescue mission.

Pride be damned.

Thor had approached her shortly after ending the phone call with Siovon. She'd been ecstatic to see the little beast — a familiar face she considered friendly. Though he'd bombarded her with questions regarding her emotional state, she'd given him vague answers until he got the message that she wasn't in a very talkative mood. Instead, she'd convinced him to see what he could do about tracking Sal's invisible scent — or at the very least find the demons who'd kidnapped him.

Naomi made it farther past the tree line than she and Sal had done beforehand. She didn't know where she was going, but she knew one of the clansmen would catch up to her sooner or later. She just hoped they wouldn't kill her before she stated her case.

As expected, the overwhelming presence of an ancient aura surrounded her, making every one of her hairs stand on end. She came to a stop in the middle of a small clearing, peering around the darkness. She squinted her eyes to see better, but her feet were suddenly kicked from under her. The impact of striking the ground caused the breath to be knocked from her lungs.

The tip of a cold blade touched her throat, keeping her from standing. From under the hood of her cloak, Arson's amber eyes were narrowed in contempt. "I warned you not to return. Did you think I would not keep my word?"

Naomi gulped, but it wasn't fear that kept her in place. It was the fact that she was desperate to save Sal, and in doing so, she'd put her own life at risk. "I need your help."

"I've assisted you once already. You are overstepping your bounds." Unlike earlier, there was an emotion in her tone — annoyance.

"Arson, please. At the auction house, The Oracles took Sal. I need to find him before…before…"

Arson made a sound of disgust. "Your problems have nothing to do with me, girl. This is the last time I will tell you. Leave my territory at once, or I will not be so lenient."

She sheathed her sword and turned her back on Naomi, as if trusting her dark threat would work. In truth, it almost did. Almost.

Naomi shifted to her knees, tears pricking the corners of her eyes. "Arson, I'm begging you. Please help me save him. I'll do anything. *Anything*"

Arson's steps faltered and she turned an irritated look over her shoulder. "Why do you even care if anything happens to him? From what I've gathered, you've rejected his advances. The man bared his heart to you, and in return, you declined him."

Naomi sniffled, digging her nails into the dirt. The words felt like acid on an open wound, because they were true. Though she'd convinced herself that she had a plausible reason for denying Sal, it was her own cowardice that prevented her from accepting his feelings. He was nothing like Reinaldo. Hell, he wasn't like any man she'd ever met before. Despite her contempt for his lifestyle, she'd gotten to know the real side of him.

And she loved every bit of it.

She heaved a deep sigh, feeling drained. "I care because I'm his truemate. All this time I was too afraid to admit it to him or myself, but I see now how selfish and stupid that was. If anything happens to him before I can tell him, I'll—" Her voice cracked and she hung her head in defeat. It was embarrassing to confess her feelings out loud, but it couldn't be helped. The words just spilled out. She only wished she'd had the courage to tell Sal.

The stretch of silence between them had Naomi's cheeks heating. No doubt the mighty clan chief was looking down at her in ridicule, as if her feelings were something to be laughed at. Hell, had their positions been switched, she would have been disgusted at the sight of someone blubbering over some man.

"Fine," Arson said in the softest tone. "Get up."

Startled and confused, Naomi glanced up to see the other woman had moved to a crouch before her. Her expression was sympathetic—almost sad in a way. "You'll help?"

She gave a single nod. "I will, but in return, you must swear to tell him how you feel—no more fear, no more excuses."

It was an odd request, but Naomi didn't care to think it over. All she could focus on was the relief that such a powerful chief was willing to help her save Sal. "Thank you."

Arson nodded again. "Tell me everything that happened."

Naomi wiped her nose and stood. She made sure to relay every detail, finishing with, "When we crossed the gate to this realm, his scent disappeared. I searched every building, stall and store. It's like they just disappeared."

"Then there must have been an imp among them who created a portal."

"I didn't sense any magic being used."

Arson pondered that for a moment. "Are you sure they were The Oracles?"

Naomi frowned. "I'm positive. Each of the ones I fought had the insignia tattooed on them. I assumed the ones taking Sal had it too."

Arson rubbed her jaw. "Those aren't normal tattoos. Those bastards have hunted in my territory in the past. They've even taken a few of my clansmen, which I didn't take too kindly to." At Naomi's slow nod of understanding, she continued. "I was able to get a few answers from a couple of them. Their tattoos and jewels contain masking spells. It hides their scents."

As Naomi thought it over, she realized it *was* strange that she'd only followed Salvator's scent. Even when she'd fought her assailants, none of them had left any tracks. They could have been ghosts, for all she knew. "They must have placed a pendant over Sal then," she murmured. "That's why I lost his trail."

Arson shrugged. "It's my guess as well."

Remembering the thin necklace Chè had given her, she retrieved it from her pocket and held it between her and Arson. She placed it around her neck and lifted her eyebrows in question.

Arson shook her head. "Just like that, your scent is gone." Her eyes dropped to the ground. "What is that?"

Frowning, Naomi spotted a folded piece of cloth. "I don't know." She picked up the rough material. Her frown deepened at the set of numbers written on it. It was too long to be a phone number and had too many consecutive numbers to be deciphered as a code. She flipped it over, not understanding what it meant or where it came from.

"Let me see that," Arson murmured. After taking a look at the cloth, she handed it back. "Those are coordinates not far from downtown."

Naomi frowned and pulled out the GPS on her phone. A few seconds of typing in the numbers proved Arson to be right. She narrowed her eyes in suspicion. "How did you know that?"

"I have lived here for quite some time."

Still suspicious, Naomi clenched the cloth between her fingers. "I don't know where this came from, but—"

She cut herself off at the memory of the man at the market. She hadn't thought much of his rudeness when he'd been the one to bump into her. However, thinking back to that moment, he could have very well been the one to place the cloth in her pocket. It was the only time someone had been close enough to touch her, other than Sal.

But that only raised more questions. She didn't know who he was or what his intentions were. For all she knew, he could be working with The Oracles and leading her to a trap. He could have been the one responsible for taking Sal.

Gritting her teeth in annoyance, she shoved the item back into her pocket. Trap or no trap, it was the only clue she had. If it led her to Sal, she didn't care what kind of obstacles lay ahead. Rescuing him was all that mattered.

Arson was quiet as she eyed Naomi. "What?" she demanded, feeling unease at being scrutinized.

"I was speaking to you. Do you often zone out like that?"

Naomi rolled her eyes. "It's an old habit. Are you ready to go?"

With another single nod, Arson started back to the golf course.

"Wait. Don't you need to let your clansmen know you're leaving or something?"

Arson didn't break stride. "They are aware. Look around."

Naomi did as she'd been told, going still at the dozens of pairs of eyes glaring at her. She hadn't even sensed them, nor had they made a single sound. "A definite *Children of the Corn* vibe," she muttered. "Are they coming with us? Because the car I sto—I mean, borrowed, is only able to seat four."

"They will remain here to guard our territory. This will not take long."

Though her voice still lacked emotion, the sureness behind her words made Naomi wonder just what the hell was going through her mind. The Oracles were large in number and proved to be pretty decent fighters. They were also damn hard to find. Two women against an entire group of demons armed and ready to kill didn't seem like something to be confident over.

Then again, Arson's calm presence exuded an aura so powerful that it had made Sal wary, and he was a Royal—one of the strongest vampires out there. She had a feeling that even a pinch of that power in battle mode was enough to wipe out an entire city.

Settling in behind the wheel, Naomi rolled the car to a stop a half hour later. Despite her driving like a bat out of hell, not one flash of lights from law enforcement had been in sight. Getting out, they followed the rest of the GPS signal on foot. Minutes later, they came to a dead end.

I don't understand, she thought in frustration. It was still early in the morning, with the tiniest crack of sunlight peaking over the horizon. She and Arson stood at the exact spot where the GPS had led them, yet there was nothing.

Nothing but a billboard advertising some fast food chain.

Scowling at the sign, Naomi double-checked that the coordinates on her phone matched the one from the piece of cloth. Perhaps she'd misinterpreted the situation. Perhaps that old man had planted it in an attempt to lure her away from the true place where Sal was being held.

Or maybe it wasn't from him at all, and the cloth had no true meaning.

Behind her, Arson tapped her foot on the ground. "There's a train moving below us."

Naomi faced her. After listening for several moments, she shook her head. "I don't hear anything. How do you know?"

"I can feel it."

Her words were so simple yet had no meaning. That was Arson's way, she supposed. The woman didn't speak in riddles, thank God, but she didn't explain herself either. It was exasperating.

"The Metro?" Naomi asked, glancing around the empty street. Save for a few closed shops, there wasn't much to suggest an entrance underground.

Arson nodded and led Naomi back the way they'd entered. Though the vampire was fast and almost invisible with the way she clung to the shadows, Naomi was right on her heels. Less than ten minutes later, they slowed to descend a set of stairs illuminated by flickering lights.

A handful of humans walked in the opposite direction, sending them curious glimpses. It wasn't surprising. Still wearing their cloaks, they probably looked like creepy members of a cult.

Or perhaps they were struck by Arson's beauty. Though there was a certain standoffish atmosphere around her, it didn't at all ebb the fact that even for a vampire, she was stunning. Other than a slight crack of a smile or a tiny twitch in her eyebrows, her face always bore a serene mask. It was like she had no emotions at all. She was the true image of regality.

With a small shake of her head, Naomi followed Arson until they reached an empty platform. Well, empty save for two humans sleeping in a corner.

Arson tilted her head to peer down one side of the tunnel then the other. After silent moments of uncertainty, she nodded to her right. "This way." She hopped down from the platform and waited for Naomi to do the same before padding through the darkness.

Nervousness caused Naomi to stroke the hilts of her blades for comfort. Though she was fond of the dark, she couldn't see very well in it. She usually relied on her senses and the moonlight to guide her way, but being underground with nothing but miles of inky blackness sent chills over her skin.

That, and the fact that she had no idea who Arson was, yet she was following her to God knows where.

"Our weather channel predicts tomorrow will bring light showers," Arson said, breaking the silence. "It'll clear up by sundown."

"What does that matter?" Naomi demanded, squinting her eyes to make out Arson's shadowy form. She wished she'd had time to charge her phone, but the GPS had drained her battery. A flashlight would be much appreciated.

"I sense you are feeling anxious at the moment. I've read that small talk can help with these situations. I am attempting to ease your worry."

For a moment Naomi wondered if perhaps the other woman had bumped her head or something to mention such a daft thing. *Small talk?* They were on a mission to save Salvator from a dangerous group of people who harvested organs and hid from other demons and she thought idle chitchat was an appropriate measure to take? And talking about the weather, no less.

"You're a weird one," Naomi muttered.

Arson made a soft sound, almost like a chuckle, but she didn't say anything else. Naomi shook her head. It was impossible to understand the clan chief. She had a reputation for killing demons who trespassed in her territory, and she wasn't open to helping outsiders — including any of her king's sons. Yet she'd shown traces of gratitude and compassion over Naomi, then left the safety of her clan to help a stranger.

It was beyond confusing.

Then again, Arson could very well be the one leading her into a trap. After all, her sudden change of heart didn't make any sense.

Naomi's suspicion was confirmed when Arson came to a halt before a narrow crack in the wall that hid another set of stairs spiraling downward. "I believe we're directly under the coordinates from earlier."

With lightning-fast movements, Naomi withdrew her gun and aimed it at Arson. "How do I know this isn't a trap? That you aren't working for them?"

Slowly, Arson turned around. Instead of looking angry or indifferent, humor danced in her amber eyes. "I could say the same," she drawled. "After all, you're the one who found a mysterious set of coordinates in your pocket that led us here. That was convenient, don't you think?"

Naomi didn't waver. "Perhaps, but if you thought I was deceiving you, why did you decide to come along?"

"I knew you weren't, but even if you tried, we both know you would never succeed."

"Fine," Naomi grumbled, not wanting to admit the truth in her words. As much pride as she had in her skills, she didn't think for one moment that she'd ever stand a chance against Arson. It didn't take a novice to sense the dramatic difference in power. Most creatures would be wise to keep their distance. "Just answer me this. Why did you agree to help me? You don't know me, nor do you owe me any favors."

For a long time, Arson was silent. She was so silent that if Naomi hadn't been looking at her, she would have thought the vampire had run away. It was hard to tell what she was thinking, since her face didn't give anything away.

When she turned her back on Naomi, she took a step toward the stairs. Then, she sighed. "I lost my truemate a very long time ago, but the pain continues to live in my heart. It's...unbearable, truly unbearable. Therefore, if it is within my power to save someone from experiencing that type of suffering, I will do what I can."

Her words were sincere. Though she still hid her emotions, the pain in her voice had Naomi lowering her gun. She wanted to ask more questions but she refrained. She knew firsthand how difficult it was to open up about her past, let alone to a complete stranger.

Besides, if she were being truthful, she didn't want to know what it felt like to lose the man she loved. Just the thought of it made her chest tighten with pain. She hoped she could reach Sal before it was too late.

Heaving a deep sigh, she followed Arson down the stairs.

* * * *

The sound of fretful whispering followed by a yelp jarred Sal from his nap. Well, he thought it was a nap — a lovely one, at that.

In his dream, he'd been lounging poolside at a beautiful resort somewhere on the coast of Spain. The sun was bright, but somehow it hadn't burned when it touched him. His eyes had been glued to Naomi, who'd been stripped down to nothing more than a sexy one-piece bathing suit. Stepping out of the water, she was all cool confidence as she strolled up to him, swinging her hips with every sensual step. Just when the action was about to start, reality sank in.

He growled in annoyance and shook his loose hair from his eyes. As his vision adjusted to his surroundings, the memory of being hit over the head and dragged to an unknown location came back. "Bloody hell," he murmured.

Silver bands held his arms together above his head while he dangled above the ground like a piece of meat in a slaughterhouse. That explained his numb limbs and sore back, as well as why his wrists felt like they were on fire. The burning metal singed his skin, but thankfully the cuffs were mixed with other elements to dull the pain.

Still, the longer they remained touching him, the worse it was going to get. Not only that, but it prevented him from teleporting.

The room he was in wasn't very big. In fact, it was no bigger than a broom closet, with a glass wall separating him from the group of demons huddled on the other side. It also wasn't soundproof, for he could hear every bit of their hushed conversation.

"Is she insane?" one man demanded. "He's a Royal vampire. We can't keep him here. Our whole organization will be compromised."

Another one responded, just as frantic as the first. "He's a fucking Gordano. If Cyrus finds out, we're all dead."

Sal smirked. At least some of them had a brain. If the fact that he was a Royal didn't shake them enough, every demon on the planet at least knew that Cyrus wasn't a man to be toyed with, especially when it came to his children.

His humor dwindled, however, when he remembered that Naomi had been with him. Though The Oracles had attacked him first, he remembered hearing her call after him just before he'd lost consciousness. Fear gripped his heart at the thought that something had happened to her, but the reasonable part of his mind soothed that she was okay. He could still feel her through their bond.

He frowned. Actually, she was pretty damn close. It was like a game of Hot-and-Cold. Once the truemate connection became active — and was strengthened after sex — the two could feel when one or the other was close or far away. The hole in his chest that acted as a beacon of sorts shrank with every passing minute. Either she'd been captured and was locked away somewhere in...wherever the hell they were...or she was on her way to him.

For those who'd been mated for a long time, it was said that they were able to share thoughts with each other. He wished such were the case so he could warn her to stay away.

The thought made him snort. Well, not that she'd listen. She was so stubborn that she'd never listen to a word he said, even if it was for her own safety. While it was troublesome and bound to stress him out, it was one of her more admirable traits.

Still, the thought of her taking on these demons alone worried him to no end. He had to get free and find her, before she did something stupid.

And regardless of how lethal her prowess was, charging into a chamber of morality-lacking demons of unknown strength was, without a doubt, stupid.

"Oh my God," someone murmured, "he's awake."

Relaxing his expression, he grinned at the trio now gawking at him with wide eyes. "*Salvete*," he greeted.

The smell of their fear was pleasing. *Serves them right.* He peered over them all, taking in their features to determine which would be the most susceptible to his charm. The two men weren't very brawny. One wasn't even five feet tall and the other was thin as a rail.

The third member was a woman. Human, but a witch. Though she was just as afraid as the other two, it was clear from her scent that fear wasn't the primary reason for her lingering glances at him.

Though he could charm multiple beings at once, the silver sapping at his strength made him stick to caution. Decision made, he curled one corner of his lips into a smile that had enthralled hundreds of women over the years. "Well hello," he purred, trailing his gaze down her small frame.

Even with the distance between them, he didn't miss her shudder. Enemy or not, she wasn't impervious to having some fun with her captives. Not that Sal would ever let it get that far, but surely Naomi would forgive him for mild flirting if it meant freeing himself.

Before he could even use his charm, however, a shrill voice had the three going still. "What the hell are you doing standing around?"

Sal hung his head and feigned unconsciousness just as another woman came into view. "Wake up, vampire," she demanded, knocking on the glass.

When Sal didn't flinch, one of the men spoke up. "Milady, what do you plan to do with him?"

"What do you think? I'm not just going to let him roam free, only to come back after us."

Someone made a sound of shock. "B-but he's a Royal!"

The woman scoffed. "Is that supposed to scare me? Besides, the big guy downstairs will be pleased to have another one to feed on. It's been a while since he's had a fresh batch of Royal blood. All that means is more money for us."

They went quiet after that, though Sal didn't miss the way their fear spiked. *The big guy downstairs? What the hell does* that *mean?*

He cracked his eyes open a smidge. The woman who seemed to be in command was tall with dark shoulder-length hair, though she wore a mask that was painted red on one side, black on the other. He bit back a laugh. It was rather dramatic, like a villain in a superhero comic.

Then he remembered Arson mentioning The Oracles having a leader who wore a mask — a fury, at that. He wondered if perhaps that was the woman in question.

She planted her fists at her hips. "Where is the girl? I demanded that they both be brought in."

The three looked at each other in nervousness. "Well, she...um, she kind of...got away," the witch admitted.

The blast of anger that exploded from the woman was damn near palpable. She brought her hand across the witch's cheek, hard enough for the smack to echo off the rocky walls. "What do you mean she got away?" she shrieked. "Every fucking time I get close to capturing that cunt, you pathetic worms let her get away."

Sal tensed. *Is she talking about Naomi?*

"W-we're sorry," the shorter man cried, backing away. "Thomas was in charge of getting her, but she killed him and the others."

"You and your excuses," she growled. "Naomi thinks she's so tough. Her luck will run out soon enough."

The witch stood, holding her palm to her bruised cheek. "Do you think she will go to Cyrus? She seemed rather close to the vampire."

"Don't be ridiculous. I know her well enough. She's too proud to ask for help. She'll come for him alone, and when she does, she won't be any match for us." She pointed at the men. "You two keep a close eye on him and make sure he doesn't try to escape. Come along, Lily. I have a task for you."

"Yes, madam," the three said at once. Sal watched the women leave and waited until a distant door opened and shut before lifting his head.

Their conversation made him eager to get free. Sal had a sinking feeling that the woman had some kind of connection to the missing Royals. While that was enough to cause concern, there was a more pressing issue in his mind. He didn't know what was going on or what sort of relationship the woman had to Naomi, but it couldn't be anything good. However, she was right about one thing. Naomi really was too proud to ask for help, and if she was on her way to him with no backup, he had to get to her side before he lost her for good.

Chapter Fourteen

"What's the plan?" Arson demanded on a low whisper.

Naomi crouched next to her behind a large boulder. Several paces down the wide hall, four armed demons leaned against the wall, talking among themselves. They looked far too casual. She shot Arson a surprised look. "You're asking *me*?"

"Of course. This was your idea, after all."

"Yeah, but you're a clan chief. Don't you have a book of attack plans or something?" At her slow blink of disbelief, Naomi grunted. "I don't do these things."

"Aren't you an assassin?"

"How did you—?" Naomi bit off her question with a soft sigh. "I never have a plan. I just kill who needs to be killed then leave." When Arson gave another hard blink, Naomi shook her head. "Don't give me that look."

Arson looked heavenward. "Young people these days," she muttered. She peeked around the boulder and concentrated on the demons.

"What are you doing?" Naomi demanded.

After a moment, the demons' chattering stopped and Arson rose. "Let's go."

Naomi stood as well, going still with shock to see all four demons lying on the ground, fast asleep. "What… What the hell did you do?"

She faced Naomi. She waved a hand at them. "Tell me what you see."

Frustrated at the delay, Naomi took uneasy steps toward them. All four lay on their backs looking far too peaceful for their own good. Then, studying them closer, horror filled her.

Arson gave a solemn nod. "They are only kids, barely into their teen years. snatched from the streets and beaten into this life. Though they carry The Oracles' mark, none of them have blood on their hands…yet."

She brushed past Naomi on her way to the door beyond them. "Killing them would have been simple, yes. They are untrained. They were commanded to guard this hall only because they are disposable. Most of the older ones have grown into what they are, and I suspect they are beyond saving. However, had you killed these little ones, would you have forgiven yourself? Would you be able to live with knowing that, to them, this is the only home they know? That they are only following someone else's orders?" When Naomi didn't answer, only continued to stare at the kids with parted lips, Arson shook her head and walked off.

"How did you know?" Naomi murmured, walking behind her. Each step over the sleeping bodies felt like lead weighing her down, guilt over almost killing such younglings twisting her stomach into knots. "How were you even able to put them to sleep? Vampire charm only works if you speak, but you didn't. It's like you read their minds and just—"

Naomi bit her words off and stopped dead in her tracks. Arson did the same, but she didn't turn around.

Hadn't she thought it was unnerving how the older woman seemed to know everything that was going on? How she was able to guess what was on Naomi's mind before anything was said? Not to mention that every time Arson looked at her, there was some kind of mild fluttering in the back of her head.

Naomi had assumed it was just because of Arson's age that brought on such wisdom, but the creeping suspicion that it was so much more had her going back to one answer.

"*Arson, can you read minds?*" Naomi thought the question rather than saying it out loud, but it worked.

"Yes," the chief responded in soft tones. "I can."

"But how is that possible? I didn't know regular vampires could—" And just like that, the puzzle snapped together. Her powerful aura, her intuition, her regal presence… It all made sense. "Oh my God. You're a Royal, aren't you?"

Arson stared up at the ceiling. "Naomi, it's imperative that no one finds out about this. Do you understand me? I need you to not tell a soul."

Naomi swallowed hard. It felt like a betrayal to keep such an important revelation from Sal and Siovon, but if anyone knew how to keep a secret, it was her. There were so many things she wanted to know, so many questions that continued to pile up. Yet, at the same time, she knew now was not the time or place. Besides, she had a feeling that Arson explaining her reason for secrecy was something far too deep to be shared with anyone.

"You have my word," Naomi promised. "I won't tell anyone."

"Thank you," Arson whispered. "Let's go save your mate."

With that, they continued on their trek.

Along the way, there'd been more than a handful of people they'd had to kill, but none that were innocent. Naomi didn't think she'd be able to stomach having to injure a kid, even if it was their intention to kill her.

Back in the guild, there had been no age limit on their targets. At one point, there'd been a political figure that had paid to have his rival's entire family wiped out, including the young children. Naomi had been the top prospect for that particular job, but she'd declined, which had resulted in a beating or two from the guild masters. It was their rule, after all. Refusing a kill ended in some kind of punishment. However, she'd made it her personal rule to never hurt a kid. She wasn't all cupcakes and rainbows, but she wasn't a complete monster either.

She didn't know how much time had passed before she and Arson came to the end of a T-shaped hall, both ends holding a set of doors with a narrow glass window allowing a peek on the other side. The one on the left revealed another corridor. Up until that point, the underground hideout had been carved into the rocks, but everything beyond the door consisted of white tile flooring and plaster walls painted a dull gray.

The opposite door contained a large room. As she peered through the window, she counted over thirty members forming a circle around a man wearing nothing more than loose-hanging shorts. The rest of his skin was red and black from an array of bruises and bleeding wounds. His legs shook with the strength it took to stand, and when he bared his teeth, only one fang showed, the other was replaced by a gaping hole. However, it was clear he wasn't going down without a fight.

The hatred in his eyes made it clear that he wasn't a willing participant in whatever was going on in there.

He faced off against two men the same size as him, and though they were injured, their condition was nowhere near close to being as worrisome as the vampire's.

Beside her, Arson's features were tight with anger. "Naomi, you go on ahead. I'll catch up with you soon."

Naomi blinked in surprise. "Are you sure? There are a lot of them. I can take — "

When Arson looked at her, there was nothing friendly about the smile she flashed. Her eyes burned bright, and the dangerous power swirling around her intensified, making Naomi take a wary step back. "No. This one is on me. Go on."

After only a slight hesitation, Naomi nodded and continued down the corridor. She'd only taken a few steps, however, when distant screams of agony ripped through the air. The chill from Arson's powers made Naomi's breath fog, but she rubbed her arms and continued on.

She didn't know what the hell had made the woman so angry. Perhaps that male vampire was someone she knew — or maybe she just had a personal dislike of seeing her fellow brethren abused. Then, if that were the case, why did she allow her clan to attack anyone who crossed her lands — including other vampires?

Naomi shook her head, deciding it didn't matter. Nothing about Arson was simple to figure out, and if she spent all day trying, she'd never get to Sal. The woman was too big an enigma.

Touching her chest, Naomi was silent as she edged her way down the maze of corridors. Though the overhead lights were dim and far enough apart to cause shadows like those in a horror film set in a creepy hospital, it provided enough light for her to see where she was going, for which she was thankful. She relied on her connection to Sal to lead the way, for each step closer to him warmed her heart.

When she entered another door, she came across a three-way hall. There were no signs telling her where to go, nor were there any lights beyond that point — just total darkness.

She rolled her eyes in annoyance, though she had to give it to The Oracles. They were a creative bunch. Whoever was behind the architectural design of the underground hideout had some skills. She didn't know how much time had passed since she and Arson had ventured inside, but the labyrinth of passageways twisting this way and that made it impossible to guess how big the place really was.

Eyeing each of the dark halls, she listened for any sign of life. When that didn't help, she concentrated on her connection to Sal. The resounding tug urged her to go left. Sighing, she took off, relying on her other senses to guide her through the vast emptiness. After a while, she breathed a small sigh of relief when she caught Sal's scent.

Her relief was short-lived, however, when she realized it was his blood.

Willing her legs to move faster, she fought back the fear threatening to rise. Instead, she sent a silent prayer that she'd make it to him in time. It was the first time in her life that she'd ever turned to religion for a favor. Hell, she didn't even know which god she'd prayed to, but she hoped one of them would show mercy.

After a while, she spotted a distant light at the far end of the corridor. Though she still couldn't hear anyone moving around, she withdrew a dagger from her thigh. When she emerged from the darkness, she slowed to a stop to find herself in what looked to be a trophy room for a hunter. Roughly the size of a basketball court, the floor had a scattering of fur rugs, wooden tables, glass display cases and a handful of rustic furniture. The heads of several animals decorated the walls, and multiple stuffed corpses had been turned into statues to be placed around the perimeter.

Upon closer inspection, bile rose in Naomi's throat when she realized that more than a few of the wolves, wild cats and bears had been actual shifters. She was willing to bet everything she had that the fur rugs had come from the pelts of other demons. It was beyond sick.

The light in the room was courtesy of two hanging chandeliers, but they were both made from different-sized bones. She did her best to not think about what poor creature or creatures they were made from.

Glancing around the room, she spotted a metal cage over in the far corner, one that was far too small for the half-naked male stuffed inside. "Sal!" she cried, running to him.

He didn't look at her, nor did he move a muscle at the sound of her voice. "*Dios*, Salvator," she whispered, grasping the bars pressing against his skin. "Are you okay? Are you hurt?" He didn't answer, still huddled into himself like a small child hiding in a closet.

"Damn those bastards," she growled, anger rising in her chest. She jerked the bars, testing their strength. She then walked around the cage until she found the lock. Picking it with a thin blade was quick work, so when she heard the click, she wasted no time in yanking the door open and reaching for Sal. "Come on. Let's get you out of here."

Sal kept his head down and stood on shaky legs. Naomi slid her arm around his waist to help him balance, worry tying all sorts of knots in her gut. She looked him over, taking in the multitude of fresh scars and bruises. "I'm going to kill every last one of them. I swear."

He still said nothing, only keeping his head down. His silver hair didn't hold its usual glossiness as it hung in stiff strips over his face, and his skin was less pale than it should have been. Blood loss tended to blanch the skin, yet the opposite occurred on him. Still, she didn't waste any more time pondering it. Whatever torture he'd gone through must have been brutal. It only made her that much more eager to sate her rising bloodlust, but she kept it at bay. She had to get him somewhere safe and clean first. "Can you teleport at all?" she asked him. "We—"

Her words were cut off on a scream when an arrow pierced the center of Sal's forehead. Everything seemed to play out in slow motion. She watched in horror as the man she loved disintegrated into a pile of ash, leaving nothing but his underwear behind. The arm she'd used to hold him up hung in the air, now covered with dark flakes of her deceased lover.

"No!" she screamed, falling to her knees. "Salvator!" Hot tears flooded from her eyes as she picked up handfuls of his remains. When the ashes fell from her hands, she hugged herself and sobbed. The bond she had with Sal remained intact. It was the only bit of connection she had to him, but watching him die right before her eyes brought forth a pain that left her feeling raw and helpless.

"Well, this is rather pathetic," a woman drawled in a heavy Hispanic accent. "All the waterworks over some man. Sofia would be so disappointed."

Naomi stiffened. She knew that voice. The hateful '*Do not ever return*' was something that had circled in her mind every night for the first few years of her exile.

Still on her knees, she raised her head to meet the dark eyes of a woman who looked so much like her mother. Shock, anger and sorrow filled Naomi as she peered at her aunt, the one bit of flesh and blood she had left in the world, the one who'd turned her back when Naomi had needed her most. "Elvira," she murmured, her voice cracking. She picked up a handful of Sal's ashes. "Why? Why would you do this?"

Elvira snorted. She entered the room and made a gesture with her fingers. Several men and women followed her to circle Naomi, in case she tried to escape. "Partially for revenge, with an equal part of boredom. It was a pretty entertaining show, watching you be reduced to a blubbering pile of nothing. You used to be a proud girl, my dear."

Naomi ignored her taunts and wiped her eyes with her sleeve. Her aunt had always had a mean streak, but most furies did. Plus, as a council member, Naomi had just assumed her aunt was tougher than others, due to her high rank. "What do you mean revenge? I haven't done anything to you. If anything, I should be the one holding a grudge."

Elvira scoffed. "Your very existence ruined everything I'd worked so hard for. Let me tell you a little story." She made another gesture with her fingers, and without hesitation, the male closest to her rushed to slide a chair over to her. She sat and crossed her legs, looking far too comfortable—as if killing someone's lover before their eyes was an everyday occurrence.

The thought sickened Naomi. Though all her kills had been clean and done in solitary places, she'd never once felt remorse over targeting someone who'd had a spouse waiting on them to return home. She hadn't sympathized with those brokenhearted men and women, had never once thought about what type of repercussions it would cause. She'd only been focusing on completing her task before moving on to the next contract.

In that moment, however, she wished she could take it all back. Empathy and compassion were traits that had always eluded her, but not anymore. Losing Salvator was the single worst feeling in the entire world. The thought that she'd never get to see his charming smile or hear his suave voice or feel his gentle caresses ever again was just…agonizing.

"Hey, are you even listening to me?" Elvira asked in annoyance.

Naomi blinked to the present, realizing that her aunt had been speaking. That explained the distant buzzing she'd heard while lost in her thoughts. "Does the council know about any of this?" Naomi demanded. "I'm assuming your lack of wings mean they banished you too."

"Don't kid yourself." She untucked the amulet around her neck, the one that matched Sofia's. "This baby doesn't just hide my scent. Those hair-brained fools have never suspected a thing."

Making sure she had Naomi's undivided attention, Elvira folded her arms and glared. "Your mother and I used to run this trade, you know. Together, we were unstoppable. Of course, we had to be careful so the council wouldn't catch on to us, but for years, she and I would go out and distribute our trophies to The Shade shoppers."

When Naomi took another glance around the room, the thought of her mother participating in skinning demons and mounting their heads and such sickened her to no end.

Taking in her look of horror, Elvira grunted. "Relax. Sofia didn't have the stomach to do any of this. Instead, we sold fury stuff—feathers, potions, armor. Nothing hardcore. Even so, the money we made from it was astounding. In just one year we were the top sellers, with the added bonus of concealing our identities. We started The Oracles to hire lesser demons to gather other goods from around the world. Everything was perfect."

Her wistful tone over what Naomi assumed to be fond memories soon hardened. The glare she shot Naomi could have opened the very gates of hell. "Perfect until *you* came along. We'd dominated our competitors, yet when we were at the peak of our glory, Sofia was selected to participate in the childbearing ceremony. I urged her to decline but, of course, she was adamant. She'd always expressed an interest in contributing to the community and raising her own, and as her sister, my presence beside her through the entire ordeal was required. That meant our business — everything we'd spent years working so hard for — was going to be thrown away for nothing."

Naomi frowned at the insult. Elvira had been a prominent figure in her life from birth to exile. She had so many memories of her aunt, ones she'd always thought to be special bonding moments. Looking back, however, she was able to see that such wasn't the case. Her aunt hadn't just been mean. Her casual teasing of Naomi had been genuine insults. Her harsh way of punishing Naomi for errors during training hadn't been tough love. The glares and constant belittlement of everything Naomi did hadn't just been from the woman having a bad day.

"I had every intention of continuing with our sales," Elvira muttered, "but my presence would have been limited. That would have been tolerable. However, that wasn't enough for Sofia. She always feared the council would find out, so when she threatened to turn both of us in, I realized that my very own sister could no longer be trusted. From there, I devised a plan to get back at her for ruining what we had. It was a plan that required a test of patience, but oh, was I willing to wait."

When she grew quiet, Naomi's suspicion rose. "What plan?" she demanded, hoping her pounding heart couldn't be heard. Here was the truth she'd longed to discover for years, the truth that she'd been determined to find at the risk of her very own life. "What did you do?"

Elvira leaned forward with her elbows on her knees. She grinned, though there was nothing warm or kind behind it. It was more like she was baring her teeth, and the malicious twinkle in her dark eyes warned Naomi that her aunt was evil through and through. "I needed a special creature to help me, someone whose DNA would remain dormant until their offspring reached maturity." She chuckled at her own cunning. "Hell if I remember what his name was, but after bribing the man into donating his sperm, it was smooth sailing. I switched out Sofia's donor sperm with his, and from there, it was a waiting game."

Naomi had to swallow the lump in her throat several times. So, the rumors weren't true after all. Her mother hadn't been tricked by an incubus, nor had she willingly given herself to one. It was shocking, to say the least. However, the worst part of it all was that, as much as she loved her mother, she'd spent so many years blaming her for letting an incubus knock her up when, in reality, the one she should have hated was Elvira.

Her aunt chortled with glee. "It was a fool-proof plan, a true stroke of genius. Honestly, I had to clap myself on the back for that one. Watching you grow up getting along with the others was the best part. You had so many friends. You'd trained so hard, thinking you were one of them. Your face when the truth came out was absolutely hysterical. No one ever knew until you went crazy and fucked that male like some wanton slut." Elvira's laughter was a mockery to the shame and horror Naomi felt. "Sofia was horrified, but the fact that she didn't push you away or treat you any differently only aided in making everyone believe she really had been seduced. I pushed for her to be executed, and I would have taken you down too, but her pleas for us to spare your life made the other councilmembers outvote my decision."

She sat back in her chair and spread her arms out wide. "When I sold you to Reinaldo, I figured you would die by his hand eventually, so that would have been the end of that."

As Elvira rambled on about her picking back up on making The Oracles the top sellers again, her voice grew distant to Naomi's ears. All she could think of was that her entire life had been filled with hatred of the wrong person — and for the wrong reason.

She'd hated herself for being born and causing her mother's death. She'd hated her mother for doing nothing to fight back against the council. She'd hated her entire community for turning their backs on her and letting her suffer at the hands of Reinaldo. She'd hated the Spaniard for being a cruel monster who preyed on weaker women. She'd hated spending years being bitter at the entire world.

However, every bit of that hate circled right back to Elvira. Her own aunt had betrayed her and her mother. All the heartache and pain Naomi had endured had been because of Elvira.

And yet because of her, Naomi had met Siovon, which in turn had allowed her to encounter Salvator. Though she'd wanted to keep her distance from the start, there was no denying the attraction that had bound her to him since she'd first laid eyes on him. After years of being alone and despising everyone around her, the stubborn vampire had become such a vital part of her life. He'd been a headache most times, but she couldn't deny that she'd been happier at his side than she'd ever been in her life.

And now he's gone.

Those four words whispered through her mind over and over again. Salvator was gone. She didn't even get to tell him she loved him. He'd died thinking she didn't care enough about him to accept him as her mate.

Elvira's cackling mingling with the others' in the room lit a fire in Naomi — a fire that roared to life and caused her heart to race. She dug her nails into the fur rug beneath her, and when everything in sight turned a dark shade of red, she threw her head back and bellowed to the high heavens. That was the only warning The Oracles had before she hopped to her feet and grabbed the nearest one.

Chapter Fifteen

It was a useless battle, for Naomi had given in to the darker side of her heritage. Blood splattered across her face, but her heart pounding in her ears drowned out the sound of their screams as she slaughtered them one by one. She didn't use her weapons, nor did she falter when the last standing member threw a knife at her that planted in her calf. She disposed of him with ease before facing the woman who'd taken everything from her.

Elvira's eyes were wide with terror as she took in her fallen underlings. "S-stop, Naomi—"

In the blink of an eye, Naomi threw a punch at her, but she missed. Elvira hadn't dodged it or anything, but it was like some unknown force had pushed her fist away at the last moment. Growling, she tried again and again, but to no avail.

Elvira chuckled and punched Naomi in the gut, making her double over in pain. "I knew that charm would still work." Grabbing Naomi by the neck, she tossed her across the room like a ragdoll across the room.

Naomi slammed into the wall with enough force to knock several mounted heads down. Her aunt withdrew a handgun and aimed it. "Have you forgotten, my dear? Even though you're banished, lower-level furies are incapable of harming councilmembers. You can't touch me."

"No, but I can."

In a blur of speed, Siovon hopped on Elvira's back and slammed two blades into her chest. She screamed in pain and tried to shake Siovon off, but the little siren held fast until Elvira fell to the ground.

It had happened so fast that it took several minutes for Naomi to understand what she was looking at.

Surprised, she stood and met her dearest friend. The red cleared from her vision, making her aware of the blade still jammed in her thigh. She jerked it out and dropped it.

"Naomi, are you all right?" Siovon asked, her violet eyes filled with worry.

"You...stabbed her," Naomi murmured, eyeing her aunt.

"Well, yeah? She was about to kill you."

"What about your pacifism?"

Siovon snorted. "She's not dead, so I'm still good. Besides, that bitch deserved it."

"Bloody hell," someone grumbled while stepping into the room. Naomi peered at the entrance as Cyrus strolled into the room, looking every bit the king of vampires, with an elegant floor-length toga draped over his large frame. His eyes were hard as he scanned the litter of dead bodies. Some had disintegrated to ash while others had been reduced to a puddle of black ink.

Three of them had been human, so their bodies would remain as is.

"I told you," Siovon chirped with a proud grin. She grabbed a handful of Elvira's hair, making her grunt in pain. "Naomi, what do you want me to do with her?"

Naomi sighed and looked to the ground as she touched her chest. "It doesn't matter. Sal is gone. She's already taken everything from me."

Siovon and Cyrus shared a look of confusion. "What are you talking about?" She jerked her thumb over her shoulder. "Sal's right over there. The boys found him hanging in a cell."

Said 'boys' filed into the room until all six of the Gordano brothers stood around her. Naomi's heart exploded with joy when she spotted Sal holding on to Lucian's shoulder. With wide eyes, she crossed the floor and threw her arms around his neck. He stumbled back a step before hugging her waist.

"Well, hey there, dove. I—"

Naomi cut him off by crushing her lips to his. It was a desperate, heart-lurching kiss that she poured everything she had into. When she pulled back, she grasped his chin and tilted his head this way and that. "Are you okay? Are you hurt? Did they touch you?"

"I'm fine, Naomi," he murmured, tugged her wrists away. "What's gotten into you?"

"I saw... I watched her kill you." She pointed to the pile of ashes. "You—"

"This is an animation spell," Siovon announced, grabbing a pinch of ash and rubbing it between her thumb and forefinger. "It was just a dummy replica— like a paper version of him. It looks like she was just messing with your head."

Naomi blinked, dumbfounded. She eyed the ashes, then Siovon, then Sal. "So, it's really you? You're alive?"

Sal gave her a comforting smile. "As alive as a vampire can be. My arms are a bit sore, since they strung me up in silver, but as you can see, I'm perfectly fine."

Heaving a deep sigh, Naomi leaned into him and closed her eyes. She savored the warmth of his arms wrapped around her. She should have known by the connection that he was still alive. Not once had it disappeared, which should have been a dead giveaway that she'd been fooled. However, in that moment, as she'd watched his body fall into a pile of ash, logic hadn't existed.

One of the twins—she couldn't remember their names—popped a stick of gum into his mouth and grinned as he took in the pools of blood and dead bodies. "I see we didn't have to come here after all. Remind me never to piss you off."

Someone scoffed, and Naomi eyed the brother she hadn't seen before. Well, that wasn't true. He looked somewhat familiar, but he hadn't been with them during the fight back in Rochester. "As if that's even possible. You and Julius can't go two minutes without annoying someone…anyone."

Lucian growled and pulled the sword from his back. "Enough. I sense another vampire approaching."

"A powerful one at that," Cass murmured, drawing a long knife from his thigh.

Though everyone was scattered around the room, Cyrus took a step forward, as if to guard them. It figured. He was by far the strongest one of them all.

Naomi lifted her head from Sal's shoulder as she recognized the opposing aura. "Oh, don't worry. That's Arson. She came to help me."

"What?" Cyrus demanded, whipping his head around to fix her with a hard stare. Naomi wasn't intimidated by anyone, but damn if the king's stern gaze didn't make her want to hide under a rock.

"Dove, how on earth did you get Arson to agree to such a thing? She wouldn't even let us into her territory."

"Wait a minute," Lucian grouched. "Clan chief Arson?"

"That would be correct," Arson stated, stepping into the doorway. She looked as regal as ever with her face set in her usual mask of serenity. She gave Cyrus a tiny nod. "Greetings, my lord."

Cyrus straightened and tilted his head to one side. "You're Arson of the southern Quebec clan, huh. We have yet to formally meet."

"Indeed," she murmured. And that was that. She didn't apologize, nor did she explain why she'd refused to meet with him in person.

The disbelieving stares on the rest of the Gordanos would have been comical if not for the tension in the air. Even when in a calm mood, Cyrus had an aura that was tangible enough for humans to sense, making all creatures wary of his presence. However, Arson's was just as strong, and the way it clashed against her king's made it damn near hard to breathe.

"You mean to tell me that 'he' is a 'she'," Julius murmured in bewilderment.

Arson met Cyrus' intimidating glare with a look of nonchalance. However, for the first time since meeting her, Naomi noticed a flicker of...something...deep in her eyes. It was fleeting, but if she didn't know any better, she could have sworn it was…longing.

But when she blinked, it was gone.

Arson trailed her gaze over the Gordanos one-by-one, though it was impossible to tell what she was thinking. When her eyes met the youngest, they lingered for several long moments. As Naomi looked between them, she remembered why she'd thought the young vampire had looked so familiar. It wasn't because she'd seen him somewhere before. It was because his eyes looked so much like Arson's—an exact replica, in fact. They both shared the glowing amber irises. Even their facial features looked similar, with the diamond-shaped angles and natural red lips.

Spinning around, Arson made to exit. "*Not a word to anyone, Naomi.*"

The telepathic command made Naomi jump, but after remembering her promise to not bring it up, she sent the thought back to Arson. "*I promise.*"

"Wait," Cyrus commanded. Arson paused and glanced over her shoulder with a questioning stare. He crossed his arms. "The next time I send a letter requesting your presence in my court, do not send your clansmen in your place. Am I understood?"

She made a soft sound of humor. "Very well, Your Majesty. I will do what I can." With that, she strolled off.

"Disobedience should not be tolerated," Lucian grumbled, sheathing his sword when her aura started to fade. "She is far too arrogant."

Siovon chuckled and nudged him in the side. "Pot, meet kettle." She eyed Elvira, who struggled to keep her eyes open. The blades still embedded in her chest wouldn't kill her, but they prevented her from attacking. Naomi assumed they'd been dipped in some kind of paralyzing potion that the siren had concocted. "Now, what to do with you. What do you think, Naomi?"

Elvira spat out a mouth full of blood and glared. "You may have ruined my plans, but no matter what you say or do, the council will never let you back in."

Naomi shrugged. "I don't care."

"Of course you do," her aunt scoffed. "That's the only reason you're here."

"Nope. I only wanted to know the truth about my mother — and thanks to you, I got it."

She flashed a triumphant grin through bloodied teeth. "So, what? Now you plan to kill me? Go right ahead. It won't change anything."

"I have a better idea," Sal murmured, throwing his arm over Naomi's shoulders. He looked at his father. "She mentioned her master would be pleased to have a fresh batch of Royal blood — my blood. Does that sound familiar to you?"

Cyrus' eyes widened a fraction. "Indeed, it does." He kneeled before Elvira and tilted one corner of his lips in a smile that was far from amicable. "You and I have much to discuss, fury. *Much*."

All traces of smug bravado left Elvira in an instant, being swiftly replaced with fear. Before she could utter a word, Cyrus locked eyes with her and charmed her into falling asleep.

Naomi blinked in confusion. That had been...easy. Elvira wasn't a weak fury, so she shouldn't have been susceptible to a vampire's charm. Hell, most demons with a strong mind were able to fight it.

Reading her expression, Sal chuckled. "Father is very, very old, dove. Not many creatures are able to overcome his will. He can make Lucian cluck like a chicken if he wanted."

"Like hell," came the older brother's response.

Sighing, she turned to him and took in his appearance. Other than his ruined clothes and a bit of dried blood from a healed wound at his temple, he looked unharmed and as beautiful as ever. "Are you okay to teleport?"

His eyes crinkled when he smiled. "Where do you want to go?"

"You can't go anywhere yet," Lucian commanded, glowering from across the room. "We still have to talk about—"

"Lucian," Siovon chided on a harsh whisper. She gave a not-so-discreet head bob in Sal and Naomi's direction. "Let them have some privacy."

He scowled. "Privacy for *what*? They don't need— Oh," he murmured, glancing between them once more. He cleared his throat. "I take that back. You two, go and get some rest. We'll meet back at father's place in"—he peeked at Siovon—"a week."

"A week?" Darius demanded, crossing his arms. "Why the hell—?"

"Believe me," Cass murmured, slapping a hand over his brother's mouth. "A week is being generous."

It was clear Darius still didn't understand what was going on, and truth be told, neither did Naomi. However, after going through the gripping fear over almost losing Sal, she didn't want to waste another precious moment.

She turned to him. "Let's go home."

Surprise flickered in his eyes. "Home?"

"Yes," she whispered, holding on to his hand, "home."

He closed his eyes, though the burst of happiness in her chest told her that her words had pleased him. "As you wish." With that, he flashed them away.

* * * *

Naomi had no idea when she'd fallen asleep or how much time had passed when she cracked her eyes open. The last thing she'd remembered was Sal teleporting them to his lair—a two-story estate on hundreds of acres of private property that was more cozy than luxurious. They hadn't said much, instead took turns cleaning each other before drying off and falling onto his bed.

The events of the previous hours must have worn them both down, for they'd fallen asleep in each other's arms without exchanging any words.

Yawning, Naomi stretched and let out a soft moan when several joints popped. Then, she sat up, frowning to find herself all alone. The opened drapes revealed it was nighttime. That made sense. It had been early in the morning when she'd been reunited with Sal, and it hadn't even been noon by the time they'd flashed to his home.

Slipping out of bed, she rummaged through his dresser until she found a satin button-down shirt. It was the closest bit of casual wear he had, which made her snort in humor. She'd be shocked if he even knew what a regular T-shirt was.

Exiting the room, she eased her way through his large home, admiring his lush furnishing and décor along the way. She followed his scent, and it didn't take long for her to find him outside on a balcony. The patio faced his backyard, which consisted of an inground pool, a gazebo with outside furniture made for entertaining guests and acres of up-to-date landscaping.

Wearing nothing more than white gym shorts — *how shocking* — he was facing away from her while leaning on the railing. His silver hair was left loose to flow halfway down his back, and when a gentle breeze caused the silky strands to flutter, her breath caught in her throat.

He really was the most beautiful man she'd ever seen.

And she loved him.

Swallowing hard, she moved to stand next to him. "It's beautiful here," she murmured.

"Indeed," he responded, peering down at her. "I love the quiet serenity of it all."

"A big city boy like you? No way."

He snorted in amusement. "It's true. While my clubs are my treasures, even I like to escape every so often — to disappear to a place where others cannot disrupt my peace."

Naomi tilted her head to one side. "You don't invite guests over for parties or barbecues or whatever you suburban people do for entertainment?"

His eyes twinkled with humor. "This home in particular is, and has always been, just for me. I do not even invite my family over."

"Wow. Why so much space if it's just you?"

He was quiet for a while, and she could sense the humor fading. He returned his attention to his yard. "I suppose you could say it's a reflection of how I've always felt inside." At her confused look, he sighed. "When you analyzed me a few days ago at The Lotus — quite brutally, might I add — you said I only use my wealth and clubs as a way to hide from my insecurities. You were right. Even though I'm a Royal vampire, I'm not like my brothers. When people see them, they are filled with apprehension and respect. Even my sister evokes fear in others, and she's just a half-blood. Yet when people look at me, their first thought is that I'm just a…a…"

"Gaudy pretty boy?" she offered when he was at a loss for words. "Arrogant dandy? Clueless womanizer?"

"Bloody hell," he grumbled, shaking his head. "Is that really what you thought of me?"

Instead of answering, she waved that away. "Go on."

He sighed again. "No one has ever looked at me and wondered what's beneath my appearance. It's gotten to the point where I don't even know what's there anymore. I have no idea who the real Salvator Gordano is, and every time I step foot onto this estate, I'm reminded of that fact."

"Beautiful on the outside, yet empty and cold on the inside," Naomi murmured. "I get it."

Sal nodded. "Because of that, this estate has become a safe haven for me. It's the only place in the world where I can relax and find myself. And so, to protect the bit of peace it brings me, I don't allow anyone in."

"But you brought me here."

He glanced at her out of the corner of his eye. "I did. You said 'home'. To me, this is home, and I… I wanted to share it with you."

His sincere words warmed Naomi from her cheeks to her toes. She peered down at the pool water to hide her smile. In truth, it didn't matter where Sal would have teleported them. To her, *he* was her home. They could have gone to a rusted old shack in the poorest corner of the world, yet so long as he was at her side, she would have been content.

"You know," she said, facing him. "I don't know who the real Naomi is either. For years, I've been this killing machine fueled by hate and anger and guilt. Facing my aunt, however, relieved me of those burdens. I feel…new. Don't get me wrong. I'm not some cleansed do-gooder who wants to hug every creature in sight." At that, Sal chuckled, which in turn made her smile. "However, if I'm being honest, I want to know who the real Salvator is." When he turned to her with wide eyes, she nodded. "We both have some soul searching to do, so why not do it together?"

His throat worked when he swallowed. "Naomi, what are you saying?"

Nervousness filled her, but she took his hand in hers and met his surprised gaze with determination. "I love you, Sal. I'm not so good with colorful words or romantic poems or any of that bullshit, but I love you. I'm sorry I didn't have the courage to tell you sooner, but I—"

Her words were cut off when Sal pressed his lips to hers in a bone-melting kiss. She framed his face with her hands while he wrapped his arms around her waist. When he pulled back, they were both breathing hard.

"By the gods," he whispered, leaning his forehead against hers, "I never knew hearing those words would bring me such joy. I love you too, dove."

Naomi closed her eyes and exhaled a sigh of relief. "I'm ready."

"Hmm? For what?"

She opened her eyes. "To become your mate…if you'll have me."

Time seemed to freeze in that instant. Neither of them blinked as they locked stares. All the emotions she'd been fighting since meeting him came rushing to a head, causing her heart to race. With her enhanced hearing, she caught the stuttering of his own heartbeat.

It was all new to her, but she didn't complain one bit. Opening up to anyone was something that had never come easy to her. The last time she had, she'd ended up with a broken heart and a mountain of guilt that had lasted for decades. With Sal, however, she couldn't fight it anymore. She didn't want to. He was the one man she was destined to be with, and even if their truemate bond hadn't deemed it so, everything about him called to her in the most primal way.

She wanted him — every bit of him. The fear of getting hurt would always remain, but she knew he would do everything in his power to ensure her happiness.

Placing a tender kiss to her forehead, he took her hand and led the way to his bedroom. Each step caused licks of excitement to shoot through her, and by the time she stepped over the threshold, her pussy was already slick with her eagerness.

Sal turned to her, widening his eyes as he inhaled the scent of her desire. "Delicious," he growled, pulling her into him.

Naomi wrapped her arms around his neck and kissed him with all the passion she could muster. He backed her against the nearest wall, all the while working the buttons of her shirt. He was three snaps in when he gave a frustrated growl and ripped the fabric in half. "Fuck it," he murmured, dropping the torn material to the floor.

Standing naked before him, she had not even a shred of insecurity as she let him drink in the sight of her. He emboldened her. He made her feel like the most beautiful woman in the world, even with her scars.

They'd become a part of her, and he made it clear with his touch that he loved every one of them.

He roamed his hands over her, fondling every stretch of her skin with fervency. She busied herself pulling down his shorts, which he happily kicked away in his haste. He was the very picture of perfection with his lean muscles and smooth skin. The curved erection pointing at her begged to be touched, to which she obliged. She took him in her hands, stroking from tip to base, while she used her other hand to fondle his sac.

Meanwhile he cupped her breasts and squeezed, then dipped his head to kiss her again. There was nothing sweet about it, and when his extended fangs nicked her, she returned the gesture and nipped at his lower lip. He drew in a sharp breath, but it was clear from the rough pinching of her nipple that it had turned him on.

"I'm sorry, Naomi," he groaned, rocking into her when she squeezed his cock. "I can't hold back much longer."

"Then don't," she shot back, trailing her tongue over his jaw and down to his throat. She gave another light nip. "I need you."

He gripped her thighs and jerked them up, making her lock her legs around his waist. With one easy motion, he thrust inside her, pinning her to the wall. There was no pause, no hesitation to allow them both to adjust. This was something they both wanted. No, *needed*.

It wasn't just her succubus side. Even without that part of her blood, Sal brought forth a desire in her that demanded only his touch. He hammered her into the wall with fast strokes, as if the moment he faltered would mean the end of the world.

"Sal," she moaned, dragging out his name. "Do. It. *Now*."

"Yes," he growled. Without breaking speed, he angled his head to kiss the pounding vein at her throat. Then, he bit.

Like the first time, his bite was pure bliss. She gasped at the feeling of him drawing her lifeforce into him, each pull tugging on her very core. He moaned against her skin, and with obvious effort, he withdrew his fangs, only to bite into the skin at his wrist. "Drink," he commanded, breathing hard as if he'd run a marathon. Still, he continued to pound into her.

Naomi wasted no time in latching on to his wrist. The metallic taste of his blood was revolting, but she drank until his wound sealed shut. He bit the skin open once more and made her drink more, which she did.

She wasn't sure how mating ceremonies between demons worked, but the tingling in her veins followed by the rush of emotions from Sal let her know it was complete.

He made a pleased sound deep in his chest then kissed her. When he slowed his speed, he angled his hips in a way that had his dick brushing against a sensitive area within her. However, it was when he reached between them to toy with her clit that she felt her orgasm looming.

"Gods, you're so wet," he growled. "Come for me."

That single, sexy command did it for her. She stiffened and threw her head back as she cried her release. Sal caught her scream with a scorching kiss, and several moments later, he groaned as he spilled into her.

Panting and barely able to stand, he carried them to his bed, though his legs shook the entire time. When they fell onto the thick comforter, they both chuckled.

"That was incredible," Naomi breathed, throwing her arms over her head.

Next to her, Sal mimicked her position. "It was," he responded. "What do you feel?"

She paused and focused her attention on the feeling of completion in her chest. "You."

He smiled and turned his head to her. "And what do I feel like?"

She returned his smile and placed her hand on his cheek. "Home, Sal. You feel like home."

"As my mate, you know that you're a Gordano now, right? That means my family is now yours. You'll never again be alone."

Feigning a contemplating look, she tilted her head to one side. "Even Tweedledee and Tweedledum?"

He laughed, a pure sound that she'd never thought would cause her heart to melt—banal as that may be. "Yes…even the twins."

She heaved an exaggerated sigh. "For the rest of eternity, huh?"

"It's too late to back out now," he chuckled, fully facing her. He leaned forward to plant a lingering kiss on her lips. "You're all mine now."

With a smile, she rolled him onto his back, while she straddled his waist. "Don't worry, Sally. I have no intention of giving any of this up."

It was true. Opening up to Sal's family was going to take some time, but they had an eternity to work it out. Besides, she loved Sal, and she was more than willing to accept everything about him. That included his motley crew of strange siblings and one intimidating father.

Chapter Sixteen

"Ready? Lift on three. One. Two. Three—"

Andreas shoved the twins out of the way and hoisted the remaining five cardboard boxes stacked on top of one another. "Move aside, amateurs," he taunted, carrying them into Ava and Marc's new house with ease.

"Show off," Darius called after him.

Naomi grinned. It had only been a few weeks since she and Sal had become mates, but his family had accepted her with open arms, as if they'd known her for ages. She still wasn't used to the constant chattering and being invited out for family dinners and such, but they were growing on her, little by little, even the twins from hell.

Next to her, Sal threw his arm over her shoulders and led the way inside. The mansion was beautiful and beyond huge, but she expected nothing less from the Gordanos. They threw their money around like it was nothing. Unlike the rest of them, however, she didn't think the extra space was unnecessary for Ava and Marc.

She'd learned that the two had been wanting to open their homes to abandoned children. Having been supportive of their dream, Cyrus had purchased their new house, and after spending the previous few days moving furniture in, all that was left for the family to do was unpack their boxes.

Naomi had also been amazed that after Cyrus had found the children Arson had put to sleep back in The Oracles' hideout, instead of punishing them, he'd taken them under his wing with the promise to turn their lives around. They'd been terrified — and still were, to an extent — but under Ava and Marc's care, they would get to live relatively normal childhoods, along with Anais and Selene. At the moment, however, they were under the watchful eye of Cyrus' Guard to ensure they weren't going to attack anyone.

She'd developed a new level of respect for the family. They were a group of powerful Royals who could seize the world if they wanted to, yet they were a merciful, loving bunch. They were also annoying as hell at times, but all families were. Not that she knew how regular families acted, but she was grateful to be able to be a part of this one.

Shaking her head, she met the rest of the Gordanos out on the back patio. Marc, Lucian and a tiger-shifter she had yet to be introduced to were arguing as they struggled to put together an outside playset. Though they were too far away for her to hear what they were yelling about, she could only guess that the three alpha males refused to listen to each other and work together.

"They're fighting because they're all accusing each other of losing the instruction manual," Siovon laughed, taking a sip of the mimosa in her hands. She offered Naomi a glass. "Now they don't know what to do."

"I'll go see if I can help," Sal chuckled. He kissed Naomi's forehead and made his way to the other men. "Come along, Julius."

"What? Why me?" the younger twin demanded. Still, he rolled his eyes and followed, leaving behind Naomi, Siovon and Ava.

Ava laughed, a mischievous twinkle in her emerald eyes. "I wonder how long it'll take them to realize that I have the booklet."

Siovon snickered. "We'll be here all night."

"Naomi," Ava said, "I've talked to Cass about his gym. He has a position available to teach martial arts classes. It's a full-time position, and he says more women sign up than men."

Naomi blinked in surprise. "Really? You think he's willing to hire me?"

"Why not? You can kick some serious ass, and you're his first choice," Ava said.

"Well, of course," Siovon crooned. "Where do you think she got it from? What do you say?"

"Well…" Naomi thought about declining but thought better of it. In truth, while she still had to fully let go of her insecurities, the thought of teaching others how to defend themselves was inviting. While Sal had more than enough wealth to provide them with comfort for years to come, she'd been wanting to take up a job to make up for all the extra free time she had now that she no longer worked for the guild. "That actually doesn't sound bad. When can I start?"

"As soon as you're ready," Cass said, exiting the house. "I meant to talk to you myself, but I see my sister has beat me to it."

Said sister chuckled at that. "Sorry. I'm just so excited about everything."

"Meet me there tomorrow evening and we can get your paperwork signed. I'll be taking this." He reached behind Ava and plucked the manual from her back pocket. She giggled at his stern look. Nodding to them, he made his way to the other men, who were still fighting over the playhouse.

"Isn't this great?" Siovon said with a sigh of contentment. "I never would have imagined life being like this just a year ago."

Naomi smiled in agreement. "Neither would I."

"Ditto," Ava added. "It's hard to even picture what would have happened if I hadn't met Marc. I wouldn't be here with my family, and who knows how far Mikhail would have gotten if we hadn't figured out his plans."

Siovon grimaced. "I'd still be chained down, forced to be a blood donor." She glanced around. "Where are Anais and Selene?"

"Dad has them. He's guiding Anais around the house to help her get familiar with everything. He's leaving little scent markers to make it easier for her to find her way. As for Selene, he refuses to let anyone else hold her when he's around, not even Marc."

"It's adorable how much they've been bonding lately. Him and Anais, I mean."

Ava nodded, a pleased smile curling her lips. "I know. Believe it or not, he's really great with kids. He's a big teddy bear, but don't tell anyone I told you that.

I'm so happy she's getting used to everyone." Then, she frowned. "I hate that I couldn't wipe all her memories."

Naomi tilted her head to one side. "Wipe her memories? Why would you do something like that?"

Siovon and Ava gawked at her. "You didn't know?" At her blank stare, Ava fidgeted with a loose strand of her hair. "Anais is a Royal like us — a pureblood, at that. There's someone she calls 'Master' who has kept her and several other Royals captive for the gods only know how long. All this time we've thought we were the only ones alive, but there's an entire community of them down there, yet we…" When her voice started to get louder with anger, she closed her eyes and inhaled several deeps breaths. "Anyway, Anais is a teleporter like Sal, but she can cross worlds. That's how she was able to escape, but she'd seen so much carnage before going blind."

She kicked at a pebble. "Marc and I spoke with her and she agreed to allow me to block her memories until she's older, but I can only do a little bit at a time. There's just so…much."

Siovon gave her a comforting pat on the back. "Well, on the bright side, with Elvira in custody, hopefully we'll have a lead soon enough."

Ava sighed and looked up at the night sky. "Yeah, you're right." She peered at Naomi with worried eyes. "Are you sure you're okay with that? I mean, she is your aunt and —"

"Let me stop you right there," Naomi cut in. "As you people so ruthlessly forced upon me, I realize that blood doesn't make someone your family."

Siovon flashed a wide smile. "Naomi Sofia Morales, that is the sweetest —"

"Oh, shut it," Naomi growled. Though these people no longer saw her as a heartless badass, she still had an image to maintain.

Siovon chuckled and shook her head. "Since we're talking about Elvira, I am curious about something. How the hell did you manage to find where she was hiding? Not even Thor could locate them, and you know how good he is at detecting things like hidden doors and whatnot."

Naomi scratched her head. "It was the strangest thing. That night when Sal and I had gone to The Shade, this rude-ass man bumped into me. I didn't think anything of it, but when I met up with Arson, that was when I realized he'd snuck a note into my pocket with a set of nearby coordinates. From there, Arson pointed out the Metro running underground, so we followed it until…" She trailed off and shrugged.

Siovon and Ava both wore confused looks. "This man just happened to bump into you and drop a hint into your pocket?" Siovon asked. "That can't be a coincidence. Who was he? How did he even know what you were looking for?"

Naomi lifted her hands in confusion. "You're asking the same thing I've been wondering for weeks. I've never seen him before, and I have no idea why he helped. However, if it were not for him, I doubt we would have even made it to Sal."

"Well, what did he look like?" Ava asked. "If you remember his face, Julius can draw a portrait so we can try to identify him."

"I don't. It happened way too fast, and most of his features were in shadow. However, I do remember he had a very distinct scar." She demonstrated by drawing an invisible line over her face. "It was slanted from his temple, over his left eye and down to his upper lip."

Siovon stiffened, and if Naomi wasn't mistaken, her dear friend had gone a shade paler. "What color were his eyes?" she asked, her voice tight.

Naomi frowned, squinting her eyes in remembrance. "Um, one was blue and the other was brown. Well, I think that's it. I just know they weren't the same color." When Siovon released a shaky breath, concern swamped her. "What's wrong?"

Siovon dropped her mimosa glass and sank into one of the patio chairs. "That's Khan," she whispered.

At the sound of glass breaking, the others stopped bickering and peered at the women. Lucian, taking note of his mate's stricken expression, charged toward them.

Ava glanced at Naomi with worry, but she could only shake her head in confusion. "Who is Khan?"

For several long moments, Siovon didn't say anything. Then, she glanced up with tears in her eyes. Naomi had never before seen her friend cry, which only made her more worried.

"He raised me," she said, her voice breaking. "That man who helped you...was my mentor."

* * * *

Southern Quebec

Lynx didn't say a word as he followed the silent group of vampires leading him through a mausoleum-style building that housed a good majority of the southern Quebec clan. The entourage wasn't needed, for he'd memorized the way to Arson's private library long ago.

However, he knew they were there more for her protection than worrying he'd get lost. Not many people had ever met her in person — or even seen her from a distance — but that didn't mean they didn't want her head. The reputation surrounding her and her clansmen was seen as a challenge to other vampires and demons. She didn't have a large territory like other chiefs, but the mystery shrouding her lands and her determination to keep them out only seemed to call more attention to make outsiders want to know what the big fuss was about.

So, to the men and women forming a wall around him and watching his every move, he was an outsider. The fact that he was the king's right-hand-man only made them more anxious.

Fortunately for them, they had no reason for concern. Lynx was a wise vampire. Though he was formidable in his own right, he'd never be a match for Arson. Hardly anyone was, so only a true fool would try to attack her. Hell, even if he wanted to, the moment he so much as twitched his fingers, her clansmen would tear him apart.

Not that he wished Arson any harm, regardless. She'd been someone he'd considered a friend for a very, very long time, and his loyalty to her ran deep — so deep, that he'd never told a soul about her. Keeping his relationship with her a secret from his king felt like a betrayal of the worst sort, yet it couldn't be helped. He'd made a blood vow to never reveal the truth about Arson to anyone — not even to the one man who needed to know.

And so, in order to prevent his secret from being detected, he only visited her once every few years — or sooner, if the king sent him to deliver a message to her.

When the group stopped before a set of stone doors that had been crafted centuries ago, they allowed him to enter, though not without making their contempt for him clear through their menacing scowls. He ignored them and stepped over the threshold. The doors closed behind him with an echoing boom.

In hindsight, he'd always admired their fealty to Arson, as well as her devotion to them. Others might think of her as cold and heartless, but it was impossible not to respect her. She was a good chief who cared for her people. She'd move mountains if it meant their safety.

Though nowhere near as large or lavish as Cyrus', the library was still rather impressive with its multitude of books and scrolls lining the floor-to-ceiling shelves. Arson sat behind her desk, looking as poised and refined as ever.

"Lynx," she greeted, though her tone remained impassive, "what can I do for you tonight?"

He strolled across the carpet to her but didn't take a seat when she indicated one of the chairs opposite her. It was going to be a quick visit, he knew. He could sense that she wasn't in the mood for talking. "So, you finally got to see him. How was it?"

Though most wouldn't have seen it, Lynx caught the brief surprise that flickered in her amber eyes. "I knew you would ask that." She placed her chin in her hand, her expression becoming one of contemplation. "It was bittersweet, I'll admit. I was foolish for even going."

He snorted. "Yeah, you were. Someone could have discovered the truth about you."

"Indeed." With her free hand, she drummed her fingers on the desk in thought. "His hair has gotten so long. He used to hate that. He'd always kept it cut short. I'm relieved Andreas is doing better now, also. He looks healthy. The others, as well. Lucian and Salvator have found their truemates. It makes me feel at peace."

Lynx watched her in silence. It was the first time in a long time he'd seen her even remotely close to being happy. She'd always kept a tight leash on her feelings to portray herself as an emotionless chief, but he knew her well enough to see beyond her façade. He saw how lonely and empty she felt inside. Yet even though her sadness remained, she seemed...lighter. It was as if those short minutes she'd gotten to see Cyrus in person had made her content with life.

He scrubbed a hand through his hair. "It's been centuries. You can—"

"Don't go there," she cut in. Her expression reverted back to its aloof state, though she wasn't able to hide the pain behind her eyes, not from him. "You know why I can't go to him. Remaining here in the shadows is all I can do. It's the only way to protect all of them."

Stubborn woman, he thought in annoyance. When she snorted after hearing the mental insult, he sighed. "Very well. The reason I'm here is to inform you that the decennial chief assembly will be held at the end of January. Cyrus demands everyone to be in attendance—including you. Failure to appear is a direct challenge to the king's authority. That means you cannot send your clansmen in your place again."

Arson breathed a soft sigh. "I'm aware."

"Does that mean you'll come this time?"

She shrugged. "It sounds like I have no choice but to oblige."

Grunting, Lynx turned around and headed for the exit. Her dry tone made it hard for even him to figure out whether or not she was being honest, but he shrugged it off. It was damn near impossible to persuade her into following the rules. If there was something she didn't want to do, she wouldn't. She was obstinate that way.

Pausing at the door, he glanced over his shoulder to stab her with a hard stare. "You know, I have been at Cyrus' side for many, many years. I've seen parts of him no one else has ever witnessed—not even his children. Believe me when I say you aren't the only one who has grieved all these years. The only difference is, you know exactly why you're both suffering."

She looked to the side, though he didn't miss the flash of guilt that crossed her features. "This is the path fate has chosen for us. We cannot change it. You know what would happen otherwise. Now, if that is all…"

It wasn't all, but Lynx knew that tone meant it was the end of the discussion. He gave a sad shake of his head. "Just think on it. This time, it will be different. See you at the assembly, Vivinna."

With his message delivered, he took his leave.

Long after Lynx had left, Arson continued to stare after him in annoyance.

'See you at the assembly, Vivinna.'

She hated when he called her that and he knew it, yet he did it after every single visit. The name was a constant reminder of a life she'd given up ages ago. It was a slap in the face of the heartbreaking choices she'd had to make.

It couldn't be helped, she assured herself. The fate of the world had rested on her shoulders, and in a desperate means to save the man she'd loved, she'd done the only thing she could think of at the time.

Sighing under her breath, she swiveled around in her chair to face the tall window showing her the starry night sky. Though she knew she was going to regret it, she allowed her mind to wander for a moment.

It had been centuries since she'd last seen Cyrus. He was still as beautiful as ever, though, as she'd mentioned to Lynx, his hair had gotten long. He used to always keep it in a short style, but now it flowed down to his knees in a river of black silk. He'd also filled out much more, growing from a young athlete's build to that of a man who'd spent years toning muscle definition. His physique had been hidden under the elegant togas she knew he preferred, but only a fool would assume he was anything less than a powerful warrior. Also, way back then, he'd carried a mighty aura, but it was ten times more intense now that he was older.

She smiled in remembrance, but it was a sad tilt of her lips. He didn't remember her, of course. There hadn't been even a flicker of recognition in his pale gaze as he'd stared at her, only mild curiosity and a bit of annoyance at her nonchalant attitude toward him. To him, it had been the first time they'd met, though it was better that way. If his memories ever returned, it would only spell trouble — not only for her, but for the rest of their kind as well.

And Andreas...

Her heart throbbed when she stared into the eyes that were so much like her own. He hadn't recognized her either, but that was also for the best. She'd read his mind. He'd just found out the truth of his birth — half of it anyway. He'd learned that he was Cyrus' blood son, though he hadn't told anyone yet. He was eager to find his birth mother, but there would not be any kind words or tears of joy. He hated her with a passion, and he was ready to tell her why.

He was confused, but he hated not knowing why he'd been abandoned as a baby. Hell, Arson hated it more. It had been beyond difficult to give him up in the first place, yet it had been the only way to save him.

How could she explain that to him — to any of them?

Lynx had said things were different — and that was true enough — but she didn't dare for one moment allow herself to believe things could go back to the way they used to be. It was impossible.

When a painful pricking stung the corners of her eyes, she realized it was time to move on — again. Those were all thoughts she couldn't dwell on anymore. The pain they brought would weaken everything she'd worked and suffered for.

Things are better this way. I did the right thing. Those were the same words she'd chanted to herself over and over again for millennia. So long as she pretended to believe them, no harm would come to those she cared for most. That was Vivinna's old life, and she was long dead. She no longer existed.

In her place, Arson had been born — a Royal vampire with no past and only a bleak future. Her clan was the only thing that mattered to her now.

Cyrus and Andreas, she thought one last time before sealing them from her mind for good, *please forgive me*.

Chapter Seventeen

The image of that Amazon woman refused to leave Cassander. The desire to see her one more time, to just strike up a conversation with her and find out her name at least would not go away. He'd ventured to his gym far more times than was necessary, yet after that night, he was convinced that fate had drawn them together somehow. It was much too early to conclude that she was his truemate, but damn if it wasn't a pressing thought in his mind.

It could very well be his desperation and longing to find someone to end his loneliness, or it could simply be a matter of lust. After all, he'd always had a thing for women who could kick ass, and based on the strength and skill she had shown, he'd popped a tent out of the blue.

Maria had been a gentle soul, the total opposite of what he usually went for, yet fate had chosen her. Despite their opposing beliefs and the lack of things they'd had in common, he'd loved her, regardless.

She'd been his truemate, after all, and it had been impossible to resist the call to claim her as his own.

Even today he still loved her and mourned her memory, but it had been centuries. He'd moved on to an extent, yet a piece of him had died with her, and he feared it would never return. Even thinking about another woman felt like a betrayal, and that should have whipped him out of his musings, but it didn't.

Sighing, he continued going at the hanging punching bag. Of course, it was the same room in his gym that the other woman had occupied. As much as he'd warned himself not to, his body had gone against his demands. Curse it all.

The thought only frustrated him more, making him attack the bag with far more vigor than was necessary. Every punch left behind deep grooves, but he didn't fret. They were tailored to take such damage. Besides, he was just getting started.

After that warmup, he switched to working out his legs and arms on the weights. It wasn't until the early morning hours were creeping up that he decided to call it quits.

However, he had to admit it felt good to get in a session. Somehow, working out in a public gym felt better than when he did it alone at home. He took the time to replace all the metal weights, then cleaned up after himself.

After a quick shower in the men's room, he slung his backpack over his shoulder and made to exit. Most demons were nocturnal, but the gym was open twenty-four hours for those who didn't mind the sunlight, so more than a handful of stragglers remained.

He exited through the front doors then hopped in his vehicle. Instead of going home right away, however, he took a slight detour to the overnight supermarket. While he no longer ate human food, he had to stock up on some chow for his new puppy.

The thought made him roll his eyes. He'd never been a fan of dogs, but the mutt had wandered into his backyard. Since his lair was on an unfenced stretch of forestry filled with traps to keep out trespassers, even the wildlife knew not to venture there. They could sense his dark presence and instinct would ward them away.

The wolf pup, however, had seemed to be unconcerned with the predatory threat. Alone, it had ambled right into a deep pit. Cass would have been happy to have left it there, but the helpless whining had touched a soft spot in him. He'd rescued it with every intention to send it back to wherever it had come from, but the little beast had refused to leave his side since then.

And so, he had a puppy. A wild wolf puppy, but a puppy no less.

When he pulled into the parking lot, he heaved an annoyed sigh and stepped out. It was inconvenient things like this that made him regret his decision to keep it. Pets demanded so much time and attention, and while he was a homebody, that didn't mean he wasn't busy. The little beast was sure to cause him a headache.

A half hour later, he exited with a cart full of puppy supplies — a collar, food and water bowl, two bags full of toys, a traveling kennel, a large pillow for sleeping, shampoo and the gods only knew what else. If there had been a picture of a dog on the product, he'd tossed it into the buggy. He was thankful for the invention of self-checkout, for the cashier would have given him some strange glances, for sure.

Shaking his head in disgust at himself, he placed his items in the back seat. Just as he was about to hop inside the driver's side, he paused at the sound of a faint scream on the far side of the parking lot. Though it had come from a dark area that the lights couldn't reach, he narrowed his eyes at the sight of two figures fighting in the shadows. Even from the distance, he couldn't quite see what was going on, but the flailing arms of one of them was a sign that someone was being attacked.

Another quick glance around showed that he was the only other person in the lot.

Slamming his door shut, he darted across the pavement, tensing when the scent of human blood filled the air. As he drew near, he watched the victim's body go lifeless as someone drank from her neck.

"Stop," Cass growled, clenching his fists in preparation of a fight.

The demon yanked away from the human and glanced at him approaching, and Cass' steps faltered when he identified her as the Amazon he'd been hoping to find—the beautiful woman he'd spent far too much time daydreaming about.

Seeing her was like a sucker punch to the gut. The glazed-over look in her dark eyes cleared, and she blinked in confusion at the sight of him.

A crimson trail of blood slid from the corner of her lips to her chin, and she peered down in horror at the human woman swiftly losing color in her arms. "No," she breathed. She dropped the human and pushed away to stand. "No, no, no. *Fuck.*"

"What did you do?" Cass breathed, staring at her in disbelief. "*Why* did you do this?"

"I didn't mean to... I just... No, I'm so sorry. I'm sorry." Tears filled her eyes, the sour scent of her desperation almost choking with its intensity. "I'm sorry!" She turned and dashed into the darkness.

"Hey, wait," Cass called. He made to go after her, but the dying woman on the pavement made him think better of it. He crouched down beside her and checked her pulse. It was weak, but steady, meaning she hadn't been completely drained. He pulled out his cell phone and dialed for an ambulance.

He squinted into the darkness after the Amazon. She was long gone, but if he followed her scent, he'd be able to catch up to her before her trail disappeared.

He looked down at the helpless human then cursed under his breath. He couldn't just leave her there. They were so fragile, and since he'd failed to stop the Amazon in time, guilt made him remain in place. He shook his head and brushed the woman's hair from her forehead.

The sight of her lying pale and weak reminded him far too much of his dead mate, and he had to squeeze his eyes shut to prevent the old memory from forming.

She whimpered, but he used his charm to calm her fear. "Sh-h, sh-h... You'll be fine. Sleep now."

When her nerves calmed and the ambulance's sirens could be heard growing near, he gently laid her on the ground and returned to his vehicle. He didn't leave right away, however. Instead, he waited until the EMTs arrived and tended to her, then he drove off.

The Amazon was lucky he'd intervened in time, but what would have happened if he hadn't? Hell, how many others had she attacked and killed before then?

However, she hadn't seemed to know what she was doing at first. It was like she'd awakened from some sort of trance when he'd called out to her, and the remorse written on her features and causing her voice to tremble had been far too honest to be a trick. It confused him to no end, but what was more pressing was the issue that what had just transpired were the tendencies of a Rogue in the beginning stages. He'd seen it happen far too many times in the past.

If that were the case, her bloodlust hadn't set in all the way, so she was aware that what she was doing was wrong. However, if he didn't find her soon, it was only a matter of time before she truly slipped over the edge of insanity.

"Bloody fucking hell," he growled, gripping his steering wheel with enough force to make it crack.

It just figured that the one woman he'd been attracted to for the first time in centuries could quite possibly be a murderer. Not that he was a damn saint himself, but attacking innocent humans and feeding from them until the point of death was an absolute crime punishable by execution, no ifs, ands or buts.

Pulling over onto a side street, he parked his truck and exited, then darted across the street. A few sniffs and he caught on to the blood trail. He followed it with determination, turning down several alleys until her scent grew stronger.

Relief filled him for a moment, but he pushed it aside. He was a terrible man. While a part of him wanted to believe he was searching to reprimand her for almost killing a mortal, that was complete bullshit. Every bit of him suffered a primal urge to find her simply to sate the curiosity that had been plaguing him since he'd first laid eyes on her.

Pathetic, he growled to himself. *Pathetic, pathetic, pathetic.*

Still, he pressed onward. Her trail led him to a less crowded corner of the city, a quiet neighborhood with narrow townhouses that had seen better days. Quiet, but it was clear this was the side of town one didn't want to get lost in. The top of the street was just the start of a long drive into the slums where tons of gang activity happened that wound up on the news, more often than not. The businesses lining both sides of the street turned into rows of two-story houses with small fenced yards. Those dwindled into older-model townhomes that went on for three blocks. Beyond that was an old, rusted playground that sat between the last house and the duplex project homes.

Cass slowed to a stop in front of one of the middle townhouses. The blue paint was faded, several shingles were missing and there were bars on the windows. A small fence separated this property from the neighbors, but the metal was rusted and one side of the chain had long ago fallen down to intermingle with the weeds around it.

He frowned at the sight. Though he didn't venture out much, there was no denying that he was used to living a much more lavish lifestyle. Though he wasn't half as flashy as some of his brothers, he wasn't accustomed to seeing such a disarrayed neighborhood.

It was clear that this neighborhood was one that was less favored by both the inhabitants and the city. Though the individual residences were considerably nicer looking than the project homes farther down the road, it wasn't much competition, that was for sure. This entire division looked ready to puff out its last breath. Even the narrow street had long ago given into the elements, containing a pothole every few feet and cracked to the point where weeds had broken through.

Scenting the air, he made sure that he'd followed the correct trail. Sure enough, the blood led him right around the back of the house. He sent his shadow out to try to detect a trap, but there was none. Hell, this street alone was inhabited only by humans, as far as he knew.

Melting into his shadowy form, he crossed the street and moved to the back of the house. He paused for a moment to listen for anything out of the ordinary. Assured that he was in the clear, he slipped under the back door and took on his physical form.

To his surprise, the inside was far nicer than the outward appearance. The first thing he noticed was that there was a distinct scent of lemon and faint bleach, as if the place was cleaned often. As he took silent steps through a tiny kitchen, an opening on his left revealed a small living room with an old tan couch, a rustic coffee table and a single armchair, all facing a large bay window that would give a view of the street outside if the curtains had been opened.

No TV, no pictures on the wall, no bookcase, not even a single sheet of paper on the coffee table… There were just those three bits of furniture and the beige carpet they sat on, but nothing that really gave away the woman's personality or her tastes in décor.

If this is even her house, he thought. He wondered if such was the case — or if it was just a hiding place.

Following the blood trail, he spotted a set of stairs near the front door. The first step creaked under his weight, making him pause. He once again shifted into his shadow form and headed up the stairs in total silence. Once on the landing, he straightened, glancing around. There appeared to only be two bedrooms and one bathroom.

With slow, cautious steps, he followed the trail into the bedroom at the end. The door was cracked halfway open, allowing only a glimpse inside. As he neared, the scent grew stronger, making him swallow.

It crossed his mind to call out to her instead of sneaking around like some creep, but he assured himself that it was necessary. The element of surprise was his specialty.

Besides, after witnessing what he had, he could very well turn her over to Lucian. As the clan chief over this territory, he was responsible for disposing of vampires who went against his rules.

Steeling his resolve, he took another step forward, but paused when the floor creaked again.

He stiffened, and the subtle shift in the air was the only indication that he'd screwed up before something slammed into the back of his head. He fell to the ground, and just before unconsciousness claimed him, his blurry vision spotted the Amazon.

"I'm sorry," she murmured, crouching beside him, "but I really need that money."

The Lucifer Brothers:
The Devil is my Boss
Makayla Roberts

Excerpt

"I quit!"

The shout was followed by the furious slamming of a file cabinet. Rhys Lucifer stood near the door, the only exit in the spacious office. Well, not unless one counted the floor-to-ceiling windows, though he doubted his employee was mad enough to jump to his death. "Come now, Ivan. We can talk about this."

The male whirled around, narrowing his eyes in disbelief. "Talk? There's nothing to talk about!" He slammed another drawer then used one arm to sweep his personal belongings off his desk and into the cardboard box he held under his other arm. "Seven months of utter hell."

"Well, we are in Sheol," Rhys drawled, not at all helping the situation, "which is technically what's referred to as—"

"I know where the fuck we are," Ivan snarled. He pointed a shaking finger at Rhys, his Russian accent thick with his madness. "This job is… It's… I don't even have the words for it, but I quit! No demon in their right mind should ever agree to this position. I don't know what I was thinking."

Money, no doubt. Money and power, Rhys thought. It was the same with everyone who was brave enough to take on the job as his COO.

Rhys grunted and shifted his weight to one leg as he watched his chief operating officer march around the mahogany desk to stalk across the room, his box tucked a bit too tightly under one arm. His eyes were desolate with dark circles that spoke of restless nights, the uncombed toupée atop his head lopsided. There was a shadow across his jaw, making it clear that he hadn't shaved in several days, either.

"I'll admit it's a...difficult position, but—"

"Difficult?" Ivan echoed on a bark of laughter. "I've had less than fifteen hours of sleep in the past week." He waved his free arm to indicate the piles upon piles of paper stacked on the floor. The movement caused his toupée to slip from his head and fall onto the desk, not that he seemed to notice. "All this work is far too much for one person to do, and between the board meetings, employee requests and upcoming events—never mind that with the wars going on topside, the mortal death tolls increase each day. No way, man. I quit! I'm done."

Rhys shifted his weight to his other leg, mild panic welling at the notion that the employee he needed the most to help him through these critical times was quitting on him. *Again.* "Ivan, please. Think about what you're doing. What about the Séance Convention coming up? I can't go it alone, and you're the only one with the proper knowledge to accompany me. Plus, there's no time to train anyone to fill your position before then." He paused. "I'll give you a bonus. How does an extra four thousand sen sound?"

Slowly, Ivan turned to face Rhys. His irises changed from black to red, a sure sign of a pissed-off demon. It didn't matter that Rhys was his boss or that he was the oldest son of one of the most important men in the underworld—nor did it seem to matter that, at six-three, Rhys had a good foot and a half on him. The look he was receiving was one of pure disgust.

In fluent Russian, Ivan jabbed a finger in the center of Rhys' chest and said, "Fuck that convention, and you can shove your money up your ass."

He snatched his toupée off the desk and slammed it on top of his head. Then he marched out of the office.

Chin dropping to his chest, Rhys watched Ivan storm down the maze of cubicles lining the floor and to the far side, where a bank of elevators sat behind a set of glass doors. His now-former employee tapped his foot as he waited for one of the elevators to arrive. When it did, he stepped inside and faced Rhys and the multiple pairs of eyes watching him. Then, just as the doors slid closed, he raised his hand high and gave them all the bird.

And that was it. Ivan was gone, having quit after only seven months. Rhys shouldn't have been shocked, since the man before Ivan had resigned after an even shorter time. *Hell's bells.* He'd taken over this portion of the family company twenty years ago and, in that time, he'd lost double the number of COOs. Not that any of them had been particularly good at their job, but *someone* needed to fill the position, and the majority of them had all the qualifications.

Now he was back at square one, with large shoes to fill and less than two weeks to do so. *Just freaking terrific.*

With a dull throb forming between his brows, he exited the office and closed the door. When he glanced at his employees watching him with wide eyes, he snapped, "Get back to work!" There was an immediate clack of keyboards as everyone did as commanded, no doubt fearing he was in a firing type of mood.

He relaxed his expression to one of ice, striding across the floor to the elevators. Gods below, he needed a damn drink. No, he needed the whole bottle and then some. It'd been a long-ass day, and it wasn't even eight o'clock yet, damn it all.

Stepping onto the elevator, he pressed the arrow going up with far more force than needed. The ride up was four floors, but it may as well have been the entire thirty-plus that made up this wing of the building. When the doors opened once more, he stormed out, heading for his private office.

He rounded a corner and his secretary perked up. "Good morning, Rhys…" She trailed off, her smile waning as she took in his fuming expression.

His steps never faltered as he strode past her. "Pull up a list of this division's employees and compile a separate list of those qualified to take Ivan's place."

Kelle's eyes widened a bit. "Yes, sir," she responded, swiveling in her chair to face her computer. There was no hesitation, no questions asked, just swift obedience, which was one of the reasons Rhys had hired her a decade before. He was a man who gave orders and expected them to be carried out to the fullest. Otherwise, someone ended up demoted — or fired.

And that was just him being polite.

With a deep sigh, Rhys entered his office. He skipped his desk and opted for the black leather sofa across the room.

Ten days. He had ten days to dig through his employees to determine which one would be qualified enough to take on the job of COO. Granted, it was a tough spot, but the benefits that came with it were incredible compared to positions of lower status. Anyone should feel honored to be promoted, especially in this line of work.

As his mind began to wander, there was a sharp knock at the door. The trespasser didn't wait for a response, proceeding to open the door. With another deep sigh, Rhys didn't bother sitting up. There was no point. He already knew who it was. With his heightened senses, the familiar scent of eucalyptus and antibacterial hand sanitizer was always a dead giveaway that his younger brother, Quin, was nearby. The man was a germaphobe. It would have been laughable, given his large six-six frame, but the sad truth behind it was one only the three brothers knew.

And, of course, the smell of dark cinnamon spices soon followed, signaling the entrance of his even younger brother, Thorne. They were the only two beings at Elysium Underworld Corp who possessed the balls to intrude on his privacy without permission.

One of them let out a low whistle as they made themselves comfortable in the matching leather armchairs around him. "Looks like the rumors are true," Quin commented, a touch of humor in his deep voice. "Your officer walked out on you again."

Rhys grunted, squeezing his eyes shut in frustration. "At the most inconvenient of times," he growled, annoyed with the entire situation. And, from past experiences, he was about to become even more so. His brothers usually came to enjoy watching him soak in misery, torturing him with their ill-conceived jokes.

"Any idea who you're going to get to replace him?" Thorne asked, though his tone suggested he couldn't give two shits.

"Not a clue," Rhys retorted. He didn't know a quarter of his employees, truth be told. There was no point in making much effort when people were always coming and going. The handful he did know were the important ones he had to deal with throughout the week, like Kelle and Ivan.

"It sucks, brother. I feel for you."

Rhys flipped his brother off, eliciting a dark chuckle. "If you two aren't going to offer any help, you can just get the fuck out."

"Hey, there's no need to be rude," Quin drawled. "We actually *did* come to help. I did, anyway. Thorne is here to be his usual self."

"Damn right," Thorne crooned.

Rhys shook his head and straightened to peer at his brothers. Though the three couldn't be more different personality-wise, the similarities in appearance made it clear that they were related. All three of them had the same dark brown hair. Unlike Rhys, who kept a short clean cut, Quin's was a bit longer, the ends curling just under his chin. Thorne, however, wore his to his shoulders, several of the thick strands shot through with natural blond highlights from prolonged exposure to the sun topside. All three had brown eyes, though Quin's were lighter in color, more along the lines of toffee, and Thorne had golden flecks around the pupils. Rhys' jawline was more defined, but Quin's lips were fuller and Thorne's nose was crooked, after having been broken one too many times.

And though they each had two six-inch-tall, curved horns rising from the tops of their heads, the spiraling patterns engraved on them were similar, but not the same, having appeared after they'd reached maturity.

"How the hell do you two know that Ivan quit?" Rhys demanded. "It hasn't even been a full twenty minutes since he walked out."

"Oh, you know," Thorne responded, throwing one leg over the arm of his chair. "Word travels fast around here. Rumors spread like wildfire among the office geeks."

Quin snorted. "For sure. Plus, someone uploaded a video of the whole thing on Fangsbook. It's already gotten a thousand views."

That much was true. Not about the video, but the other bit. Though every day was busy for his employees, they still made time to babble and converse. Secrets never lasted very long. "So, you two merrily shirked your duties to help me find a replacement?"

Quin shrugged, the thick muscles making up his shoulders rippling under his button-up shirt. His usual attire wasn't a full business suit like Rhys preferred. His brother always wore slacks, khakis or dress pants with either a polo or a button shirt tucked at the waist. Thorne, on the other hand, didn't even try. As the head of the field workers division, he spent a lot of time topside and was always active, so there was no need for him to dress as professionally as Rhys and Quin did. Still, Rhys had encouraged him several times over the decades to do so, to set an example for his own employees.

He'd ignored him, of course. As the youngest, Thorne had always been something of a wild child, the typical rebellious bad boy who broke all the rules and did what he wanted. Sitting across from Rhys, he was dressed in ripped jeans and a black T-shirt with some rock band logo on it. *Yeah, real fucking professional.*

"Pretty much," Quin answered, leaning back in his chair. He formed a triangle with his hands, drumming his fingers against each other in thought. "Between the three of us, it shouldn't take more than an hour to scan through your workers. We'll start with the higher-ranked ones then move on to the lower levels. We can separate them into two piles—the maybes and the rejects."

Rhys snorted. "You make it sound as though they're nothing more than test subjects."

Quin shrugged. "In a way, they are. You've had four COOs quit in the last five years, and the numbers beyond that are even more pitiful. It's a tough position, so you need someone with a stiff backbone. And no offense, but most of your people are—"

"Weak," Thorne suggested.

"That's a polite way of putting it."

Rhys rolled his eyes and stood. "They may think the job is overwhelming, but it can't even lift a candle to the shit I have to deal with."

"True," Quin and Thorne said in unison.

Rhys ambled out of his office, rounding a corner to approach Kelle. She was focused on her computer monitor. Without looking at him, she said, "I've filtered out anyone with excessive absences or tardiness, anyone who's worked here for less than five years and anyone with complaints, suspensions, demotions or write-ups against them."

Rhys gave a curt nod. "Excellent. How many does that leave us with?"

She glanced up at him with sympathy. "It didn't even cut the list in half. There's two thousand, nine hundred and thirty-nine left."

Rhys' tiny flare of relief was squashed. No wonder she'd moved so fast. There was hardly any trimming she'd had to do. "Terrific," he grouched. "Reschedule any meetings this morning to after lunch. Then divide the list into three sections, one each for Quinton, Thorne and me."

Kelle nodded. "Yes, sir."

He returned to his office, reclaiming his seat on the couch. "The list has been narrowed down to a little less than three thousand. You might as well get comfortable, boys."

Both grunted, but he knew they truly didn't mind helping, no matter how much they enjoyed mocking him. They knew the stress that came with his job.

There were four main regions in Sheol—otherwise known as the underworld located beneath the earth—and each was ruled by a major family name that had been around since its birth. Elysium Underworld Corporation was a business in the Elysium region, of course. Rhys, Quinton and Thorne were all Lucifers, the three sons born from Damien Lucifer. As a way to better organize the constant arrival and departure of mortal souls, a thousand years ago Damien and two other family leaders had built massive corporate-style buildings in their separate regions to better control and keep track of the souls sent there.

Similar to the other three regions, entire cities had been built around EUC, which had influenced the creation of similar formations topside. That was right. As much as the humans believed that they'd thought of everything, the very world they knew had been taught to them by demons long ago, and only a select few mortals were aware of the truth.

After coming of age, Rhys had taken over EUC when his father had retired. As his brothers had gained the knowledge to join him in management, the business was then divided into three main sections to ease his workload—the Fielders, the Processing Center and the Soul Distribution Center.

Thorne was CEO of the first. The Field workers included reapers and charons. The reapers—aka angels of death—were assigned to mortals who were on the verge of dying, whether from illness, failing health or even the unexpected piano falling from the sky. They gathered the souls of dead mortals topside and brought them to the charons. Similar to Charon of Greek mythology, charons were the demons who walked between the human and demon world, delivering souls to EUC.

That would place them in the Processing Center, which was controlled by Quin. There, the souls were detained in a vast holding cell and processed for paperwork. The admin took down every bit of information about the soul, collecting every thought and action from the moment they had been born up until their death. Once the paperwork was complete, it was sent to the Soul Distribution Center, which was Rhys' division.

Charged with uploading the paperwork into specialized databases designed to keep track of every soul born and reborn, it was the SDC's job to make sure the information taken from each soul's past life was properly formatted. Finally, at the end of each day, all the paperwork was to be typed into a report that went through one final stop for organizing, to make sure each soul was dispersed correctly.

One of three things happened to a soul after that. If a mortal died before its time, it would be given a second chance at life, in which case charons would carry the soul back to the reapers to return to their human bodies before the corpse became damaged. The other two options determined if the soul could be reborn or would be destroyed.

Very rarely did the latter happen. When a soul was to be reborn, the COO looked over each one and decided where to distribute it. For those who had lived a life over-indulging in one of the seven deadly sins, they would be faced with some sort of punishment, needing to work for several months or years to earn their freedom to be reborn again. From there, the soul would be confined and transported to Asphodel to receive its sentence. The souls who had led good, meaningful lives were at the top of the list to be reborn into another mortal form, so would be sent off to The Meadows. Or, as Thorne called it, 'Hippie Land', for the serene atmosphere that gave souls the impression of being in 'heaven'.

Still, it was up to Rhys' COO to go through the thousands upon thousands of souls on the paperwork sent in weekly to make the decision on each soul, as well as assist in overlooking the rest of the division to make sure everything ran with ease.

Yeah, they were *very* large shoes to fill, and since Rhys had more than enough of his own problems to deal with, he didn't have the time to begin sorting through the paperwork himself. Free time just didn't exist in his life anymore.

A knock sounded, making Rhys blink to the present. "Enter," he commanded.

Kelle strolled in, her short legs clad in bright pink nylons, crossed the distance to where all three brothers sat. "Here are your lists, sir. I've organized them according to who has worked here the longest."

Thorne whistled in appreciation. "Impressive," he complimented, surveying Kelle's small frame in a way that indicated he wasn't just talking about her work.

Kelle narrowed her dark eyes, giving a toss of her hair to make the bite mark on the side of her neck evident. It was a symbol of her mating, making her off-limits to any other demon. Kelle was a wolf shifter. Like most other demons, wolves mated for life, and they were damn territorial. Not that it would stop Thorne from hitting on one of them, but Kelle was devoted to her mate.

Thorne grinned, wiggling his eyebrows at her. "I can bite just as hard as your mate, Kelle."

She rolled her eyes, turning her back to stroll away. "Even if I wasn't mated, that's a big fat 'hell no'."

"Fifty refusals eventually turns into a yes," Thorne called after her.

Just before exiting, Kelle turned to flash red eyes at him. "Given that you've fucked half your employees and just as many in our and Quin's divisions, I repeat. Hell. *No*." With that, she slammed the door behind herself, her heels clapping against the marble flooring as she stormed away.

Rhys shook his head. Thorne had once broken the heart of one of Kelle's friends. He could have been forgiven had he shown remorse, but, of course, such an emotion always seemed to elude him. Thorne was even less fond of emotional attachments than Rhys, though, unlike him, his brother was a dick about it.

Thorne chuckled, turning back to his brothers with a wide grin. "She totally wants me."

Quin shook his head in dismay. "You and I must have different definitions for the word 'want', brother. The look she gave was pure venom."

Thorne shrugged. "She'll come around. They always do."

Rhys waved aside their banter. "Let's get to work, if you two are done."

Both brothers shifted to focus on the stacks of paper before them. For several moments, the three of them just stared and stared…then stared some more. Three men. Three five-inch-high piles to sort through.

What. A. Drag.

Home of Erotic Romance

Sign up for our newsletter and find out about all our romance book releases, eBook sales and promotions, sneak peeks and FREE romance books!

About the Author

Makayla's love for reading began at the age of twelve when her mother introduced her to the world of mystical creatures. From then on, she discovered a talent for turning her own imagination into words. From fanfictions to short stories to full-length novels and novellas, if she wasn't focused on school activities, she was either reading or writing.

Raised on the coast of Mississippi, Makayla juggles her everyday life between work and being a mom. In her free time, she enjoys binge watching criminal suspense shows, shopping, painting, wood burning, and of course, working on her books.

Makayla enjoys writing stories with strong elements of romance, adventure, and paranormal. Vampires, shifters, fairies, dragons—she loves them all!

Makayla loves to hear from readers. You can find her contact information, website details and author profile page at https://www.totallybound.com